L.B. DUNBAR

www.lbdunbar.com

Other Books by L.B. Dunbar

<u>Sterling Falls</u>
Sterling Heat
Sterling Brick
Sterling Streak

Parentmoon

<u>Holiday Hotties (Christmas novellas)</u>
Scrooge-ish
Naughty-ish

<u>Road Trips & Romance</u>
Hauling Ashe
Merging Wright
Rhode Trip

<u>Lakeside Cottage</u>
Living at 40
Loving at 40
Learning at 40
Letting Go at 40

<u>The Silver Foxes of Blue Ridge</u>
Silver Brewer
Silver Player
Silver Mayor
Silver Biker

<u>Sexy Silver Fox Collection</u>
After Care
Midlife Crisis
Restored Dreams
Second Chance
Wine&Dine

<u>Collision novellas</u>
Collide
Caught

L.B. DUNBAR

The Sex Education of M.E.

The Heart Collection
Speak from the Heart
Read with your Heart
Look with your Heart
Fight from the Heart
View with your Heart

A Heart Collection Spin-off
The Heart Remembers

BOOKS IN OTHER AUTHOR WORLDS
Smartypants Romance (an imprint of Penny Reid)
Love in Due Time
Love in Deed
Love in a Pickle

The World of True North (an imprint of Sarina Bowen)
Cowboy
Studfinder

THE EARLY YEARS
The Legendary Rock Star Series

Paradise Stories

The Island Duet

Modern Descendants – writing as elda lore

Dedication

For Loving L.B. (on Facebook) – you keep me grounded and sane, and filled with laughter and stock in #sexysilverfox images.

Chapter 1
Put a Ring on It

[Janessa]

"What are you doing in here?"

My eyes leap up to the mirror over the dresser to meet the rich brown ones scowling back at me. The depth of his voice doesn't match his face. He's smooth and handsome, almost pretty, with silver at his temples and a clean-shaven jaw. His question is a good one.

What *am* I doing in this town?

What am I doing in his house?

What am I doing in his room?

Staring back at him, I slowly lower my hand to my belly. The fingers of my right hand struggle with the item on the left. I shouldn't be in here. I shouldn't have done this.

"Who are you?" he growls.

"I'm Jan," I say, struggling on the name as I admit a partial truth. I should clarify, but I don't want to get my mother in trouble. With all she's sacrificed over the years, I don't want her to lose this job working for him. I don't need to ask who he is. I've heard plenty about him.

Charlie Harrington, mayor of Blue Ridge, Georgia.

"I asked you a question." His voice softens a little, but the command is clear.

"I heard you," I snap, still tugging at my left finger with my right ones. I can't believe this is happening to me. It's what I get for being curious.

Mami sent me over here so she could go with Papi to the doctor. I didn't want to be here, and my eyes wandered when I was supposed to be picking up the bedroom. Make the bed. Straighten the pillows. Fresh towels in the bathroom. Toss the laundry in the washroom. I wasn't the housekeeper, and I didn't want to act like one. I didn't want my mother to be one either, but she'd dedicated her entire life to cleaning up after others. It was what she did. She even did it for my brother and me.

"You still haven't answered my question. I'm giving you to the count of ten before I call the police."

Dear Lord, he's acting like I'm a child, but I've done something childish. I couldn't help myself. I just wanted to know what it would look like, but now I'm struggling to remove it. My right fingers tug as the skin on the knuckle of my left bunches.

"*One. Two.*"

The louder he counts, the more I sweat, and my ring finger swells. His voice isn't helping either. It's deep and rugged, clashing with the sharp suit and open-at-the-collar dress shirt. He wasn't supposed to be here. Mami said he left for work.

"*Three. Four.* What are you doing?"

My eyes lift back to the mirror, watching him stalk closer to me in the reflection. He's almost to my back, but his aroma precedes him. Manly and woodsy like this area. I didn't grow up in a place quite so lush with foliage and greenery. Texas was more dry dirt and barren. Dull brown, actually.

His presence overshadows my childhood memories. His chest nearly presses into my back.

"*Five. Six.* I'm still waiting." He pauses, and then his body language shifts. "Are you trying to steal something?" His pitch elevates. His brows pinch, furrowing his smooth forehead, and I glance up at him again through the mirror, but he's not looking at me. He's scanning the top of his dresser, which is relatively clean for a man. He's not a bachelor; this I also know about him. He's a single father who lives in this large house with his only child, Lucy. My mother is her nanny along with her other responsibilities.

Thick hands land on my shoulders, and he spins me to face him. My back collides with the tall bureau, and I glance up at him, captivated by his eyes. The brown isn't dull like desert sand, but earthy and rich like turned soil. His mouth curls downward as he continues to scowl at me.

"I wasn't stealing anything."

"Then what are you doing with your hands?" A brow tips again, the look almost playful as if he has something more to say, something mischievous to add, but he stops himself.

Lowering my head, I lift my left hand and hold the back to him so he can see what I've done.

"It's stuck."

He stares at my finger, focused on the gold band with a large emerald and two smaller diamonds on either side of the gem. It's simple and beautiful—a priceless antique, I imagine.

"Where did you get that?" His voice lowers, the rugged sound turning rough and menacing.

"I swear I wasn't stealing it. It was sitting in the dish." He has a small bowl with coins and such on the dresser, and the ring sat inside with the collection of items. "I slipped it on." I exhale. "I shouldn't have done that because now I can't get it off."

With my right fingers, I tug once again, but my left knuckle is already red and raw from my aggressive efforts to remove the item.

"I should call the police," he states, and he's within his rights. I can explain, but again, I don't want to get my mother in trouble. She says Charlie's a good boss, fair and kind, and I don't want to put any blame on her for this situation. I'm the one who slipped on the ring, and I'm the one who can't get it off.

"Please don't. Just…Just let me get this off my hand, and you'll never see me again." I'm good at being in the shadows. I've done it most of my adult life, married to a man who'd rather pretend I didn't exist, at least not exist with intelligent thoughts.

Just stand there, Janessa. Look pretty.

Charlie grips my hand, and I instantly react when I shouldn't. Something charged and prickly races up my arm, and my heart skips a beat as though it's been jump-started even though it's already racing.

Without a word, he tugs me forward, and I stumble after him. He drags me to the bathroom off his master bedroom and shoves my hand into the sink. He turns on the faucet with his free hand, and the water almost hurts it's so cold. Reaching forward for the green bar of soap, he works at my hand, coating it in a thin lather. More woodsy fragrance permeates the air around us.

He drops the bar in the sink and massages my finger, but the ring isn't moving.

"I don't have time for this," he snaps under his breath and rinses my hand, working his fingers over mine to wash away the soap. Once satisfied I'm free of sudsy residue, he lifts my hand, droplets of water sliding down to my wrist, and he opens his mouth.

"What…?"

Before I can finish my thought, my ring finger is inside the warm cavern between his cheeks. He closes his lips over the digit, and his tongue circles around my finger. Within seconds, his teeth scrape the length of my ring finger. He pauses at the tip like he's pressing it with a kiss and then tugs my hand free as if it offended him. Leaning forward, he lifts his other hand and spits.

The ring drops into his palm, and he stares at the sparkling emerald with the almost white diamonds on either side of it. I tug at my hand still held within his, but he doesn't release me. He glances up at me instead.

"This was my grandmother's," he states as if I asked, which I didn't, but from the puzzled look on his face, I sense its value is more than something on a price tag.

"It's beautiful," I whisper, staring down at it, and then slowly, I lift my eyes, and we lock stares again. We're standing in his bathroom, a space clearly occupied by only a man. The scent of aftershave. The woodsy soap. The dark towel over the rod. His eyes aren't leaving my face, but slowly, he loosens his hold on my hand. There's a question in those eyes. He wants to know more than who I am and what I'm doing in his room, but I won't give him answers. He's too similar to what I left behind, and I'll never go back to where I was, who I was.

Once I sense I'm free, I draw back my hand, turn for the door, and race for the hallway. He calls after me, but I take the stairs two at a time, hopping down them as if I'm a teen instead of a forty-something woman trying to flee a man's home, hoping to get away scot-free from both his house and those rich, haunting eyes.

Chapter 2
Single Daddy

[Charlie]

"Dad, are you listening to me?"

"What? Sorry." I zoned out almost immediately as my ten-year-old chatters about her day. My mind returns to the woman I found in my bedroom this morning. The woman I haven't been able to stop thinking about. Her eyes matched the emerald stuck on her finger. Brilliant and bright green against her tan skin, the color captivated me, and then I recall the ring.

My grandmother's ring. It's a simple ring compared to the others my grandmother owned. Call me old-fashioned but my grandmother was important to me, important to all the Harringtons. As one of five grandchildren, the ring probably should have gone to Mati as the only sister in our clan, but I inherited the ring because Charles was the male version of Charlotte, my beloved grandmother's name. My name also comes from my mother's obsession with Roald Dahl when we were children. Charlie and his chocolate factory. Momma jokes she knew I'd be a leader like the young boy hanging out with his grandfather for a day in that candy factory.

"Who else can be trusted with all the secrets?" She often whispered that to me as a child as if we had secrets to be held. Us Harringtons are pretty much an open book. Our great-great-grandfather started brewing beer in the backwoods of this area and calling Georgia home before Georgia had a name, or so the old family folklore goes. Once brewing beer was legalized, Pap, my grandfather, established the brewery, and when it became legitimate for craft brews to be sold, Giant Beer Company was born under the nickname of my eldest brother, George Harrington II, or Giant as he's called. His size fits the name.

"Dad," Lucy drones, and my attention snaps back to her.

"I'm sorry, Pint." I used to call my daughter half-pint because of her tiny stature. As she was born a preemie, we almost lost her, and I hate the immediate memory that Angela hadn't wanted our daughter in the first place. I no longer call Lucy half-pint as she's quick to remind me the term means something small and inconsequential, and she's nothing of the sort.

"I'd rather be demonstrative than diminutive," she told me one night as she was learning her vocabulary list for school, and I marveled at the intelligence of someone so young. She's mature in some ways because of her position—daughter of the town's mayor without a mother—but as she whines my title for the third time, I'm reminded she's still a child.

"Dad, you aren't listening."

"I'm sorry," I say again. "Start over. You have my full attention." I cup her cheeks in my large hands as I lean over the island counter. Focusing on her eyes, I try not to be distracted by the fact they match Angie's blue and not my gray-brown.

"So I made a new friend today in art camp, and I want to ask her over to swim."

This isn't a big deal although I'm hesitant of new people in my home—case in point, this morning. Blue Ridge is a tight-knit community, most of us having grown up together, but the town's size has nearly doubled in my four-plus decades in the area. Though the economy thrives under my reign as mayor, it comes with all sorts of headaches as I balance the locals' desire to remain small town and the growing developments for tourism.

"I don't see how that will be a problem. Let's speak with Rosa."

Lucy's face drops.

"What? What's wrong with Rosa?"

"I love Rosa, but I just thought you could be there instead." I have a rule where my housekeeper or myself must be present to supervise when another child comes to my home. It's just a way to protect my daughter, and something I learned from friends in the political culture.

You never know who will go through your child to get to you. Sometimes, I feel silly about the rule, but I'd never let anyone use my child.

"Pint, you know I can't be at every playdate, especially with as many as you have." Lucy is a popular child, not necessarily from her status as the mayor's daughter but because she's so open and accepting of everyone. She twists her lips, another reminder of her likeness to Angela.

"Maybe Gran can be there instead," Lucy sheepishly suggests of her grandmother, my mother, and my brows pinch. *What's wrong with Rosa?* The woman has worked for me since before Lucy's birth. She's practically family.

"I guess we could ask Gran, but what am I missing here?" My hands slip from my daughter's small cheeks.

"Vega's mother wants to be present for the playdate as well." Lucy smirks at me like this is a conspiracy. *Vega?* What kind of name is that?

"Well, she sounds like a smart woman." I nod to emphasize my point. I'm definitely not hanging out with some other kid's mother for an afternoon. Being a single father is difficult enough because some women think I'm desperate and lonely. "I'll call Gran and then have Rosa set it up."

Lucy looks pacified for the moment, but she still scowls a little at the suggestion.

"What else is bothering you, Pint?"

"Mom called. She wants to know when I'm visiting this summer." Lucy looks down at the countertop. "Do I have to go?"

Angela lives in a high-rise in Philadelphia. City life was her dream and politics her mission. When I said I wanted to be mayor of my small town, she begrudgingly agreed as it was a steppingstone on the path to something bigger, only I stayed on the first rung of the ladder to success. Things fell apart after a few years, and she left, returning to the city where we met. Through the divorce agreement, Lucy has a two-week visit every summer.

"Pint, we've been over this. It's only for two weeks."

"But it's always awful there." As a kid raised in this large house with land, and the woods surrounding the area, high-rises and gated parks don't cut it for my daughter.

"It's only two weeks," I remind her, but my chest aches at the thought. Fourteen days is a long time without her, even if I'm guilty of not spending as much time with her myself. Her head nods, acquiescing to the decree, and the guilt doubles.

"Let's call Gran about that swim date," I suggest, hoping to redirect her. "And I'll see what I can do to be there for a bit."

The smile I receive almost blinds me. There's nothing I wouldn't do for my daughter, and if I need to suck up a half hour to meet this new friend's mother, then that's what I'll do.

Chapter 3
Poolside Plan

[Janessa]

As I sit on the patio around the pool, I hold my breath. I've been assured that Charlie isn't home and won't be present for this supervised playdate. Richard can't reach me here, but I didn't want Vega going to anyone's house without me inspecting the place first. Little did I know I'd only be going a few feet from my mother's home when Vega mentioned swimming with her new friend from art camp.

My daughter is ten and used to a lusher lifestyle than the confines of my parents' coach house, but I'm hoping to give her a better life, here or wherever we settle next. She'd been spoiled by her father until ulterior motives came to light. He wanted to pit her against me. Thankfully, Vega is smarter than him.

"So Lucy mentioned you recently moved here," Elaina Harrington asks me. She's Charlie's mother, and while my own mother explained she'd normally supervise a playdate with Lucy, Charlie suggested his mother be present instead. Elaina is beautiful in that classic Southern belle mystic of *how does she still look so young when she must be over sixty*? My own mother looks well past her age, having worked hard all her life to please others and to support my brother and me, but my father still tells her she looks beautiful every day. "Where did you move from?"

I could fib a little, like when I said my name was Jan. Instead, I decide a general truth won't hurt.

"Texas." I don't offer more, and Elaina's brow twitches just a bit, waiting on further explanation.

"And what did you do there?"

I was the arm candy of my husband, I want to snap, but I bite my cheek. "I was in marketing." It's not a lie. I went to college and got my first job in sports marketing for a Major League Baseball team. Then I met Richard Swank, center fielder for Houston. Pretty boy, all-star, notorious player. Adulterer. The list could go on and on. He refused to let me work once we married, citing I'd be too enticing for others. He worried about me leaving him. *Oh, the irony.*

"Anywhere I've heard of?" Elaina asks, keeping up the small talk.

"I don't think so," I offer, knowing she might recognize Richard's name if she's into baseball, but Elaina Harrington doesn't come across as a sports fan.

"And where are you working now?" Her eyes question something I'm unable to answer because I don't have a job yet. We've only been here for two weeks, and I haven't pursued any employment. I'm trying to make things as normal as possible for Vega, like registering her for a summer art camp.

"I'm still looking for something," I mention, my eyes lowering. I'm not embarrassed I've been a stay-at-home mother for ten years, but shame washes over me anyway. I don't feel I have any other skills, having lost out on furthering my career and continuing to network once Richard demanded I stop working.

"Perhaps, I could help. I have a few connections in town." She winks good-naturedly at me, and I'm certain she has several well-meaning connections, but I don't want any favors. She begins with her list anyway. "My eldest son runs the local brewery that we own. Another runs Blue Ridge Microbrewery & Pub. Charlie is the mayor, as I'm sure you are aware." She smiles politely, proud of her offspring's accomplishments. "My other son is…estranged from the family at the moment, but there's also my daughter, Matilda. She's a women's volleyball coach for Northeastern Georgia University." She gives a dismissive wave as though she isn't quite as proud of her daughter's achievements. "But I don't know how interested you'd be in sports."

I bite the inside of my cheek. She has no clue how much my life revolved around them before.

We both turn at the sound of hard-soled shoes snapping against concrete, and my breath catches. My hand grips the armrest of the outdoor dining chair where I sit as I turn to face the person approaching.

"You?" Charlie hisses, his eyes instantly latching onto mine, and I'm caught in his gaze like a fish snagged on a hook.

"Charlie, we were just discussing you," Elaina interjects, standing to greet her son whose eyes don't leave mine. He isn't even touching me, and my skin prickles like yesterday morning.

I'm hyperaware of a young girl's squeal, calling out, "Dad!" A small, wet body rushes past me, and without a care to his suit, he stoops to catch his daughter. Lucy. "Dad, you made it!"

"Wouldn't miss it," he states in that too deep voice with a hint of untruth. I bet he's missed a few important moments in his daughter's life. Richard missed several of Vega's. A meeting. A practice. A woman in a hotel room. "Wanted to meet your new friend. And her mother."

His eyes don't leave mine as he presses a kiss to her temple and sets her back on her feet.

"Dad, this is Vega. We have the same birthday. Isn't that so cool? And she's going to go to school with me this fall." The excitement in his child's voice turns my head to Vega who has also left the pool and stands near my knee. I reach for her damp back and rub. I haven't decided if we are staying or not.

"Yeah, so cool," he mutters, still watching me when I glance up at him. "Charlie Harrington."

He extends a hand to shake mine, remembering his manners.

"Jan." I pause. "Jan Cruz." I've shortened my given name and use my maiden name.

"Pleasure to meet you," he fakes again in that rugged voice as our hands touch, and that current shoots up my wrist like it did when he touched me the other day in his room.

"What were you saying about me?" he questions, releasing my hand and turning to his mother.

"Ms. Cruz is new to the area and was telling me she's looking for a job. I was listing off all my connections."

"Yes. Elaina Harrington is better than LinkedIn," he jokes, giving his mother a teasing grin. He's close to her. It shows in the way he looks at her. A good man treats his mother with kindness. It's sweet but unnerving. "What line of work are you looking for?"

"I'm undecided at the moment." I sound like a kid heading off to college without a plan when I'm a forty-three-year-old woman…without a plan.

"Well, I hope that works out for you." He isn't mocking me but teasing once again, and I smile despite myself.

"Dad, come swim," Lucy begs, tugging at his hand.

"I can't, Pint, but I promised I'd stop by, remember?" Lucy releases his hand. "Dinner," he states the reminder, and Lucy nods, then turns for Vega. "Race you."

The two sprint for the pool while Elaina calls out, "Walk. Don't run." When her head turns back to face us, the weight of her stare is heavy as she glances from me to Charlie.

"I think I'll go get us some fresh iced tea." Patting Charlie's arm after she stands, she says, "Take a seat and meet Ms. Cruz."

Once his mother's gone, he turns to me and lowers into the seat across from mine.

"What are you doing here?" he growls under his breath as he leans forward, placing his arms on his knees. He's too good-looking in that suit. Too clean-cut and smooth. Despite the darkness of his eyes, they gleam.

"Your mother invited us." It isn't exactly true. Lucy invited Vega and said I needed to attend as well, which is fine as I wanted to be here to learn more about my daughter's new friend. The assurance of Charlie's absence made it easy to accept the invitation. I should have known better.

"Have you been in the house? How do I know you didn't try to steal something else from me?" His accusation stings, and sass gets the better of me.

"Want to strip-search me?" Holding out my arms, I sit straighter in my seat, and Charlie's eyes travel down my body like a slow glide down a waterslide. I'm wearing a sundress that lays over my thighs and thin sandals on my feet. Charlie takes his time, making it obvious to slip over the slope of my breasts down to my waist, and along my legs to the cross of my bare knees.

"Don't tempt me," he mutters, and my head tips.

"Search my bags," I snap, placing my arms on the armrests.

"How do I know there isn't a whole posse inside wiping me clean while you distract my mother out here?"

"I think you've watched too many crime shows, Mayor. Besides, I'm not a gang member, but thanks for stereotyping me."

He leans back in his seat and swipes a hand through his hair, which is longer on top and trimmed close to the scalp near his ears. His temples are graying. It's a sexy look on him.

"I apologize. That might have crossed a line, but then again, so does thievery."

"Thievery?" I snort. "Big word."

"Yes, I use them occasionally." He stares back at me, but he grins just the slightest bit, and a dimple curls at the corner of his lip. "It's very mayorly of me."

I chuckle. Reaching inside his suit jacket, he pulls out his cell phone. I'm assuming he's checking the time, but then he says, "Give me your number."

"Excuse me?"

"If you give me your number, I can share mine, and you can contact me about a job. I might have a connection or two myself." He winks like his mother did. *Yep, too smooth.*

"I'd prefer to just find something on my own but thank you." Nervously, I swipe down the length of my short dress and cup my knee cap. My response surprises him as he holds the phone in his palm, primed to take my digits.

"You don't want help?" A singular brow lifts, and the dimple disappears.

"I'm good," I say, waving a hand. I don't want anyone connecting themselves to Vega and me. I need to do this on my own. I *want* to do it on my own terms.

"Well, Ms. Cruz," he states formally, returning his phone to his jacket and standing. Surprising me, he leans forward, bracing his hands on the armrests of my seat, bracketing me in. He lowers even farther, as if he's going to kiss my cheek, only he speaks in my ear. "If ever we should meet again in my bedroom, I hope you're naked and willing in my bed and not stealing from me."

Chapter 4
Parks and Recreation

[Charlie]

"What's this?" I ask as I enter the conference room in the mayor's building. The structure is an old house on the opposite side of First Street near the other municipal buildings for the town. This office has history, one I tried to eradicate when I took the position by allowing my law firm—Harrington & Rathstone—to move here. We remodeled, giving the historical landmark new life. The dining room became a conference room, and it's where I stand, puzzled as I see Jan Cruz sitting at the oval table within.

A gathering of the town council members circle the table as well.

"It's an interview for the new Parks and Recreation Director," Bryce Norton says. Sally Maywood held the position forever until she passed away in the spring. Her ideas were antiquated, but as much as I wanted Sally to go, I never had the heart to fire her. Our little town needed some updates, though, not only in this building but also in the activities and adventures provided to tourists and locals alike. It was an all-encompassing job, and the position was open to interpretation and creativity.

However, I wasn't certain I was open to Jan Cruz obtaining the position. When Jan was at the house a week ago, my mother didn't share anything she'd learned about our guest. Then again, I hadn't asked too many questions because an inquiry of my own would lead to a setup from my mother. She loves to play matchmaker.

Jan. The name doesn't fit her. Something says Jan is too simple for her. She looks complicated. She has secrets just under the surface of that beautiful skin and those mesmerizing eyes and knowing she has them makes my skin prickle in a conflict of curiosity and caution. I've had enough scandal in the past. I don't need to invite more into the mayor's office or my life.

The other members of the town council stare at me, waiting for me to either comment or take a seat. I don't typically attend interviews, but I want in on the decision for the new Park-Rec person because they'll be working closely with me at first. Charity Bernard, my assistant, sits at the table to take notes along with Scarlett Nugent, Gretchen O'Leary, Wyatt Hubner, and Bryce.

The only open seat is next to Jan who sits near the end of the table. I don't run a hierarchy with an *I'm the leader* attitude but allow for more of a roundtable discussion with me as the final decision maker. We already had the monarch wannabe running this town when I was child. Kip Chance, Denton and Dolores's father, was a tyrant.

Jan forces a grin my way as I take my seat, and the interview continues with the typical requests for experience, references, and accountability. How will she handle herself in an XYZ situation? Her knees are bouncing under the table, but the upper portion of her doesn't move as she keeps her hands folded on the tabletop and answers without a quiver in her voice. But her legs—those long limbs crossed with a shoe dangling off her toes—are distracting the heck out of me.

Sitting forward, I slide my seat a little closer to her and then reach my pen under the table to poke her thigh. A hand on the knee is something I'd do with a fidgeting Lucy when I needed her to sit still, but I don't dare touch Ms. Cruz. One, because I don't trust my fingers on her skin. The previous times I've touched her, the charge racing over my fingers was like getting zapped from an outlet. I know about these things as I did stick a key in a socket on a dare from my older brother when I was a child.

Secondly, I'm one comment away from a sexual harassment complaint. I can't believe I said what I said to her beside the pool. *Naked and willing in my bed.* I don't know what came over me, but when she flinches from the stroke of the pen tip on her thigh, I realize I know exactly what came over me.

Her.

I haven't been able to stop thinking of her for days. That long dark hair and those bright green eyes with light cappuccino skin and perfect white teeth. Not to mention, she's curvy. Hips. Breasts. Backside. A real Jennifer Lopez clone and I'm drooling. Today, she wears a tight skirt and loose blouse with her hair pulled to her nape and eyeglasses. She's a vision, and I'd let her play naughty secretary with me any day.

Jesus, get a grip. I retract the pen and scrub at my forehead with two fingers. I haven't heard half of what she's said in this interview. Something about sports marketing. A love for recreation. And then there's a question of where she lives.

"I'm staying within the town proper as per the qualifications for the position." The answer is vague, terse, and direct, and I'm not certain it's within our right to question her further, though her address should be on file with the application. We do require our council members to live within the boundary of town, not up in the woods or down the ridge in another city.

"Well, I'm just curious…" Gretchen O'Leary states, but I interject.

"Thank you. If those are all the questions the council has for Ms. Cruz, perhaps we should wrap this up."

"We have another interview at one thirty," Charity announces to the group, and Jan's shoulders fall. She wants this job, and Charity was out of line to reference others.

"Thank you for your time." Jan smiles graciously at the council and twists for her bag at her feet.

"If I might have a word alone with Ms. Cruz. Let's take a break for a few minutes before the next appointment. Coffee's in the kitchen." Charity keeps the coffeepot full, and the cabinets hold endless donations of cookies and treats for meetings and such. Never one to turn down a cookie, Wyatt is the first to excuse himself, and the remainder of the council follows.

I turn toward Jan once the door to the kitchen is closed, but she's already out of her seat and heading for the double doors leading to the front hall. Circling the table on the opposite side of her, I cut her off before she reaches the exit.

"Hey," I say, stretching my hand for her and then retracting it. "I want to apologize for what I said the other day. It was inappropriate and uncalled for. I just want you to know I don't make a habit of soliciting women into my bed."

"Don't you mean seducing?"

"Wasn't aware inviting you to my bedroom was appealing." My voice drops, and her breath catches. "Not that I'm trying to be seductive or seducing or anything. I just wanted to say I'm sorry."

When she blinks up at me, those green eyes steal my thoughts. I'd like to seduce her, but that would be a terrible idea—the worst idea—especially if she gets this job.

"How exactly did you get this interview?" I question, and she shifts the bag on her shoulder.

"I filled out the application."

I chuckle as there's no way it was that simple, especially as she avoided one specific question near the end. "Where *do* you live?"

"Are you asking as a part of the interview, Mr. Harrington, or for seductive purposes? Because if it's the latter, you're crossing the inappropriate line once again."

"Let's see," I say, stepping closer to her. "And what line did you cross by being in my bedroom in the first place, slipping on my grandmother's ring, and then dodging quickly out of my house, only to show up a few days later on a swim date with your child?"

Her nostrils flare like a bull ready to pounce, and for some reason, I want her to jump. I want her to leap at me, so I have cause to lay her out on this dining room table and have my way with her. That tight skirt does nothing to conceal the outline of her body. The rounded hips. The dip to her waist. The swell of her ass. My hands twitch to touch her, preparing for the combustion if she gave in to me.

"I'm not at liberty to answer."

Staring down at her, I scoff. "At liberty? What does that mean?"

I shouldn't trust her. She was trying to steal that ring, yet when I reflect on it, she didn't try to run with the ring on, and of all the things in the bureau, the antiquated jewelry has the least monetary value. I had it out to get it cleaned for Lucy.

"It means I'm not telling you, and I already apologized for being in your room and trying on the ring."

"Yes, but *why* were you in my room in the first place?"

Her bright eyes drift to the side, and her pouty lips curl inward. "I'm…I'm not at liberty to tell you that either."

I snort, but for some reason, the counsel rests on this question for the moment.

"What about running away from me?" My smile curls, hoping to convey I'm teasing her, but her eyes shift, darkening the green from grass to pine.

"I'll never apologize for running, sir."

Sir? *Don't call me that.* Now another body part is twitching, and it wants under that skirt. My mouth waters, and I lick my lips. Her eyes trail the motion, and I wonder if she feels a pull to me like I do her. It was there before. In my bedroom. In my bathroom. Beside the pool.

Has she stepped closer to me? My suit pants will do nothing to contain the developments happening within.

"Are we finished here?"

When I step back, waving a hand for her to leave, I realize how close we stood. My front feels cold with her absence, and my dick still stands at attention, longing for relief. It's been a long time since a woman has had this kind of effect on me. Since the divorce, I've had a couple of one-night stands, but no one I would trust near Lucy.

I watch the sway of her ass as she slips through the two pocket doors that disappear into the wall. When she turns to slide them back in place for privacy, her eyes find mine, and we stare at one another. I'm reminded of those smoldering moments in movies when the elevator doors are about to close and all will be lost.

"Mr. Harrington," she states.

"Jan."

+ + +

"Tell me again how she got the interview?" I ask of Charity, my loyal assistant of ten years. Her father is a powerful man as the local judge, and he's the one who recently put the bug in my ear about running for Congress.

Charity sighs. She's a pretty woman with brunette hair and blue eyes, but nothing that has ever tempted me. We've worked side by side as professionals for a decade, and I'm reminded of the adage about work wives. Charity is mine. I've spent more time with her than I did with Angela my entire marriage.

"Your mother." She smiles with a shake of her head, understanding the relentless pressure of Elaina Harrington. "She got Gretchen to give the woman a shot."

"What's this business about an address?" For some reason, I'm worried we're interested in a homeless woman. Not that the woods around us don't cater to a few homeless camps, but I can't hire a woman living out of a car. Then again, this could be the break this woman needs. How did my Rosa get ahold of Jan for the playdate with Lucy and Vega? Jan refused to give me her phone number. Does she even have a phone?

Things about our secretive applicant aren't adding up, and I'm back to wondering if I should trust her. But for some reason, I want to pull her into my arms and let her know she's safe here. Then again, the things I want to do to her body as well as my suggestion to join me in bed don't scream safety.

I'm an idiot.

Chapter 5
Baseball Under the Lights

[Janessa]

I'm not surprised when I don't hear from the council after a few days and decide I'm desperate enough to apply for a job at the local diner—Wine&Dine. The old diner has a new interior, or so I've learned, and it reminds me of a roaring twenties dining car on a train.

"I'm here about the help wanted," I say to a buxom blonde in a waitress outfit.

"The application's online." She speaks proudly. "We're doing things differently nowadays." Her eyes sparkle like she knows a secret or she's smarter than me. Both might be the case, but she smiles warmly and holds out a thin hand. "I'm Hollilyn. Hollilyn Harrington."

"You ain't a Harrington yet," an older gentleman sitting at the counter remarks, and Hollilyn turns on him.

"You mind your own business, Jerry Stunner."

Jerry what? The name does not fit the portly man who narrows his eyes at Hollilyn.

"Well, when's he going to marry you then?"

Tension swirls between them, and I'd think I'm witnessing a lover's quarrel if it weren't that Jerry looks about fifty and Hollilyn looks like she wants to kick his ass.

"He'll marry me when he's ready," she says, placing her hands on her hips, and Jerry huffs.

"Wonder if it'll happen before he gets you pregnant again," Jerry mutters not so subtly under his breath, and Hollilyn turns away from him, crossing her arms.

"Don't pay him any mind. He's crotchety because he can't get laid even by his wife."

"I get laid just fine, thank you," Jerry states a little too loudly for the crowd within the diner, and another man who looks like a rock star interjects.

"Jerry, let's keep your sex life to yourself, okay? Hollilyn, help this woman." He smiles at me, and I almost fall over. Charm is written all over him. What's with the men in this town? Then I look back at Jerry and find some normalcy. Not everyone is breathtaking.

"Anywho, if you go to our website." Hollilyn pauses to hand me a menu and point out the site name on the bottom of the card. "There's an application. What's your name? I'll look for it."

"Jan," I say, getting used to calling myself by such a name. "Jan Cruz."

"Got any experience being a waitress?"

"Does working in a bar in college count?" I sheepishly offer. The last time I waited tables was over twenty years ago, and it wasn't food I was serving.

"Sure does." She smiles, and I take the menu she offers. "Good luck."

"You won't need it," Jerry interjects. "No one wants to work with this sourpuss. You'll get the job."

"Oh, Jerry, you just shush," Hollilyn says to him, waving a menu in his face, and he smiles despite the insults he's been slinging at her. Hollilyn winks at me, and it seems like a friendly enough place to work, but I really want the Parks and Recreation job instead.

+ + +

It's dark by the time I head home, and the quiet and bleak drive up the mountain matches how I feel. I need to work, and I need to earn money. I can't keep living off my parents' generosity, and the weight of their hospitality presses on me. Their home is not what Vega is used to, but she's been a good sport about it. It was difficult to leave behind her friends and our house, but she understands. She was a witness to the life her father led.

After I park my father's truck in the drive and walk toward the house, I see lights shining over a row of bushes that mark the edge of the yard. The hedge stands taller than my head, but the illumination is too bright and too close to the coach house.

What the heck?

Circling the dense bushes, which my father purposely keeps tall and wide, I walk a short concrete path to find a tennis court. The lights in question are a string of outdoor Edison bulbs lining each side of the tall chain-link fence. Only the person inside the fence is swinging at baseballs, not playing late-night tennis.

I watch for a moment as Charlie tosses a ball in the air and then swings a wooden bat, the crack so familiar. The ball soars a short distance, colliding with the fence on the opposite side. I take in his stance and the curve of his backside. He has a nice backside in loose athletic shorts. He's wearing a snug gray T-shirt with a trickle of sweat down the back. A baseball cap on his head backward tops off the look, and my eyes are looking.

"That's one interesting batting cage," I say, unable to help myself, and then I freeze.

Shit.

I've just exposed myself.

Charlie quickly turns to face me, his eyes wide. Then he shakes his head.

"Good God, you've gone from thieving to stalking." He laughs after he speaks, resting the bat on his shoulder.

"I'm not stalking," I snark.

"No, just wandering around my property in the dark."

I can't explain where I was really going, so I tease, "Would you believe I was in the neighborhood?"

"That's a terrible pickup line," he says with another chuckle in that deep tone he has.

"I'm not trying to pick you up," I snap.

"Oh, then what are you doing here?"

"I'm staying nearby, and I saw the lights."

His brows lift. "Another pickup line and a lie."

I'm actually not lying for maybe the first time since I've met him, but he doesn't need to know the truth. He doesn't believe me, and he has no reason to, either.

"Are you a friend of Cora's?" he suggests, mentioning the woman who owns the house next to his. Mountain Spring Lane is unique in that it's a gravel road with only three antebellum homes on it. The Harringtons, this Harrington—Charlie as he lives in the town-sanctioned mayor's house—and the Conrads. A river runs behind the three homes, and the road dead-ends on the other side of Cora Conrad's house. I don't know Cora Conrad personally, but Charlie doesn't need to know that yet.

"Sure," I say, not denying or confirming anything about Cora.

Charlie stares back at me for a long minute, and my palms sweat as my fingers curl into the steel fencing. I'm not certain if I'm holding on for dear life or holding myself back because for some reason, I want to run to him. I'm that girl on the sidelines ready to tackle her man when he scores the home run to win the game, and I want to do him on the pitching mound. Only there's no mound here, not even a field. It's only a makeshift batting cage.

"Get in here," Charlie demands, and my eyes narrow.

"Excuse me?"

"Come on in here. Do you know how to hit a ball?"

"I might know a thing or two," I mock, entering the fenced area. Charlie watches me walk and notices my shoes dangling from my fingers.

"Rough day?" His voice softens as his brows pinch in question.

"Just long." I sigh. I've literally been up and down this mountain applying for jobs, and it's made me edgy. I don't want my name out there in too many places.

"Can I help?" he offers with a weak smile. He knows I don't want any favors, and I definitely don't want his pity.

"Just let me bat. I feel like I could beat the hell out of a ball," I tease. I could use a few swings, though it's been a while. "You don't strike me as a baseball player. More like a golf man."

Charlie tips his head. "I play golf, too, but why don't I seem like a baseball guy?"

"You've got the whole uptight suit thing going," I tell him although he looks good in a suit. *Darn* good. This baseball getup he's wearing works, too, though. His athletic build proves he takes care of his body but isn't a freak about working out.

"Uptight, huh?" he questions, his lips twisting as though I've struck a nerve with him. He shakes his head and glances at me. "I played baseball in college."

Charlie tosses me a ball which I catch overhand, and his brows lift, impressed with my skill. Then he hands me the bat. Stepping out of my way, I do my best to hitch the ball into the air and then swing. The ball falls to the ground at my feet, and the bat pitches me forward. I'm out of practice.

Charlie steps up behind me. Without asking permission, he wraps his arms around mine. "You need to choke up a little." His warm hands cover mine and tug my hands farther up the bat, giving me better leverage on it. He pauses behind me as my backside sticks out, and I bend my knees in a batting stance. He hisses as I accidentally nudge his front.

"Sorry about that," I mutter, but I don't straighten. Charlie steps away, and once again, I toss a ball upward, swing, and miss. I'm normally better than this, but his presence behind me is distracting. He's still too close, and I can feel his eyes roaming along my spine and over the curve of my ass. Just to taunt him, I bend forward, giving him the full view of my backside as I pick up the ball at my feet. I slowly lift, practically rolling the baseball up my leg, and then I snap upward, tossing my hair and looking at him over my shoulder.

"Was that just the bend and snap?"

My mouth falls open. "You know *Legally Blonde*?"

"I have a ten-year-old daughter."

"And you let her watch that?"

"Her mother did. She called it a study in how *not* to get a job in the legal system."

I turn to face him. *Oh my God*. I swear my mother told me he was divorced.

"Your wife did that?" I ask.

"Ex-wife and yes, she did. And you didn't answer my question." His arms are crossed over his chest, but he leans one forward and twirls his finger at me.

"I did not just bend and snap for your pleasure, sir," I state, and his eyes narrow, the dark color darkening.

"I'd like to bend and snap you for my pleasure," he says, and I stare at him. *He did not just say that*. He did not just insinuate, once again, that he'd like to do something to me, something sexual, something pleasurable, something I might enjoy myself.

Shit. I don't need this. Not now. Not him.

Charlie hangs his head and scrubs a hand down his face. "I'm sorry. That was uncalled for again."

"It was," I retort, haughty and hurt, but only because I haven't been bent over and snapped in so long, I've forgotten what it feels like. Just as I've forgotten what it feels like to be desired by a man, really desired. Charlie has that spark in his eyes like he wants something from me, something I haven't given away for a while.

I turn from him, toss the ball in the air, and nail it into the fence at the opposite end of the court.

"I take it you might have done that before," he teases, the tension around us releasing a bit.

"High school all-star and state champion softball player in my junior year," I proudly say and then realize I've said too much. I spin to face him and his widened eyes.

"And that high school was where?"

I drop the bat and stalk to the entrance. "Thanks for the swings," I mutter. I'm not answering his questions, no personal sharing, but he cuts me off before I reach the gate opening.

"Okay, I'm sorry again. No prying tonight. Forget I asked." He holds up his hands as if to stop me, as if surrendering. "Take a few more hits with me," he suggests after a couple of seconds, and I acquiesce, holding batting practice with the mayor on the edge of his backyard in the dark.

I don't know how long we're out here, but I'm thankful we don't speak much other than to talk technique or baseball jargon. It's still a risky topic. If he turned to professional teams and discussing his favorite players, I'd have to walk away again. Thankfully, he doesn't because I've enjoyed myself. For the first time in a long time, I've had fun.

"I should probably be going," I eventually say as a sheen of sweat graces my brow, and I've already tucked my hair up into a band to keep it off my neck. Fine hairs still fall loose at the nape and curl in the Georgia summer heat. It's a nice night, but I'm warm, and it's getting late.

"Yeah, I need to get up early myself. I just needed the stress relief."

"Lots of pressure being a small-town mayor?" I mock.

"You'd have no idea," he mutters, and I feel guilty for picking on him and his community.

"I'm sorry. That wasn't nice of me to insinuate your job is small potatoes, or that this town is for that fact."

Charlie laughs again. "I'm not offended." He picks up the loose balls, then settles the bat and balls inside the bat bag and slings it over his shoulder. "Let me walk you to Cora's. It's dark out here."

"It's not that dark," I say, implying the brightness of these lights. Can my parents see us? Do these lights shine into the house? This court is closer than I thought to their home.

Charlie stops near the entrance and reaches for a switch in a metal box. Flipping it down, he turns the lights off with a click, submerging us in darkness. We hold still a second as our eyes adjust. The black settles around us as the song of the crickets increases in volume.

"What was that about darkness?" Charlie teases. I chuckle nervously, and he flips the switch again, the lights rushing back on. "Shit. I'm sorry again. I'm freaking you out, aren't I?"

My heart races, and my blood pumps, but I'm not as afraid as he might think. I'm turned on. Conscious of his nearness, the hint of sweat combined with the physical exertion has my body humming as I stand close to him, not aware that I stepped up to him when he shut off the lights.

"Jan?" he whispers, looking back at me, and I lick my lips. This is dangerous. I'm alone with a man when I haven't been alone with anyone in months. He reaches out for my arm, the touch meant to be reassuring, but my skin prickles the same as it does each time he touches me. I lick my lips again, and his eyes follow the trace of my tongue. He groans, and I don't know who moves first.

But suddenly his mouth is on mine, and my arms are around his neck.

The bat bag falls off his shoulders, clanging against the concrete court, then his arms circle my back.

Our mouths move like starved people, hungry for a taste of something they haven't ever had. Our teeth knock together.

"I'm sorry," I mutter at his lips, trying to pull myself back.

"Don't be," he says, still holding me to him and backing me up to the fence. His mouth crashes to mine again, and he reaches over for the light switch.

Click.

It's the crack of a bat. The sound of a gun. The start of a race.

Hands roam. Fingers squeeze.

He fumbles with my hair. I tug at his shirt.

He reaches for a breast. I grab at his dick.

We both moan.

"We shouldn't do this," he says.

"You're absolutely right," I reply, only my mouth keeps moving over his.

My skirt rises under his hand. His waistband lowers underneath mine.

His palm reaches between my legs, and mine slips into his shorts.

Fingers enter me, and I cry out, "Don't stop."

My hand tugs at him. "Harder," he commands.

We're all heavy breaths and teasing touches, and then my underwear falls to my ankles and his shorts slide down his hips. He's gone commando, so he's lined up at my entrance, and I'm squeezing the firmness of his ass with both hands.

"Are you sure about this?" he mutters.

"Don't you dare quit," I snap, desperate to feel him inside me, feel what he could do to me. I'm on edge. I'm on fire. I'm…so full as he thrusts upward, sliding easily into me. I coat him in my wetness, which practically drips down my thighs. I'm soaked and willing and want this more than I should.

We're total strangers.

I know nothing about him, yet this…this feels like I've been missing him my entire life.

Charlie grips the back of one thigh and hitches my leg higher against his hip. His knees are bent as he pummels into me, over and over, filling me with the roughness of his thrusts. The fence rattles at my back, setting a background beat to our sexing.

"Oh God," Charlie exhales into my neck, and my fingers clutch at his ass, holding him to me. The fingertips of one hand dig into my raised thigh, and his others clutch at a butt cheek. We slip, and we slide as my channel strokes at his length. I'm so close but not yet, and I'm afraid he'll finish before me. Richard always did, walking away satisfied before I was.

Fumbling in the dark, Charlie slips a hand between us. It's awkward and desperate, but he knows what he's doing as his fingers rub my clit.

"I…oh, God." *What's this?* I've never had it like this. He's moving within me and working the nub outside of me, and I'm a bundle of nerve endings ready to burst. "Right there, Charlie."

Stating his name brings his mouth to mine, and it's all over for me. I groan against his lips with his tongue in my mouth and his dick buried inside me. With the addition of those fingers… I'm just a puddle, melting as I come undone like I've never come before.

"Jan," he says, and I still, but he doesn't notice. He thrusts once, twice, and then halts, holding himself inside me, only one part of him jolting.

Reality returns to him slowly while I'm stiff as a board with my back to the fence.

My name. It's not right, but he thinks it's something else.

"Shit, I didn't use a condom." He nearly falls out of me, tugging free so quickly, I falter even with the fence at my back. His hand grasps my upper arm, but I shrug him off me.

I'm not upset with him. I don't feel violated. I'm not even mad at the lack of a contraceptive.

"I'm on the pill," I mutter, bending for my underwear and then stepping out of it altogether. I stand upright, feeling shame.

How could I do this?

And why did I like it?

I'll never admit the truth about any of it.

"Another bend and snap," he teases, but there's no humor in his voice as he pulls his shorts back into place and swipes a hand over his head, tugging at his ball cap. We can hardly see each other in the soft glow of the moon somewhere, and I wonder if it's for the best.

I reach up and snap my fingers in front of his face like a magic trick.

"Just the snap," I say in my best spooky voice as I slip through the open gate and run toward the coach house. I hear my name called out.

"Jan!"

It's all wrong.

Chapter 6
Office Antics

[Charlie]

I totally fucked up, but I loved fucking her. It's the first crazy thing I've done in years.

Uptight. Rigid. *Goody Two-shoes Charlie*. That was me. I always followed the rules. I always did what I was told. I wasn't spontaneous, which suited Angela just fine. We had sex penciled in on a calendar. No lie.

But what I'd done with Jan had been one of the most unplanned and unexpected acts of my life. It was incredible, and then she ran away.

Why did she do that?

Perhaps it was nailing her up against a fence, my brain scolds for the millionth time in three days. I haven't seen Jan anywhere, and any attempts I've made to walk the Lane down to Cora Conrad's have been thwarted.

Take this morning, for instance. I was hoping to slip out of the house earlier only to find Lucy and Vega sitting at the kitchen island eating breakfast.

"Hey, Dad," Lucy says to me as I stop at the sight of the two girls. They could be twins from the back with the same long dark hair and thin bodies. Only Vega has the permanent tan Lucy needs to work at with her paler skin.

"Good morning, ladies," I address them both as I cross the kitchen for the coffeepot. Rosa isn't present, but she's made quite the spread for these two girls. My lips curl over the edge of my coffee cup, but my eyes hover over the rim at Vega. With those bright green eyes, she looks just like her mother. Feeling me watching her, she looks up at me, and I clear my throat.

"Vega, how did get here this morning? Did your mother drop you off?" I hate that I'm fishing for information from a ten-year-old, but I'm curious. Not only how she got here so early but also where do they live.

Vega's brows pinch, another look so similar to her mother.

"I walked," she says like it should be obvious to me and as simple as that. She holds my gaze all innocent as if it wouldn't be miles from town or anywhere else for that matter.

"Walked from where?" I press.

"My grandparents' place." Her voice is light as she returns to her pancakes for another bite.

I stare at her, still wanting more details. I wait until she glances up at me again, and Vega tips her head.

"Rosa. Henri." She states their names slowly, almost like a question. "They're my grandparents. We live with them now."

If Rosa and Henri are her grandparents, and Jan is her mother, that means…

"You live here?" *Here, as in on my own property?*

My eyes drift to Rosa who stands just within the kitchen entrance from the back hallway. It takes another minute for things to settle in.

"Jan is your daughter?" My voice rises as I stare at Rosa, who rubs a hand over the towel wrapped over her arm. She's been my housekeeper for a dozen years. We don't speak about personal stuff although she knows almost everything about me. She mentioned something about her daughter coming to visit, but her name was not Jan, and Rosa certainly never mentioned she looked like she does. She also didn't mention she was staying long enough to seek a job, which suggests permanency.

Which also means she wasn't visiting Cora that night like I thought but heading to her home—*on my property*.

"Your daughter is Jan?" I repeat the question as Rosa's dark eyes shift to the side. Her hand increases the speed in which she strokes over the towel.

"My daughter is Nessa," Rosa corrects, and I recall hearing the name.

I glance back at the child. "I'm so confused," I admit, and the ten-year-old lowers her fork to her plate and bites her lips.

"My mother's name is Janessa. Nessa is her nickname. She wants to be called Jan since we moved here."

What the fuck?

My thoughts race back to the morning I found her in my room. *What was she doing in my room?*

"Does she work here?" I gasp, not meaning to sound offensive but knowing I do.

Oh, my God. This would be more than a sexual harassment complaint. This would mean sexual harassment *as her employer*. I had sex with her. I fucked her against a fence.

My heart races within my chest, and then I take a deep breath.

Wait.

Wait! my head screams.

We had consensual sex. She wanted me. I felt it. The way she clung to me. The way she clutched at my dick. The way she took me inside her.

I stiffen, and the wayward appendage stands at attention, rejoicing in the memories, but my heart squeezes in my chest.

She must hate me.

I scrub a hand down my face.

"Where's your mother now?"

"She got a job. Today is her first day," Vega announces, glancing over at her grandmother with a cautious gaze as though she might have told me too much.

Rosa proudly beams, continuing to explain what Vega offered. "She works for the town. She's the new Parks and Recreation person. She work for you, Mr. Charlie." Rosa smiles, pride in her broken English and excitement in her face as dread fills my belly.

I'm so fucked.

Yes, you were, and you enjoyed every minute of it.

+ + +

I need to rectify this. It's what I do best. It's why I'm a lawyer first and the mayor second. I need to mend.

"Charity, can you get Ms. Cruz to meet me in my office?" It's almost the end of a workday, and Charity will be leaving soon. I don't need her to overhear what I must say to Jan…to Nessa…to whatever the fuck her name is.

Charity enters my office a few minutes later. "I'm sorry, Charlie. She says she can't today." Her brow pinches. People don't normally deny me. The town council meets when I ask. I'm not domineering, but I'm also not denied.

"Call her back. As her new boss, tell her I demand it."

Charity's brow lifts as her hands wrap around the doorframe. She's giving me a quizzical eye while a small smile curls her lip. She's still looking at me after I've turned to my computer and then glance back at her from my desk.

"Charity?"

She blinks, clearing her focus and swiftly looking away. "Yes. Of course. You demand it." Smoothing a hand over her hip, she turns for her desk in the outer office and tugs my door closed behind her. Once she leaves, I fall back into my desk chair, which rocks and pivots. My sight falls to the open mini-blinds and the late-afternoon sunshine streaming into my office. I've been on edge all day, planning out my apology and how to diplomatically explain how what we did can never happen again.

Then someone walks into my office unannounced.

"Mr. Harrington," she states, a curtness to her tone as I turn to face her. "Sir."

Fuck. When she calls me that, I want to bend her over this desk. My eyes roam her body as I swing my chair to face her direction.

Goddammit, she's wearing the same skirt from the day of the interview. Cherry red and hugging her hips, it perfectly sculpts that fine ass I had my hands on the other night and tapers over her legs, one of which was hitched against my hip as I drove into her.

"Ms. Cruz," I say as I stand. "If that's really your name."

Jan's hands come together before her as she turns her head to glance over her shoulder.

"Close the door," I command. Her lips twist, but she steps back for it and presses it shut.

The sound of the click is like a shot in the dark. I race around my desk, rushing up to her and pressing her into the barrier.

"Who the hell are you?" I mutter as her backside rests against my front, and her hands brace up against the door.

"My name is Janessa… Janessa Cruz. It's my maiden name."

"Are you married?" I feel sick. *Dear God, don't let her have a husband.*

"Divorced."

Stepping back, I allow her enough space to spin and face me with fire in those green eyes. A forest fire has nothing on the scorch she's giving me.

"Your mother works for me," I state the obvious.

"Please leave my mother out of this," she says, her voice cracking. "She hasn't done anything wrong."

"Why were you in my bedroom?" I ask, finally hoping for an answer.

"Mami needed to take Papi to the doctor. She told me you weren't home and wouldn't know who picked up your room." Her head hangs a bit. Is she ashamed of her mother's profession? Is she embarrassed she cleaned my room? *Should I be?*

"Why did you lie?"

"I didn't lie."

"Oh, really, *Nessa*? Omission is the same thing."

She turns her head, so her eyes face the other side of the room. My fingers come to her chin and force her attention back to me.

"Don't look away from me. Tell me the truth."

"I'm divorced, like I said. Coming here was the possibility of a fresh start, so I shortened my name." She pauses as my eyes search hers.

What is she hiding from me? What is she hiding from herself?

Her chest heaves, and I hear the rustle of her loose blouse over her breasts. My fingers still pinch her chin.

"I like Nessa better. It suits you."

"You know nothing about me," she snaps without sass. Her tone is one of defeat. An animal trapped. I don't want to trap her. I want to help.

"I want to apologize. The other night—"

Two fingers cut me off as they cover my lips, and her eyes close. She swallows, and I watch the roll of her throat. Her neck. Her long, pretty, needs-to-be-kissed neck.

"Don't," she whispers. "Please don't."

"Don't what?" I ask, my voice dropping.

"Don't take it away. It won't happen again. Just… don't ruin what happened."

My eyes hold hers, feeling the same way. I don't want to ruin it. I don't want to forget it. And it definitely should not happen again, I think as my hand reaches around her for the doorknob, and I turn the lock in the handle.

Another click, and it's like a whistle blew. *Play ball!* We lunge for one another, mouths crashing and teeth colliding.

"Ow," she mutters against my lips.

"Sorry," I mumble, but her hands are already curling in the short length of my hair at the back of my head, and my hand slips down her back to her ass. "My God, you're fucking perfect."

She hums into my lips, and I tug her to me. Her other hand clutches at my dress shirt. I yank her shirt out of her skirt, my hand desperate to get to a breast. Fingers curl into the cup of her bra, and I tug it down under the soft material of her shirt. She bites at my lip, and I pinch her nipple. She yelps, and I swallow the sound, pressing her into the door at her back.

"We shouldn't be doing this," she mutters as her mouth comes to my jaw, and my fingers feel the weight of her heavy breast in my hand, voluptuous and spilling over the edge of my palm. I love it.

"We shouldn't be doing this *here*," I state, lowering my mouth for that throat and licking her skin before sucking at it. I'm aware of where we stand. In my office. A public office. My secretary is on the other side of the door, yet nothing could pull me away from the woman in my arms.

She groans as I nip at her neck. "You must be quiet," I warn, and she nods as her hands lower for my belt. My fingers reach for the hem of her skirt.

"It has to go down," she whispers as she sucks on my jaw.

"What?"

"My hips are too big. I can't tug it up. It has to go down," she explains as she pulls back, her eyes meeting mine for a second. I reach behind her and lower the zipper along her ass. Then I push at the two sides and look down to find the thinnest scrap of fabric covering her in a lace so transparent it hides nothing.

"You wear that under your clothing?" I didn't see what she wore the other night because it was too dark. Today, my office is bright, and I get a good look at what I missed the other evening.

"I like pretty things," she says softly, and my mouth crashes against hers for a second before I pull back and tell her, "You're a pretty thing."

Her eyes narrow at me. She didn't like that compliment, and to prove it, her hand slips into my pants, palming my dick, and then lowers to squeeze my balls. *Fuck, that feels good.*

"You're a pretty thing," she snaps, and I chuckle as she massages me. I unzip my own pants and lower them to my hips. With my other hand, I push aside the flimsy lace and shove two fingers into her. She gasps as I easily thrust into her. She's so freaking wet.

"Ready for me?" I tease.

"Been thinking of you for days," she admits, and I can't take it. It's been the same for me. My fingers slip out of her, and I grip myself, teasing her entrance as her hands slip to my ass. She squeezes, and I push into her, filling her to the hilt. In her heels, we almost match up. *Almost.* And fuck, does she feel good.

We thrust, and we rock, biting lips and whispering shushes. Our breaths catch as I hammer into her. She lifts a leg as she did the other night, and her fingers return to curl into my hair. I pick her up under her ass, and her legs circle my hips. Struggling to cross the room with my pants near my thighs, I set her on my desk and then press her back, leaning over her.

It's broad daylight, and I'm fucking her on my desk in my office.

It's insane, absurd, and totally out of character for me, yet I can't get deep enough, can't drive hard enough. I reach between us and stroke over the spot that made her wild the other night.

"I-I like that," she stutters as we rock on my desk. She reaches up for my shirt, fisting it in her fingers as her head lifts, and she stills.

"Charlie." My name is breathless on her lips as she falls apart around me, clenching me within her, and I break as well.

Holy shit. Stars dance before my eyes despite the early evening sun in the room. My arms shake, holding me over her. Our heavy breathing is the only sound in the room, and then a knock comes to my door.

"Charlie," Charity calls out. "Charlie, are you okay in there?"

"Shit," I hiss, withdrawing from Jan—*Nessa*—too quickly. A suction sound resonates, and Janessa pushes at my chest. Scrambling off my desk, she races to the other side of the room. Her heels still on. Her thong disappearing between two globes of perfection. She bends over for her skirt, and my dick is coming to life again.

I need to get it together, I think as she looks up at me, and I point at the bathroom off my office. My fingers fumble with my shirt, tucking it back into my pants and struggling to refasten my belt. I swipe a hand through my hair and then cross the room for my office door. Taking a deep breath, I smell the evidence of Janessa and me together, and I close my eyes for a second.

God, I like her.

"Charity," I say as I open the door. "Sorry about that. I didn't realize I had locked it." She attempts to peer around me as I hold my hand on the door. I only open it as wide as I can without releasing it, which prevents a view of the bathroom.

"I just wanted to let you know I was leaving for the night."

"That's fine," I say, my voice tight and a little too high. Her eyes search around me, her head tilting. "Is Ms. Cruz still here?"

As if on cue, the bathroom door opens, and Janessa walks out looking as if nothing happened. Her hair is up when it wasn't when she first walked in, but I don't think Charity will notice.

"Ms. Bernard," Janessa states, tucking a piece of hair behind her ear.

Charity's brow lifts. She totally notices the change. "Ms. Cruz," she replies, her voice curt and sharp.

"Mr. Harrington," Janessa addresses me, walking up to me and then brushing between me and the door to exit.

"Janessa," I whisper as she walks into the outer office, and I follow the sway of her ass in that damn red skirt and ignore the glare of my assistant drilling into the side of my head.

Chapter 7
Mothers and Daughters…
and Sons

[Janessa]

I cannot believe I slept with him again. And even though I'm giggling at first with what we just did, the tears follow as I sit in my father's truck on the street outside the office. My hands shake as I start the ignition and then pull into traffic. Blue Ridge isn't a busy town, but for a small community, there seems to be an awful lot of vehicles on the road. It's a reminder that one part of my job is to learn about the tourism industry here and market to it.

However, I can't think of anything other than Charlie's commanding voice, his tender touch, and then his thickness filling me like I've never been filled before. He's everything I've never had and should not desire. Smooth on the outside, he's domineering on the inside, and it's a turn-on when it should be a warning.

Richard was like that. He was full of charm and promises.

We'll look so good together, he told me. *We're a team.*

Only that team included other players—other women, specifically—and I'd been a damn fool to stay with him.

He promised he'd change.

He'd give them all up.

Well, mostly.

There was always a catch, a clause, an exception, and Richard worked every angle.

When we divorced, it was my fault. I wanted it, not him. However, he hadn't wanted our marriage either—the sacred vows of love, honor, and faithfulness.

I will not be a fool again, I tell myself as I turn onto Mountain Spring Lane—the Lane, as it is nicknamed by the locals—and park in the coach house driveway. The coach house is nothing to snuff at, but it isn't large enough for a family of four. My parents generously allow Vega and me to sleep in the second of two bedrooms on the upper level, but the quarters are tight all around. Sleeping in matching twin beds like teenagers, I feel sorry for my daughter more than myself. I love being close to her but as a ten-year-old, the last thing she wants is to share a room with me.

"We don't have any space here," she mutters as I enter the room. Our belongings are still primarily in suitcases and boxes. I didn't allow her to bring all her stuffed animals and toys. Not that she had many toys at ten, but the animals had been in abundance. Pity purchases. Richard buying the affection of our daughter when he missed yet another school activity or an important day in her life.

"Now that I have a job, we can unpack a little better," I assure her as I step to the small closet and realize we don't have much more room in there. I only brought necessities with me. I didn't want most of what Richard had purchased over the years. When the divorce was final, I hadn't gotten much. I only wanted Vega.

And a nondisclosure agreement that I would not specify I had sole custody.

This could ruin your reputation, his lawyer told him as if his adultering ways hadn't already damaged him. The press had caught him a few times with someone *not his wife*. The notion that he'd give up his child was damning, according to his publicist. Richard disagreed.

Giving up Vega was the only decent act Richard did.

Still, I didn't trust him.

You'll never belong to someone else, he warned me the night before we left. We'd been living in the same house despite the pending divorce. Richard didn't spend much time there anyway, but that night, he'd returned.

"Are we staying in Blue Ridge?" Vega asks me, her question full of hesitation.

"Don't you like it here?"

She shrugs as she looks out the window, which has a partial view of the tennis courts.

"Abuela and Abuelo are so happy we are here." As someone who grew up with my grandmother, I've often thought Vega was missing out on an experience as my parents lived states away and never visited.

"Mami and Papi," she corrects, referring to my parents with the same terms I use. I haven't kept up with her Spanish education. She can understand me when I speak my native language, especially if I scold her in the tongue, but she has not picked it up enough to be comfortable speaking it. "And I like getting to know them, but it's still not home."

Home. Houston. The lush mountains are a far cry from the bustling city in Texas. Strangely, I like the quiet and the slower pace here. It reminds me of Mexico with my own abuela.

"Baby, we can't go back," I tell her just as I tried to tell her when we left. It's going to be better this way.

Vega nods but lowers her head for the pillow in her lap.

"How was art camp?" I ask, hoping to change the subject as I examine the size of the closet and make a mental note of how it might work for us.

"We're learning folded paper art."

"Like origami?" I ask.

"Sort of, but it's more three dimensional. I can bring my project home in a few weeks." Her voice remains sullen especially on the word *home*. I step over my suitcase and around the bed to squat before her.

"You'll still have everything you had before. School. Art classes. Friends."

Vega nods, but it's not the same. She left her friends behind. "You like Lucy, right?"

"I do. It's just she has everything I used to have, and it's hard not to mention the things I left behind."

Ah, my girl is wise beyond her years. "You can tell her whatever you'd like minus Daddy." Vega isn't allowed to mention who her father is, which is a hard compromise for a child. His denial of her hasn't quite sunk in.

"He hasn't called me."

My lips roll inward as my brows pinch, and I squeeze her hands. He won't be calling. "I know, baby. He's working, remember?"

While she isn't allowed to talk about him, I've also kept it from her that he isn't allowed to talk to her. Due to the circumstances in which Vega last saw her father, his signing over full custody included no visitation or communication. I'll only have until the end of the season before my excuses run out for his lack of contact.

She nods as if she understands he's busy. He's been too busy for her in the past, but it still stings, I imagine, especially when *all that Lucy has* includes one doting father. On the other hand, Lucy's missing a mother.

"Do you know where Lucy's mother is?" I pry when I shouldn't be asking a child.

"She says her mother lives in Pennsylvania. She wants to run for president someday."

Oh my God, that's huge. "In the next election?" I question. It's an election year, and I can't recall all the candidates.

"Lucy doesn't really talk about her much. I don't know."

I stare at my child, taking in her bright eyes, which match mine, and her hair, which is also the same midnight color. What a powerful woman Charlie's ex-wife must be, which causes me to feel even more powerless. *I'm not hiding*, I remind myself. I just wanted a fresh start, but the reality sinks in as I squat between two twin beds in the room I'm sharing with my ten-year-old in my parents' borrowed home.

I'm definitely hiding.

+ + +

Elaina Harrington corners me one afternoon.

"Jan, you must come to dinner, and you can bring your daughter."

"Excuse me?" I'm completely thrown off by the invitation, especially as I know for a fact my parents have never been invited to dinner at the Harringtons. The *other* Harringtons. The ones who own

Giant Beer Company and employ a good portion of this town in their company.

I still where I stand. I'm on the edge of the property, near the fence surrounding the pool as I told Vega she needed to be home for dinner. She'd been spending a lot of time at the younger Harrington home, enjoying the pool and the comforts of a more spacious house, but I didn't want her getting any ideas. Their house is not ours. My mother works for Charlie as does my father.

"I'm having a little party for my son, George. Giant is what we call him, and I'd like you to attend. His girlfriend recently moved to town, and we'd like to give her a little welcome to the family party."

"That sounds very nice, but I'm not family," I remind her with a teasing but forced smile. *My parents are the help*, I grit against my back teeth.

"Oh, I know, but I'm also inviting a few other people, hoping to introduce Letty to women who might be future friends." Elaina smiles at me. "As you're also new in town, I thought you might be able to commiserate with her." She chuckles at her choice of words.

"Lucy will be there, and she's so bored when it's only adults. Charlie surrounds her with them. Bring your daughter with you so Lucy has someone to commiserate with her."

I haven't seen Charlie since our romp in his office. I've tried to avoid him since then because I knew without him telling me that we should not—would not—be doing what we'd done again. As a full-time employee under him as the mayor, I refuse to think of myself under him as a man. Or driving into me like I've never had before. *His desk.* My fingers twitch at my side, fighting the urge to fan my own face with the memory.

"I'll need to think about it," I say.

"Well, think quick. The party is tomorrow evening. Say six at our home. We're the next one over." She points in the general direction of her house as if I don't know she lives there. Perhaps, she doesn't know I live on Charlie's property in the servants' quarters.

Chapter 8
Dates with Blinders On

[Charlie]

"You did what?" I bark, and my mother looks up at me from where she's double-checking her hors d'oeuvres platters.

"I invited Alyce Wright to the party."

I know exactly what this means. My mother is trying to set me up. For years, after Angela, after the scandal, she let it go that I didn't want a woman in my life. The only girl for me was Lucy, but since she failed at linking Alyce to my eldest brother, Giant, she's moved on to me. Alyce is my younger sister Mati's assistant volleyball coach (she's now the head coach) and an English teacher at the high school. She's fun, sweet, and pretty, but she's not my type. I honestly don't think she wants to be linked to any of us Harringtons, but she hasn't found a way to say no to our mother.

"What happened to Billy?" I chuckle, knowing the brother closest in age to me was skipped in the make-Alyce-a-Harrington plan.

"He has Roxanne," my mother says, a smile in her voice at my brother's live-in girlfriend. They had a bumpy start to their relationship, but all is right with their world now.

"Before Roxanne," I grumble. Mother never tried to set Billy up, and even Giant dodged these awkward situations. Tonight, we celebrate his new girl who is here to stay.

"William was at no loss for women," Mother states, exhaling under her breath at the rumors of my brother's wayward history.

"What makes you think I'm missing out on women?" Instantly, Janessa comes to mind. I have been missing out. It's been a week since I've seen her. She's avoiding me, and with my schedule, that isn't hard to do. Her office is upstairs in my building, but still, we have not crossed paths.

"Do you have a woman?" My mother's brows lift as she glances up at me.

"No," I state emphatically just in time to see the woman I'd been thinking of seconds before walk into the kitchen.

"Janessa?" Her name is a breathless woosh of air from my lungs.

"Mrs. Harrington. Mayor." Her eyes drift from my mother to me and back to Mother. She's wearing a wrap dress that hugs every curve and curl of her body, and my fingers fist. I want to outline her form, trace every dip, and slip inside her again.

"Thank you again for the dinner invitation. Is there anything I can help you with?" Janessa's green eyes shift to the platters, but Mother shakes her head.

"We have servers for tonight," she says, rounding the counter and walking up to the beautiful woman who won't look at me.

"Sounds like more than just dinner," Janessa states, confusion on her face.

"It's a party," my mother responds excitedly. She *is* excited. My eldest brother has fallen in love again after a decade of mourning his deceased wife. "Come, let me introduce you to a few of the girls," Mother says, wrapping an arm around Janessa. Turning her toward the back hall, Mother leads her out to the patio where the party is set up.

I hang my head once they leave, feeling like someone punched me in the gut.

What is she doing here? And what is Mother up to?

"You look like you could use a beer." Billy's voice startles me as I didn't hear him come into the kitchen.

"I could," I say. *And keep them coming.* My brother Billy owns Blue Ridge Microbrewery & Pub, a local favorite and a nice tourist attraction. It's located on the corner of Main and Third, right in the center of downtown, and draws quite a crowd. It also sells the family heritage, Giant Beer, which is a bonus. I'm the one who broke tradition. Well, sort of the only one. My thoughts leap to James, the black sheep and missing member of the Harrington brothers, but I only think of him for a second. My history includes going to law school, moving to Philadelphia for a bit, and then returning to run this town, not the brewery and not an establishment supporting it. My parents are proud of me despite diverging from the family business.

In the long run, you running this town will benefit us, George Harrington Jr., my father, stated when I told him I planned to run for mayor. At first, the town didn't openly support me. They wanted someone older, old-school, and who had been a consistent member of the community. I won that first election by the skin of my teeth and the promise of a pending family. Angela was pregnant. But when I ran a second time, I almost lost the town's trust because of a few things I don't want to think about. No thanks to Angela. Charity Bernard's father was a huge help in that matter. I owed Ford Bernard, which is how the congressman business started.

I see bigger things for you, son. You've done great things, but you could do even greater things for our community by stepping up a notch, Ford told me in the beginning of the year. I've been blowing off decision-making. It's already June, and with elections in November, I'm taking a pass on it this year but haven't told anyone of my conviction.

Angela was the one interested in high-stakes politics. My ex-wife is up for re-election as a senator in Pennsylvania. Her campaign is not doing well. This reminds me I owe her a phone call about Lucy's hesitation for a summer visit. I sigh when I think of Angela.

"Here," Billy interjects, handing me a beer as I've been lost in my thoughts. "Did you see that hottie Mama's escorting all over the place?"

My eyes narrow at my brother. "Yeah, I've seen her."

"She has your name written all over her."

"What the fuck does that mean?" I say as I lower the bottle I just drank from.

"Curves for miles and a Jennifer Lopez vibe." Billy winks at me.

"Just because you had a poster of her as a teen on our wall does not mean I have an obsession with her," I clarify, reminding my brother of the room we shared.

"You sure enjoyed her, though." Billy holds a fist near his zipper and yanks forward a few times.

"William, don't show your brother how you play with yourself."
Ah, saved by Roxanne. Thank God.

"Hello, Roxanne," I say as Billy's girlfriend walks up behind him and wraps an arm around his waist. He slips his around her shoulders and brings her head to his for a temple kiss.

"I'd never show my little brother what you do to me," he teases, switching up what she said.

"You're incorrigible," she states, rolling her eyes at him.

"Incredible, you mean, and that's why you love me." He gives her another quick kiss, and it's all too much for me.

"Get a room," I mutter.

"Got one upstairs." Billy turns back to me. "With a poster for whenever you're ready to loosen up that tight ass of yours." Billy chuckles, and I shake my head. He's always been the crude one in the family. As for the tight ass comment, I'm used to that, and I hate it.

My ass is not tight, I think, which reminds me of Janessa's hands on it, squeezing and teasing, and holding me to her. I swipe a hand down my face.

Fuck, maybe I do need that poster for some relief after all.

+ + +

Eventually, we're called to an elaborate spread at my parents' elongated outdoor dining table with twenty plus people. It's a mix of my nieces and nephews, plus my siblings, their significant others, and my parents. Then there's Alyce, Janessa, and Vega, clearly outsiders to this gathering, and to my surprise, Ford Bernard, his wife Rebecca, and Charity. The Bernards are one of our oldest family friends, Ford being Dad's best friend.

Dinner proceeds with a toast to Giant and Letty, and their happiness. Letty recently moved to Blue Ridge with her baby son, and the potential for more grandchildren has my parents thrilled. We learn that Letty and Giant are to be married in the fall up on the ridge, and I'm pleased for my eldest brother. He desires happiness after all he's been through in his fifty years.

As dinner continues, my mother goes into full matchmaker mode with questions for Alyce, linking her answers to connections with me.

"You love sports, right? Charlie loves sports as well. He played baseball in college."

"You love to read? Charlie's an avid reader of nonfiction. He loves history."

"You love children? Isn't Charlie's Lucy adorable?"

It's so obvious and ridiculous. Poor Alyce. She wears a weak smile beside me, knowing the routine and also knowing we already know these things about one another. She isn't from Blue Ridge. Much like Janessa, her history is a mystery, but she's been here a decade and worked with Mati and the high school girls' volleyball team almost as long. She's more little-sister's-best-friend than of interest to me, but I humor my mother and try not to make Alyce feel any more uncomfortable than things already are.

The real discomfort comes when Ford Bernard asks if I've decided to run for Congress.

The table quiets, and I feel a pleased stare from my father and a concerned one from my mother.

"This could be just what the Ridge needs," my father states, the business wheels turning in his head.

"You're a real shoo-in for this, Charlie. You check all the boxes. We could use someone like you climbing the ranks," Ford adds as my father and him tag team.

There it is again. The political ladder, only I'm perfectly happy where I am. I have a good home, a solid job as both lawyer and mayor, and it makes Lucy happy to be here. My eyes seek hers, but her head is lowered to the table. She knows what it means if I accept. She's already been through it with her mother.

"I'm still undecided," I say, playing the political game, but Lucy looks up at me, her eyes pleading with mine. She won't tell me not to run, but she's already been through enough with Angela's previous campaign. My ex-wife's brand premise is that of a single mother, only she forgot to mention she hardly sees her daughter.

For some reason, I turn to Janessa next, who sits across from me, finding her gaze on me as well.

"It's a very public lifestyle," she states, which seems like an odd comment. She reaches for her glass of wine and lifts it to her lips. Whoever she is, she has grace. The few times I've watched her walk, she moves like fluid water. She drinks her wine like it's a seduction of the glass at her lips. Her throat rolls, and I remember sucking at the delicate skin. Her lips curl over the rim of the flute, and I wonder what they'd feel like wrapped around a hard and desperate part of me under the table. When she removes the glass from her mouth, her tongue peeks out to clear her lip, and I'm ready to burst. My skin crawls. My fingers twitch. I need to touch her.

"Charlie," my mother interrupts my thoughts. "Perhaps, you and Alyce could bring out more champagne. We have much to celebrate."

My eyes leap back to Janessa, and she smirks. She doesn't miss my mother's intentions. Turning to my mother, she asks about a restroom, and Mother directs her to one off the den or another one on the second floor at the top of the stairs. Janessa stands at the same time Alyce and I do, and Janessa's eyes meet mine.

"I'll grab that champagne," I tell my mother, stepping back from the table and allowing both women to step forward.

Chapter 9
Bathrooms Are Meant for Privacy

[Janessa]

What am I doing here? I place my hands on the second-story bathroom windowsill and gaze down at the pergola covered in wisteria and miniature white lights. It's a beautiful setting with a long dining table and a lovely family, celebrating the arrival of Letty Pierson and the question of Charlie's running for Congress.

I'm undecided, he said, but his brown eyes sparked in the candlelight of the table. He wants the challenge. If his ex-wife is a senator running for re-election, they must have been a real power couple when they were together. She was certainly not arm candy to him.

My eyes fall on Alyce Wright who re-enters the backyard. She isn't necessarily arm candy either, but rather small town in a sweet and bubbly, blond hair in a curly bob kind of way, and a smile that forces you to grin in return. She's nice and perfect for Charlie. And his mother knows it.

I sigh, pressing back from the window.

I don't need to be involved with him anyway. I wouldn't want the public exposure.

Still.

I like what I know of him.

He's devoted to his daughter as she's the first person he looked at when Ford Bernard mentioned Congress. Plus, I still remember him picking her up, soaking wet from the pool, and pressing her against his expensive, crisp suit without a care. He's athletic and sweet as I learned the night we had batting practice, and he cares about his community. He's a good man with a naughty streak.

My body hums as I recall him driving into me both against a fence and on his desk. I shiver and close my eyes. I need to stop thinking about him. I'm not the right person for him.

The doorknob of the bathroom twists.

"Just a minute, please," I call out, needing another deep breath before I face their beautiful family, sharing in celebration of one family member's happiness and hoping to settle another's—Alyce with Charlie as the next congressman.

Suddenly, the door unlocks from the outside, and it swings open.

"I said—" My mouth hangs open as Charlie presses the door inward and then reaches above the frame outside the opening, tucking something above the door's trim.

"When Mati took too long, hogging the kids' bathroom, we used this to pick the lock."

"That's so mean." I chuckle.

"That's what brothers do when they have a sister." Their sister isn't present at this dinner because she's on a summer road trip of a lifetime with her fiancé.

"What are you doing?" I whisper as his presence forces me back into the bathroom, and he closes the door behind him, locking it at his back.

"How are you?" he asks.

"Oh, now you want to speak with me?" Charlie hasn't said more than casual words to me all night. No matching of special interests like his mother so blatantly attempted with Alyce during dinner.

"You've been avoiding me as well." He glares at me.

I turn my back to him, looking out the window again but no longer close enough to see down into the yard.

"Charlie, we shouldn't do this," I whisper, crossing my arms around my middle. I feel the heat of his chest at my back as he steps up to me. He had a suit coat on earlier, despite the warm evening, but he's removed it and rolled up his sleeves to his elbows, giving off a more casual appearance around his family.

"What shouldn't we do?" he asks, his voice at my ear as his hands come to my hips. The material of my dress hugs my body. It's summer weight, so thin and smooth, and the warmth of his hands radiates through the fabric.

"Charlie," I murmur, closing my eyes as the tip of his nose drags around the shell of my ear.

"I shouldn't kiss you," he moans before his mouth comes to my neck. He brushes my hair aside, sucks at my skin, and I lean into him, melting a little at the soft suction.

"I shouldn't touch you," he growls as his hands skim over my belly and easily slip under the fold of my wrap dress, feeling the coolness of my skin under the heat of his palm. His hand lowers over my front and curls between my thighs, instantly finding the dampness which pools on my lacy thong.

"I shouldn't fuck you," he states, his voice deep and rough as he pushes aside the thin strap and shoves two fingers into me. I lurch forward, catching myself on the windowsill. Hidden by the plantation blinds, I force my backside against Charlie, and I gasp as his fingers invade me, filling me.

I shouldn't want this, but I do.

"Your family has plans for you." I state the obvious. Alyce. Congress.

"And I have plans for you." His belt unbuckles, and I close my eyes, hating that I want him so much.

"We shouldn't do this here," I whisper. His family is downstairs. They're probably waiting on him.

"Here is the perfect place. You're the perfect place," he growls as his hot tip slides between the seam of my backside over my dress. Heat simmers off him through the material until he lifts the skirt portion of my dress, flipping it up my back, and then settles just outside my entrance where his fingers still work me. His other hand curls over my exposed butt cheek, smoothing over the globe. His fingers twitch, and I wonder if he'll spank me.

"I think your mother has other ideas of perfect," I say, my breath still hitching with anticipation as he teases me.

"I don't want to discuss my mother right now," he groans, leaning forward and nipping at my ear.

"What do you want?" I question. Although I don't want his answer, especially if it involves Alyce Wright or being a congressman.

"This," he states, rapidly removing his fingers and then surging into me with his thick dick. I gasp as I pitch forward, but he catches me with an arm around my waist, tugging me back to him as he fills me. My backside hits his lower abs. He hammers back and forth, delving deep as we both struggle for air. His fingers return to my clit, and I whimper.

"Shh," he whispers. "You need to keep quiet."

I hate feeling as if I'm his secret, but then again, I know all about secrets as I'm keeping several from him.

He isn't wrong about haste and silence. I bite my lip and meet him thrust for thrust. He's the one losing his grip on noise as he grunts with each smack of our skin, and the suction of us working in tandem fills the small room.

"Nessa." When he whispers my nickname, I break, stilling over him as my orgasm rushes forward. My thighs clench together as my channel holds him in. Pistoning into me, he rubs against me in a most delicious manner that brings him to the edge. He slams into me one final time, and my hand slaps at the blinds for balance as he jets off inside me. We shouldn't keep doing this…any of it. No condoms. Random places. Delicious positions.

"Charlie, you didn't use a condom again." This makes three times, and I don't know why I'm mentioning it.

"You said you were on the pill."

"Yes, but aren't you worried about—"

"I'm not worried about anything," he cuts me off, suppressing my fear.

Both his arms wrap around my waist as he lowers his chest to my back in this bent position. His mouth comes to the nape of my neck, and he kisses me. Tender. Intimate.

"I've missed you," he admits, and my eyes close again. I've missed him, too, but I can't have him.

"We can't do this," I say, steeling my heart to his body wrapped around mine.

"You're right. It's dangerous with you as an employee."

That wasn't what I meant, but he stands and slips out of me. A cloth comes between my thighs as he cleans me. Once removed, I straighten my dress and turn toward him. He's tossed the towel into the bathtub, and he's already righting his shirt.

"I'll let you go first," he says, and my stomach roils. Am I his dirty little secret? He's keeping his eyes averted, and I wonder what his thoughts are. Does he really think I'm just a good fuck? An office dalliance? Is that all he sees in me?

I don't care, I tell myself as I brush past him and yank open the door.

"Well," Billy says, his eyes on me and then glancing over my shoulder.

"Fuck," Charlie mutters under his breath.

"What are you kids up to?" Charlie's brother asks as his girlfriend stands behind him. Roxanne McAllister has wild white and silver hair and these gray exotic eyes that soften as she looks at me. A hand covers her mouth as her fingers curl on Billy's shoulder.

"Billy," she warns.

"What are you doing up here?" Charlie asks, a grizzly grumble to his tone.

"Seems I have the same idea as you," Billy teases. "I'm getting a room like you suggested."

"William," Roxanne gasps, swatting at his back as she presses her forehead against his shoulder.

"Billy," Charlie warns. "It isn't what you think."

I hold my head higher and draw my shoulders back as Roxanne lifts her head and meets my eyes. It's exactly what they think, sort of. My eyes shift to the side, unable to face her or my shame for more than a second.

"Charlie," Roxanne softly admonishes.

"If you'll all excuse me," I say, stepping into the hall without any other explanation. Billy steps to the side, Roxanne following his movements.

"Didn't need that poster after all, did ya, big brother?" Billy teases behind me as I round the bannister and step down the first stairs. I have no idea what he means.

"You're an ass," Charlie states somewhere above me as I descend.

"Nah, seems like you are," Billy says to his brother, and I bite my lip to prevent the hysteria bubbling inside me. Laughter would be preferable to the tears stinging my eyes, but neither action seems acceptable.

Chapter 10
Walkability

[Janessa]

I don't have a choice but to face Charlie a few days after the romp in his parents' bathroom. He's my boss, and I have things to discuss with the town council.

"As I said, I've run some numbers, and I'm proposing a one-million-dollar venture for a walking trail."

"A million dollars to walk along the woods?" Wyatt Hubner states. He's a portly older man who remembers the good ole days when men were men and women stayed in the kitchen. He has definitive views, and one of them is that the town does not need any exercise landscape.

We have thousands of acres of wildlife around us. Why do we need a damn park?

"Walkability is—

"Walka Billy who?" Wyatt interjects.

"Walk*ability* is a means of transportation by making a city more walkable," I explain. "Walking is good exercise." I tip a brow at his weight, and he blushes. "The budget is actually a modest estimation, but it could yield double that in revenue for local businesses. I've researched similar sized towns for comparison. In addition, I'm recommending a community center. You don't have one here, and there's an old church—
"

"A church?" Bryce Norton snorts. Bryce is a decent-looking man, roughly in his forties, but I have yet to learn what exactly he does in the community. "You can't make a church into a playground."

"I'm not suggesting a playground within the church but perhaps outside of it. The First Church just outside of town happens to be for sale, and—"

"How can a church be for sale?" Gretchen O'Leary interrupts. She's a friend of Elaina Harrington, and her presence on the town council results from being a wealthy woman without much else to do with her time. Her family owns the local funeral home. The congregation of First Church inherited land upon the death of a well-to-do parishioner, and the worship community decided to build a larger, more accommodating facility on the donated property. The former church is now up for sale. Well, the property at least, but the building is still a decent structure.

I ignore Gretchen and continue. "Based on its location, it's just off the town proper and an excellent place to start the trail as well as become a community center. It's a beautiful structure but in need of some TLC and—"

"And who is going to provide the tender loving care?" Wyatt huffs.

"There's a major construction company in town. Duncan Construction. They also own Duncan's Hardware and Lumber." I'm stating facts the council members already know.

"We are not putting a town project into that three-ring circus," Gretchen comments, and I'm lost. I glance at Bryce for clarity.

"Milton Duncan is Rehab Dad."

I stare at him. "Who?"

"*Rehab Dad*. It's a television program on HGTV. Milton Duncan along with his brother, Griffin, fix up old homes or foreclosed properties and broadcast the progress," Charlie explains without glancing in my direction. Stating this information flatly, he continues to gaze down at a pad of paper resting on his lap. He sits casually with an ankle crossed over his knee, and his tone suggests I'm ridiculous for not knowing they have a budding celebrity in their town.

"Like *Nailed*?" I question, mentioning a famous home improvement program, and Charity nods without glancing up at me. "Maybe Mr. Duncan will donate his time," I state, sitting straighter in my seat.

"We aren't a charity case," Scarlett Nugent comments, speaking for the first time.

"I didn't mean to imply we were."

"*We?*" Charity Bernard mutters under her breath, emphasizing my newness with a snort or perhaps because I'm an outsider. I'm beginning to think Sally Maywood, the person who held this position prior to me, wasn't antiquated in her ideas but hit with stumbling blocks at any suggestion she made for recreational improvement. I glance back at Charlie for support, but he doesn't look up, and I'm baffled. Proud of his town, he's the one wanting interactive improvements.

Whatever's on that damn piece of paper must be fascinating.

He hasn't looked at me during most of this meeting, and I'm actually surprised he's present. Town council issues don't necessarily dictate the mayor's attention, but then again, he seems to be everywhere. As this is a budget and proposal meeting, I suppose it makes sense he's here, but I wish he wasn't. I wish I didn't have to feel him ignoring me or fight how I want to ignore him…and lose the battle. My eyes drift to him again, but then I notice Charity Bernard staring at me.

She's a bland woman with brown hair and blue eyes. Her outfits scream uptight. I suppose with a name like Charity, she's sweet at the core. As one of three Bernard sisters—Faith, Hope, and Charity—I met her father the other night at dinner at the Harringtons. Ford Bernard not only owns a local Christmas tree farm but he's also a prevalent judge in the area. He wanted boys, and that's evident by the way he moseyed up to Charlie at dinner the other night. He wants a congressman from this community, and if I'm not mistaken, he has his sights set on his daughter being a congressman's wife.

I ignore the heat of Charity's stare and the coldness of Charlie, returning my attention to Wyatt, who is still complaining about the money.

"I think one way to find money in the community is to have a fundraiser. Perhaps a charity walk, where the money is a donation to the new walking trail in the name of the donating town member. Participants would earn a brick in the walk as commemoration of their generosity."

I pause.

"Being as you aren't from here, who would you suggest we name the community center after?" Charity Bernard questions, and I wonder if it's typical for the mayor's assistant to be present at a meeting. Then again, she is taking copious notes on all that's said, but her question is meant to stump me and remind me that I'm *not* from her precious town.

"Well, we could leave that up to a town vote. Suggest names. Maybe Sally Maywood as she was the Parks and Recreation Facilitator for decades." This has Charlie's attention. "Or perhaps a youthful community member, maybe someone special."

The silence in the room grows heavy, and I fear I've suggested the wrong thing. Charlie lowers his head, no longer scribbling or doodling or whatever he was doing on the paper before him but flattening his palm and resting it against the paper while he stares at his fingers.

"It's just a suggestion," I mutter, hoping to defuse the thick tension and move on.

"A walking trail, a community center, *and* a playground area?" Charlie lists, and I hold my breath. "And each named after someone?" He's clarifying, like a checklist of my suggestions. "And all this for a million dollars? It sounds a bit ambitious." Charlie isn't exactly cold but detached as though he wasn't altogether listening, and he's trying to catch up.

"Well, potentially. It might cost more. It might cost less." My vague answer is met with a distant stare from him. "Of course, I can look into this more. Once the town approves a plan to move forward, we will have better estimates." We'll need a landscape architect to draw plans and suggest a budget. I've researched several potential prospects, but their fees can run steep. A man in Missouri looks the most promising.

Charlie nods, glancing back at the pad of paper before him, and then notices the time on his watch.

"Ladies and gentlemen, I suggest a lunch break. Let's think about this and reconvene after the holiday."

Charlie means the Fourth of July, which is in a matter of days. What am I supposed to do in the meantime? I suppose I'm to go back to my office and stare at the summer schedule already decided for the community. *Back to the kitchen*, like Wyatt might want of a woman. I thought Charlie was more progressive than this, but I feel wrong about him on many levels.

After we'd been caught in his parents' bathroom, he ignored me more than ever despite all he'd said in the bathroom. As soon as I could, I made an excuse for Vega and me to leave, and I didn't look back. With damp panties and a rumpled dress, I did the walk of shame once again.

As we stand to break for lunch, I'm gathering my things, although admittedly I don't have a good grasp on them. I'm balancing a notebook on top of my closed laptop with pens in one hand and a diet soda in my other. I've just collected everything when Charlie's nephew and law partner, Jordan, enters the conference room.

"Did you hear the news? Richard Swank just got traded to Atlanta." His excitement is lost on me as the pens slowly trickle to the floor. The notebook slides next as my laptop slips forward. In a comical reaction of trying to catch the notebook while still holding something else in my opposite hand, my diet soda releases. As I bend forward in hopes to recover it, the laws of physics somehow keeps it upright, landing with a thunk, and the carbonated drink pops upward like a Mentos candy fountain, spraying my chest with cola.

For a moment, I remain bent over, my chin dripping, and my blouse soaked, but I can't even consider my condition. I've broken out in a full-body tremble. My fingers visibly shake as I reach for the overflowing soda can and the pens scattered on the floor.

"Janessa?"

My eyes close. This can't get any worse, but with witnesses to my mess—both physically and mentally—this is one of the most embarrassing positions I've ever been in.

A hand comes into my view and picks up the sticky soda can, and I slowly swipe at my face.

"Janessa, are you okay?" Charlie's voice softens as I look up at him, lifting as though I've strained my back. I shake my head once on instinct instead of fighting the response. Charlie's brows pinch, and my head continues to shake, hoping he takes it as a dismissal of his question instead of an admission of my emotions.

"I'm so clumsy," I say although I've never been. My teeth chatter, and the reality of the cold soda dripping down my neck hits me.

"Come here," Charlie says, setting the soda on the conference table and placing an elbow at my arm. He guides me to his office, excusing himself from his law partner. I'm holding the laptop to my chest like a shield.

I should go to my office.
I should get a new shirt.
I should leave Georgia.

Charlie stands before me once his office door is closed. Two large hands grasp my upper arms.

"You're shaking. Is the soda cold?" He chuckles softly, but it isn't that. When I look up at him, his eyes widen for a second, reading something in my expression. "Actually, you're trembling."

He steps away from me, making quick work to open a closet and pull out a dress shirt on a hanger. Walking back over to me, he removes the laptop from my clutched hands and begins to unbutton my white blouse—a new shirt now ruined by my mishap. I don't have money for mistakes like this. New clothes are frivolous but also necessary with new employment.

"Charlie," I whisper.

"Let's just get this off." He diligently returns to removing my shirt, stroking the wasted material over my neck and upper chest to remove the sticky residue and then helping me into his own dress shirt. He rolls the sleeves to my elbows and then ties the longer flaps at my waist.

"Thought I might like you in my clothes," he mutters, but I close my eyes. I can't do this with him. My mind races with images of Richard.

Instantly, I'm pulled into Charlie's chest, inhaling the scent of him. Woodsy and athletic. My arms dangle at my sides until Charlie lifts one for his shoulder and the other for his neck. I'm scooped up, cradled to his chest, and I melt against the warmth of him. If only he could protect me, keep me safe, but I know better than to rely on a man. Too many promises from Richard. Too much evidence to the contrary.

"What is it?" Charlie says as he sits on the couch in his office with me on his lap. I'm still wrapped around his neck, and I settle there, telling myself I'll only take a minute. I'll soak all this up and pretend he cares.

"Tell me what happened. You're still trembling, and you look like you've seen a ghost."

I shake my head in the crook of his neck. I can't tell him. Slowly, I loosen my hold on him, but he catches me on my sides, his hands near the swell of each breast. A hand lifts, and he cups my chin, tipping it upward so I'm forced to look at him. His eyes search mine, shifting from one to the other, and then he leans forward, kissing me with the most tender of kisses. Like a flower petal drawn over my skin. Like a butterfly tickling my wrist.

He leans back.

"Just relax," he says quietly. "Whatever it is, you're okay."

My eyes widen for a second as if he can read my thoughts, my concerns, my fears. The hand on my chin moves to my bare knee, the hem of my skirt riding up a bit as I sit on him.

"Charlie," I whisper again, uncertain if it's a plea or a warning. His hand slips between my thighs, fingertips moving in a circular motion, massaging gently at my skin.

"Relax," he says again. His voice remains steady and soothing as his hand glides up my inner thigh. "Let me help."

I don't need help, I want to retort, but my tongue can't form the words. My lids feel heavy. My core pulses. My legs separate the slightest bit, allowing Charlie's hand room to move.

"That's it, sweetheart. Let me in."

My eyes close completely as Charlie's mouth comes to mine, tender once again. His fingers inch forward and swipe over the dampness of my underwear. I should curse him for what he's doing, curse my reaction to him, but I'm weightless at the moment. I'm drifting, and Charlie is steering me. A finger curls inside the fabric of my panties and slips inward. I can only spread so far with the tightness of my skirt, and the constriction adds to the pleasure.

"Charlie," I purr as he takes his time to dip into me and then draw back. Reaching for my clit, he drags a finger over the sensitive nub before diving back into me. He repeats the movement several times, and my head lowers for his shoulder as I continue to breathe him in.

"Let me do this for you," he says, taking his time to calm me into a sweet climax and rid my thoughts for a few minutes. "Give this to me, sweetheart."

The gentle tone but commanding words brings me to a sweet release. One where my knees clamp together, trapping Charlie's hand between my thighs and his fingers inside me. I rock over them, relishing every drop and drip until I'm replete.

"That's it, sweetheart," he coos at my ear as my arms clutch around his neck, holding me in place against him.

When I finally settle, my knees open, and Charlie removes his hand. Lifting his fingers to his mouth, he sucks on them.

"I haven't had the pleasure yet," he states, licking his fingers while lifting a brow, insinuating his mouth hasn't been near my center. "I can't wait for the day when I can."

"Charlie," I mutter again, letting my hand slip down his chest as I move to sit upright. His hand comes to my upper arm, holding me still on him.

"When will that day be, Nessa? Because as much as I try, as much as I tell myself to stay away from you, I just can't." His mouth lifts for mine again, taking his time to savor me like the delicate way he just touched me. "Let me see you somehow."

"We both know that's not a good idea," I tell him, stroking a hand down his handsome face.

"What happened before?" His head tips toward the door to the conference room.

"Oh God," I mumble, struggling to pull myself from his lap. Did he lock the door? Someone could have walked in. Someone might have seen us. Someone would…tell Richard.

Once standing, I look down and see what I've done to him, his thick erection bulging in his suit pants. "Charlie, I…"

He holds up a hand. "That was all for you," he says. Leaning forward and placing his elbows on his knees, he looks up at me, those dark eyes filling with concern.

"Let me in," he whispers, but I shake my head.

"I can't," I say, and then I turn for my laptop, swipe my ruined shirt from the chair where Charlie set it, and exit his office through the conference room without looking back.

Chapter 11
Fourth of July

[Charlie]

Nowhere celebrates America on the Fourth of July better than small towns with parades honoring the local celebrities, first responders, and prominent townsfolk along with school sports teams and community groups. Blue Ridge is no different. Along Main Street, our proud parade proceeds with children on bikes and scooters or wagons pulled by parents weary in the heat, signaling the end of the festivity. The thought of a cool community center at the end of the route makes me consider Janessa's proposal for a community center and central park.

It's only been a couple of days since she ran out of my office with no explanation of what upset her. Jordan simply mentioned Richard Swank, a famous center fielder, being traded to Atlanta, and she dropped everything. My gut says something about the name unsettled her, but as I haven't seen her, I haven't had the chance to ask. I could walk myself over to the coach house, now that I know she lives there, but for some reason, I hesitate. I want her to open up to me. I want her to come to me with her secrets. And my gut also tells me that isn't going to happen.

After the morning parade, an adults versus teens baseball game is played on the ballfields near the high school, and my thoughts drift again to Janessa and her town plan. A casual field centrally located would be more inviting to locals and visitors alike. It's here that I find Janessa on the sidelines after missing her at the parade.

"Nice home run, Mayor," she teases me, her smile genuine but her eyes sheepish. I don't want to think about her walking out of my office the other day. I just want to soak up this smile. She's on one side of the fencing bordering the ballfield while I remain on the inside, but my eyes check out her outfit now that she's so close to me. White shorts hugging those hips, accentuating her booty, and a red shirt with a miniature

American flag stretches over her ample breasts. My mouth waters at her patriotism.

"You saw that, huh? How was my batting stance?" I question, and her cheeks pinken, hopefully recalling the first night we were together. Batting practice. Sex against the cage. Me inside her. Those are the thoughts I want in her head, not whatever startled her the other day.

"You have nice form, sir." My own smile matches hers. I like her like this.

"Good game, Dad."

"Thanks, Pint," I say to my mini-me who has rushed up to the fence next to Janessa.

"Dad, can Vega come to the fireworks with us?" Lucy turns to Janessa. "You can come, too. Both of you."

Huh? "Maybe they have plans with their own family tonight, Pint." There are a variety of places to view the fireworks over Bolton Lake. My family has their sacred spot, and I appreciate the privacy because it allows me a few minutes to enjoy the meaning of the holiday without any fanfare or the prying eyes of the town.

"Actually, we don't have plans, but I don't want to intrude on your family time," Janessa says, reaching out to cup my daughter's chin. The touch is tender looking and intimate, and I watch as Lucy beams up at this woman we don't know well. Janessa's soft expression and the heat in Lucy's cheeks tell me my daughter doesn't know how to respond to the affection despite the attention of myself and my family, especially my mother. Lucy isn't for want of love, but watching this woman stroke the face of my child reminds me my daughter doesn't have a mother's touch in her life.

Janessa releases Lucy's face and reaches for her own daughter, stroking a hand down the length of one of two braids in her hair. It hits me then that both girls wear a complicated yet similar set of braids in their hair.

"You two look like twins," I interject, staring from one girl to the other with their matching dark locks.

"We could be." Lucy giggles. "Remember we have the same birthday."

"Well…" Janessa smiles, biting her lips. "That really wouldn't be possible, but today you're the star-spangled twinsies."

Lucy swipes her hand down one braid dangling over her shoulder. "Miss Cruz did our hair, Dad. Isn't it cool?"

"Yeah, cool, Pint," I answer, lowering my voice as my fingers curl into the fencing. I want to touch her. I want to draw her into me and thank her for putting a beaming grin on my child's face.

"So, Dad, fireworks?" Lucy prompts, and Janessa looks up at me.

"You don't have to—"

"Why don't we pick you up at eight. Is that too late?" I suggest.

"Yes, Dad. Have them over for the cookout first?" Lucy presses.

"The cookout is Gran's party, honey. Not mine," I remind my child, wishing I could just include two more people to the guest list, but sensing Janessa might not be comfortable with the invitation.

"We already have plans with my parents for dinner, so it's no big deal," Janessa offers, a hint of letting me off the hook to Lucy's pressure. I've never had Rosa or Henri over for dinner. While I adore both of them, respect them for their hard work, and appreciate their dedication to Lucy and myself, I don't interact with them other than as boss and employer. Guilt taps at my chest. They're practically a second set of grandparents to Lucy, a pair she doesn't have on her mother's side. I'd love to toss up the entire holiday and tell Janessa to bring her parents to my place and shift the cookout there, but I can't upset my mother. This is her holiday, like all the rest, and it's the one day Giant lets Mother fuss because of his military history.

"How about seven? It's early, but we could take dessert and drinks to the lake."

"Yes," Lucy says with a bumped fist and a little tug at her side. Vega holds up her hand, and the patriotic twins high-five.

Janessa looks up at me, and whispers, "Are you sure this is a good idea?"

"As your mayor, I'm deeming it your patriotic duty to spend the evening with me." I wink, and she fights the curl of her lips. She's *so* beautiful. I couldn't have expected this evening, and I'll need to secretly thank Lucy somehow for swinging this date even though it's not really a date.

Just a man and his child spending time with a single mother and her own kid.

Yeah, and I have a mountain peak property to make me rich.

Still, I'm excited for tonight.

"See you at seven," I say, pushing off the fencing.

"See you then," she says, placing an arm around both girls and leading them off for ice cream.

+ + +

We agree to take Henri's truck instead of my car as the girls convince us that the truck bed will be a fun place to hang out. Janessa says her father won't mind, and she allows me to drive as I know the location of the private trail leading to the edge of the lake.

A beautiful large body of water just outside the town proper, Bolton Lake is the safest place on a warm night to set off fireworks. There's a public beach packed with viewers and tons of private parties held at homes surrounding the lake. Our spot is no different other than there is no home here. My mother inherited a strip of land that my parents never built on but also never had the heart to sell despite the fact that lakefront property is a commodity. I explain all this as we pull through the thickly covered archway into the clearing and park with the bed to the lake.

"Tailgater," Lucy yells, scrambling from the truck, and I shake my head, curious how my girl knows such a term.

"Uncle Billy told me that's the name of a party at a football game."

Thank you, brother Billy for corrupting the youth of America so young. I head to the back of the truck and tip down the gate while Janessa flings a couple of blankets over the metal lining.

"Dad, can we swim?" Lucy asks, bouncing on her toes. I'd forgotten all about suggesting suits, and I look up at Janessa.

"Vega has hers on. Lucy told her to wear it."

"That lake is mucky at first," I warn Lucy who doesn't like the feel of the squishy bottom on her toes, but I'm not prepared to enter the water myself. Not unless it involves skinny dipping and only Janessa and me, alone.

Lucy waves a hand at me as though it's no big deal when I know it is, and both girls give off squeals of disgust as they hit the water's edge.

"She's been such a good friend to Vega. She needs that," Janessa says as we watch the girls make their way to the deeper water.

"It's difficult for Lucy sometimes as the daughter of the mayor. She takes on the pressure of being my right-hand girl when she's still a child and not my partner. You've probably heard my ex-wife is in politics, and sometimes I worry I'm no different than Lucy's mother: the single parent in politics brand." I snort, hating the comparison but riddled with guilt that some days I might cross the same line as my ex.

"Charlie, how much you love your child is written all over your face. No one would doubt your intentions."

I look over at her from our seat on the edge of the tailgate. Her long tan legs stretch forward, ankles crossed and knees bending as she swings them back and forth. Her hands curl over the edge of the metal.

"What happened to Vega's father?"

"Charlie," she whispers.

"Why won't you talk to me?"

"I just…I don't want to ruin tonight," she says, letting out a breath of exasperation.

"I don't want to ruin anything either. I just want to get to know you. I want to understand."

"There's nothing to understand," she says, looking over her shoulder at me, those green eyes suddenly sad instead of sparkling. My shoulders fall. She's right. I don't want to ruin tonight. I want to enjoy ourselves.

"Maybe one day, you'll let me in," I whisper, and she leans to the side, bumping my shoulder with hers.

"One day. Maybe." Her teasing tone does nothing to reassure me, but after a few awkward moments of silence, I ask another question.

"Tell me your favorite Fourth of July memory," I state. If she won't tell me about her current history, maybe she'll at least tell me a bit about her ancient past. We laugh together as we share stories and recall things no longer done. We chuckle over things like rotary phones, long curly cords, and having to share phone time with siblings. We laugh about outdated clothing and how cool we both thought we looked, and we even share a memory of fated dates. Bad kisses. Missed opportunities. Thankful escapes.

"God, I hope I never disappoint you like that," I say after she tells me about one awful evening back in high school.

"I don't think you'd ever disappoint, sir," she says, turning her eyes to me. The corner of my lip curls upward.

"I strive to always satisfy," I state, and she bursts out laughing.

"That was really cheesy, Charlie." While it might have been, I'll take her reaction—the deep sound of her laughter—over and over again, giving her a million cheesy lines just to hear the richness of her. While the girls swam, we moved closer and closer to one another on the tailgate, our thighs pressing together. My hand behind her backside as I lean back. But when another vehicle pulls through the heavy brush, followed by a second one, our private time is over, and Janessa scoots away from me.

Instantly, I want to tell her to come back to my side. I have nothing to hide. I want to be with her, but something holds her back. I don't have time to question it as Billy and Roxanne exit his truck, and Giant and Letty hop out of a Giant Beer Company one. Moments like this make me miss James, even if we didn't always get along. Even my sister, Mati, is missing this year as she travels across country with her new man.

After handshakes, back pats, and hugs, I'm reintroducing Janessa to the group, and then Lucy and Vega appear, shivering and soaked from the lake.

"Where's Sadie?" Lucy asks of her cousin, and Billy groans.

"On a date, honey," Roxanne offers, and Billy exhales.

"Just you wait," my brother warns me as Janessa wraps Lucy and Vega in towels.

"Vega can't date until she's thirty-five," Janessa teases, hugging her child to her.

"I tried that one," Billy grumbles.

"Up it to thirty-seven and it might stick," I joke. Roxanne shakes her head, stroking a hand up Billy's back, and he cups the back of her neck, pulling her forward for a kiss. I want to kiss Janessa like that, open and out in public. I want to mark her before all of them. Giant's next, showing off his affection for his soon-to-be wife by wrapping his arms around her from the back and placing his hand on the baby in her arms. They make a nice family, and I sense how much I've missed out on. I never had that with Angela—a real family bond, a sensing of belonging—and I want it. I want a wife for me and a mother for my child.

My eyes drift to Janessa, watching her fuss over both girls, helping them dry off and then swearing she'll protect the front seat while they change and make sure no one looks at them in the cab while they struggle into warmer clothing.

"You've got it bad, little brother," Billy teases, handing me a beer. Roxanne walks over to Janessa, adding herself to the shield of protecting two ten-year-olds changing in a truck.

"I don't know what you're talking about," I say as Giant approaches the tailgate where I sit.

"Yeah, he didn't know what he was talking about either," Giant guffaws, picking on Billy and his denial of Roxanne before they finally got together.

"Look who's talking, Mr. Grumpy Big Giant and his years of celibacy," Billy groans at our eldest sibling.

"You were spreading yourself enough for the three of us," Giant reminds him, and I cringe. My brother was a bit of a player before Roxanne settled him.

"Yeah, well, there comes a time…" Billy begins.

"You mean, there comes a woman," Giant corrects.

"And you just want the one," Billy says, looking up at his speaking about Janessa.

"And it feels damn good, don't it?" Giant softly states, a smile in his low voice.

"The best," Billy whispers, and I hate them both.

"I hate you two. You sound like fucking chicks."

"You need to fuck a chick," Billy says, leaning forward and lifting a brow. "Then again, I know you already did that."

My fingers curl into fists around the edge of the tailgate, and I want to crack my brother over the head with my beer bottle. "Keep your voice down," I shush him.

"No shame in wanting her," Giant says, catching my eye.

"Well, she'd have to want me, and she doesn't," I whisper, looking briefly over my shoulder and catching Janessa looking in my direction.

"Oh, she wants it," Billy drones. "She wants it bad."

"You just shut it, William Forrest," I warn, sounding like Mama when she gets mad and reminding them of myself when I was younger.

"I have faith in you, kid," Giant states as if I'm still a child. "You'll come up with a plan. You always do." He winks at me as though he understands all my secrets, but I don't know what he's talking about. Roxanne and Janessa return to the back of the truck while the girls walk to Giant's to fuss over Finn, Letty's baby, and the night settles into casual teasing and soft laughter until the fireworks begin.

When Janessa settles next to me on the tailgate again, we're no longer touching in any manner, but I feel her presence. The heat of her. The spark of her skin when we connect. I almost taste her on my tongue, and I realize my brothers aren't wrong.

I have it bad, and I need a plan.

Chapter 12
Meeting Room Meetups

[Janessa]

During the night of the fireworks, Roxanne invited me to join her and a few girls the next night at Blue Ridge Microbrewery & Pub. When I arrive, the place is packed.

"Wow, this is a popular place," I say, taking my seat and trying to ignore my nerves at the crowd of people. I never worry about being recognized. I'd need to be next to Richard to be noticed. It was always a strange dichotomy. On my own, I don't stand out. I'm one of those people who look familiar, but you can't place me. With Richard, people remembered my name, let their eyes roam, and made lewd suggestions. And while Richard appreciated the appraisal, as I was the one on his arm, he raged inside with fear that I'd take another man's offer.

If you ever tire of him, feel free to pay me a visit.

Yeah, that would never happen.

"Most popular place in town," Alyce Wright states. Alyce, Grace Eton, and Roxanne are all present as I was running a few minutes late. I don't want to dislike Alyce. It isn't her fault Elaina Harrington wants to set her up with one of her sons. After a waitress takes my drink order, I quickly learn the history of how the matron of the Harrington family has been dragging poor Alyce to dinner after dinner.

"It isn't that I don't like the boys," she says of the grown men. "It's just…we don't have anything in common other than I'm friends with their sister." Alyce is the new head coach of the girls' volleyball team at the high school after the previous coach—aka Mati Harrington, the only sister in the clan—took a job coaching at the college level. I'm all for women's sports, so I liked Alyce even more when I learned this about her at dinner a week or so ago.

"Roxanne already knows their mama never tried to set me up with Billy," Alyce clarifies for me as I feel awkward on Roxanne's behalf learning about this relentless Southern mother.

"No, *my little sister's best friend romance* for you, huh?" Grace Eton teases. Grace works at the bookstore owned by Roxanne—BookEnds—and both women somehow managed to come out tonight.

"I don't really believe in romance," Alyce comments with a dry chuckle, and I notice the edge in the sound. My eyes leap up to her face, which lowers for the beer before her. Her hands slip up and down the mug. "So Jan, how do you like Blue Ridge?"

I hadn't corrected the women with my name yet, becoming more comfortable with the nickname.

"I like it just fine." I smile at Alyce, who mimics mine as I've taken her hint to change the subject. "I'm thinking of enrolling my daughter in elementary school."

"With your new job, I didn't realize you were considering leaving?" Roxanne questions. She knows I work as the Parks and Recreation supervisor.

"Well, I wasn't certain we'd be staying here at first as I struggled to find a job, but I am liking the new position with the park district. It's been a bit of a challenge, though." Who knows how long I'll keep my new job if I can't get anything approved by the town council?

Roxanne eyes me, not suspiciously, but more all-knowingly. "Must be fun working under Charlie."

Before my beer fully reaches my lips, I spit at my drink, spraying liquid in all directions, and my face heats. She has no idea how nice it is to be *under* Charlie although I've been telling myself not to think of such things for the past few days. Then again, Roxanne did catch us coming out of the bathroom together, and there really isn't any other explanation for us both being in there at the same time.

"That's right. You work for Mayor McSteamy." Grace giggles.

"Mayor McSteamy?" I question, and Roxanne shakes her head.

"Don't encourage her," Roxanne teases of her employee, but I can't be left hanging.

"Tell me," I ask Grace, who reaches for her phone and pulls up an image.

There's Charlie, in his mostly bare glory, plus dark European-cut swimming trunks with a broad white band. Six-pack on display. Tan skin. Mischievous grin. And a hard-on—thick, raised, and rugged in those tight shorts—leaving nothing to the imagination. "Someone found his ex-wife's lost phone and published this photo of him. It was eventually traced back to our own small-town mayor."

"Charlie's always had a reputation for being so clean and wholesome. Mr. Goody Two-shoes. But this image…" Alyce fans her face.

"Goody Two-shoes Charlie doesn't look so innocent there," Roxanne adds.

This small-town mayor is making a big splash in an impressive display of toned abs and tanned skin, among other parts of his anatomy. A civil servant of Blue Ridge, Georgia, he isn't what we'd expect of a mountain man. Think beards, gruff voice, and vibrant flannel, but underneath this man's flannel is a fine package, and despite missing a beard, we'd still like to climb his peak and settle on his ridge.

"Oh, my God." I laugh. "Who wrote this article?"

"A desperate woman," Roxanne states.

"A horny woman," Alyce adds.

"A woman who isn't wrong in her assessment." We all stare at Grace and then burst into laughter.

"What's so funny?" asks a rugged male voice, and we look up in unison to see the man in question. Another round of laughter fills our table. If only the writer of the article knew of his voice, they'd note two out of three puts the odds in Charlie's favor of fulfilling mountain man fantasies. Then again, I personally know how equipped and capable Charlie is.

Damn.

"Hi, Charlie," Alyce says, her voice still struggling with giggles.

"We were just discussing you," Roxanne adds as Grace sheepishly returns her phone to her bag. The bright red glow to her face lingers.

"Oh, yeah?" Charlie tips his head, eyes meeting mine.

"That's quite a package you have there, Mayor McSteamy," I state, unable to hold back.

Alyce snorts. Roxie smiles. Grace begins to shudder, and the laughter starts all over again. Thankfully, Charlie's good-natured, and the corner of his lip slowly crooks upward.

"You ladies having a good time?" Billy Harrington asks, sauntering up to our table with a grin like he knows a secret. Billy curls a hand around the back of Roxanne's neck, and she tips her face up to him. I watched him touch her like this the night of the fireworks. Leaning forward, he kisses her. It's so sweet.

"They're having a great time, looking at old pictures of me." Charlie tips up a brow at his brother.

"Mayor McSteamy?" Billy grins.

"Jan is new here," Grace states as if that explains everything.

"Just showing her the man *beneath* the man she works for?" Billy questions glancing over at Grace and then down at Roxanne. "And here I thought all the tee-hee-ing coming from this table was about a good joke."

"Looks like the joke's on me," Charlie says with a grin, but his voice grows a little tighter.

"With all due respect, sir. That picture was no joke," I state, which brings stunned silence while my eyes hold Charlie's. Then Alyce snorts. Roxie chuckles, and Grace titters with giggles once more.

Those brown eyes of Charlie's flame, not in anger but in that way he gets right before he attacks. Before the good mayor kisses me until I'm dizzy and then fingers me until I give into him. Before Mayor McSteamy gives me his impressive package and more.

Well, maybe not *more*, but I'd like to know more about him.

We did learn a bit about each other during the fireworks, and my skin itched with the desire to touch him all night, but with Vega and Lucy watching us every second, I didn't reach for him. Plus, I didn't trust myself. When we connect, I spark, and the entire night was an experiment in fighting attraction. He didn't even lean in for a good night kiss after parking in the coach house drive, and I'm thankful he didn't because I was a live wire ready to burn by the time he left us that night. An innocent peck on the cheek was going to result in him tackled to the drive.

Still, how did something like this image happen to him? As much as he's keeping a brave face, there's something pinched in his expression that suggests this wasn't a pleasant experience. His ex-wife lost her phone. What was it like with his ex-wife? Was he happy? Did he miss her?

"You ladies enjoy your girls' night out," Charlie says, lifting his drink in salute. He's holding a tall boy filled with fresh beer, but he's still wearing his suit from a day's worth of work.

He works too hard.

"Want to join us?" I ask before realizing the other woman might not want him present. It's been a long time since I've hung out with just women. Kind women. Genuine women. Not desperate housewives of famous baseball players looking to one-up each another.

Charlie shakes his head to deny my invitation, and Billy claps his brother on the shoulder. "You ladies should have Letty join you. I'll text Giant." Billy then addresses Charlie. "Stick around a bit."

"I should get home to Lucy," he says, and it's sweet that he's thinking of his daughter, but I know for a fact she's going to the movies with Vega and my mother. It's the main reason I said yes to being here myself. Only, I can't mention this to Charlie because I don't want these women knowing my mother is his housekeeper and nanny. It's bad enough *I* work for him. The thought makes me feel all kinds of wrong, which I often feel after I've been with Charlie. I mean, being with him feels so right, but afterward, the guilt and questions riddle me.

I look away from him, not able to offer what I know of his daughter's plans, and I'm suddenly embarrassed that I asked him to stay with us. Billy pulls his phone from his pocket, types something, and then sets it back in his pocket.

"I have to make a few rounds," Billy states to Roxanne, as he's the owner of this establishment. "Sadie's out with Christian." He grimaces as he mentions this information, but Roxanne smiles.

"Be good, Dad," she teases, and I gaze back and forth between them. Billy kisses Roxanne's temple before warning her not to drink too much.

"These boots are new," he tells her, and she swats at him before they both laugh. I guess it's a private joke.

As both men walk away, Roxanne explains Billy's angst over his teenage daughter dating, and Grace gives me her background. Widow. Five boys. How sad. It's evident she loved her deceased husband deeply. Being a military wife comes with great risk.

"It's been a while, though," she says, trying to end on a positive note, implying how his death was a few years ago.

"And that's where Clyde comes in," Roxanne interjects. Grace's face pinkens again.

"Who's Clyde?"

"Who wants to know?" A deep, jovial voice draws my attention as a large man steps past the table and then backs up to stand next to it. He's got a thick beard and slightly unruly dark hair along with a plaid flannel. *Hello, mountain man.* Only he looks a little disheveled, and his pants are too tight. *Are those corduroys?*

"That's Clyde," Alyce whispers with a smile in her voice.

"He's my best customer," Roxanne adds. Clyde holds out a paw of a hand and shakes mine.

"Welcome to the village. We promise not to eat the young here." He winks at me, looks up at Grace, and then walks away from the table.

"He loves graphic novels, utopian society fantasy, and Grace," Roxanne explains.

"He does not," Grace drones.

"He so does," Alyce adds. Grace's brows pinch, and her gaze follows Clyde's retreating back before glancing down at the table.

"I'm not interested," Grace says, but there's untruth in her tone. After all she just told me about the love of her life, I'd say she's scared to open up again, and I can relate.

My eyes wander to where Charlie is standing near the bar. His older brother Giant enters with his fiancée under his arm.

"Hey, ladies," Letty announces, walking up to our table after Giant releases her with a kiss. Her non-Southern accent gives away she isn't from the South. I learned at dinner that she's from Chicago and recently moved here like me. Pulling up an extra chair, she joins our little party, and more laughter ensues. It's been a long time since I've laughed like this. Bending at the waist. Tears filling my eyes. It's so good for the soul to laugh like this, and I'm…happy. For the first time in a long time, I'm content right where I am.

And then I look up to see Charlie watching me. Only my eyes catch on the large television screen behind his head. The closed captioning reads the announcement of Richard Swank being traded to Atlanta mid-season.

Something about Richard looking for a fresh start. Deciding he wants to be near family.

But Richard isn't from the East Coast. He's from Arizona.

His parents remain there where his mother is an alcoholic and his father, a notorious adulterer. Seems the apple didn't fall far from the tree, but I didn't see the signs. I believed all of Richard's pretty promises about wanting to be a better person.

"Will you excuse me a second?" I say, slipping out of my seat and heading for the restroom. I just need a minute to wrap my head around this farce.

What is Richard doing?

+ + +

After splashing cool water on my face and running my wrists under the faucet, my heart rate lowers, and I exit the bathroom. I don't know if I'm surprised to see Charlie standing in the hallway as if he's waiting for me.

"Charlie?" I question as he's peering down at his phone. I can't simply ignore him. We're the only two standing in this narrow space.

He looks up, and his eyes search my face. Those eyes. And I know what he wants.

"Charlie, I'm here with the girls. I need to get back."

"Tell them you had to call home. Vega needed you." He steps up to me. "There's a party room upstairs. Just one more time, and then we'll stop."

I stare up at him, and his knuckles swipe down the side of my face.

"I find it hard to resist you when you look at me like that," I whisper. The next thing I know, Charlie's unlocking a door for the second floor and leading me upward. The hard soles of his shoes make a racket of noise on the wood plank risers. As we enter the opening at the top of the stairs, he spins me, and my back presses against the wall.

Out of breath as though he's run a marathon, Charlie says, "And every time you call me fucking sir, my dick gets hard." His mouth crashes against mine, hungry and desperate. I can feel his words in this kiss.

One last time. Then we'll stop.

So much for the *let me in* he asked for the other night.

"And why do you respond in such a way, sir?" I murmur, attempting to pull back from his devouring lips.

"Because I want to own you, possess you, and I can't seem to stop myself. This isn't like me."

"Goody Two-shoes Charlie?" I ask as his mouth lowers to my jaw and then skims to my neck.

"Fucking nickname," he hisses into my skin.

"Those pictures show otherwise," I tease. Charlie's head snaps up.

"I don't want to discuss them." His tone is the roughest I've ever heard. As I have plenty I don't wish to discuss either, I respond with, "Whatever you say, sir."

His eager mouth returns to mine, hard and anxious, taking me like he said—owning me, possessing me—one more time.

He releases my mouth and lowers to my breasts. Pressing up my T-shirt, he tugs down my bra cup and covers my heavy swell with his mouth. He suckles and sips. His tongue teases the nipple, and then his teeth nip. I hiss, and he covers me with the bra, moving to the other breast and repeating the attention. My fingers delve into his hair, holding his head to me, massaging his scalp as I purr under the warm suction of his mouth.

I moan his name, and he releases me, not bothering to cover this breast. His mouth returns to mine, and we spin, moving across the floor until my backside hits a table. Charlie lifts my skirt and works my thong to my ankles. Then he hikes me up on the wood surface.

"Charlie?" I question as he lowers onto a chair, then pulls himself up between my knees.

"If this is my last chance, I want a taste." He reaches around to my backside and tugs me to the edge of the tabletop. Forcing my thighs to spread, he lowers his face, and his tongue swipes across the heat of me. Thick and flat, he sweeps over ready folds and then dips his tongue between them.

"Oh God," I groan as my palms cup his head. My legs dangle off the table, trembling with the effect of Charlie's mouth on my center. His fingers dig into my hips, holding me in place as I rock, unable to help the movement. Charlie catches on, and he aids me in moving against his face, his mouth working its magic as his tongue takes me.

I warn him with only the moan of his name before I explode. Like crystal candy dissolving, bursting with flavor, I come apart at his mouth, and he vigorously laps as the orgasm drags.

"Charlie, I…I'm going to go again." My voice catches, my breath hitching. It hasn't ever happened like this. "I've never…" I begin until he pulls his mouth back, stands as he fumbles with his suit pants, shoving them to his hips and slams into me without a word.

"Come. Fucking come all over me," he demands. He tugs me off the table and onto his lap to ride him in the chair. My hands grip his shoulders but move to the back of the wood seat for leverage. I drag myself up and down his thick length, the sound of us quietly reverberating in the large room. I rebuild quickly what I lost at the removal of his tongue. His thickness lashes at me more firmly than his mouth. The drag and draw of his length is deeper in this position. His mouth seeks mine, that tongue surging forward to meet mine, and I come all over him.

"Sweet heaven," he mutters, rocking back and forth. Setting a new rhythm, he's moving faster, diving deeper, and his grunts grow louder. Finally, he stills, tugging me down on him and holding me in place. His fingertips pinch at my hips as he releases, jetting off inside me.

My heart races as I rest my forehead against his.

One final time? It won't be enough. It's not like I want to walk away from this, from him. It's just that it isn't smart to keep doing whatever we're doing.

After what feels like only seconds, Charlie lifts me off his lap, and something swipes between my thighs. I step back and straighten my skirt. Charlie folds an honest to goodness handkerchief and slips it into his pants pocket as he tugs them back in place. He's hardly pulled them down. I smooth my skirt again and bend to the floor for my underwear. A hand skims over my backside and then moves to my lower back as I stand. The touch feels intimate as though he isn't ready to let me go either. Perhaps he's only helping me stand upright as my legs still tremble from what we did. He takes my thong from me and slips it into his pocket as well.

"Did you like seeing that picture of me?" The question is like ice on his tongue, and I stare back at him, surprised by his tone.

"Lost her phone, that's what the article said, right? Those images were blackmail, and when that wasn't enough, she had a blatant affair in hopes to break me."

I stand taller, wanting to reach out for him but sensing he didn't want my touch.

"And then she tried to use my child, threatening to release more images, embarrassing our daughter."

"Charlie, I—" I step up to him, but he holds up a hand to stop me from getting closer.

"She used my child to forward her political career, playing her brand as a single mother, raising a modern feminist child, only she forgot to mention she hardly sees that sweet child, and all the while holding more exposing photos over my head. Goody Two-shoes Charlie wouldn't want the scandal, and she was right, I didn't. I wanted my wife to be faithful. I wanted my child to be loved by her mother."

The vulnerability in his face and the crack to his voice break me in two.

"Why didn't you tell me the girls went to the movie with your mother?" he asks, switching subjects.

"I wasn't going to announce in front of the others that my mother is your housekeeper and nanny, Charlie." My voice drips with displeasure, and I cross my arms.

"Why not?"

I stare back at him. "Because I don't want everyone to know my entire family works for you."

"Are you embarrassed?" The question stings.

"I'm not embarrassed. My parents work hard, but I don't need the town thinking I'm shacking up with their employer, and perhaps that's how I got a job working for him myself."

"That's not how it happened," Charlie says, taken aback. "And we aren't shacking up."

"What the hell are we doing then?" I groan. Charlie looks at me for a long minute.

"Nothing. This was it." Like he has the last word. The final say. Judge and jury on my feelings for him or my body's reaction to his.

"If that's what you want," I snap, and Charlie stares at me.

"Isn't that what you want? You won't let me in. You refuse to see me. You won't tell me what happened the other day in my office or tonight as you stared at the television over my head." Charlie's voice rises. "What does Richard Swank mean to you?"

After what he's just revealed about his ex-wife, the door is open for me to explain my relationship. I could easily agree with his assessment that I wanted a husband to love me and a father for my child, but I don't open up like he did.

"It's…not your concern," I stammer, not willing to tell him.

Charlie huffs and runs a hand over his lips, the palm swiping off the taste of me on him.

My God, what he just did to me. My core pulses again. I want him. I want to comfort him about what I've learned. I don't want to give him up, but one of us needs to be strong, and it's obviously him.

"I'm going home." His tone is cool like when he explains something, a directive, a dismissive. "I'll relieve your mother, and she can take Vega home. Enjoy the night with your new friends." His words are distant, robotic even as he stands from the chair. He dismisses me as though I'm some petty constituent under him, and before I can comment that I never voted for Mayor McSteamy to conquer me as he has, he's disappearing down the stairwell.

Chapter 13
Mayor McSteaming Mad

[Charlie]

I enter my house still worked up over what I'd done with Janessa and how things ended. I didn't want to walk away like I did. I didn't want to walk away ever, but she'd been right. We shouldn't be doing what we've done. She works for me. Her parents work for me. It has scandal written all over it.

I sigh as I recall the damn pictures.

Fortunately, only one out of the fifty or so made it into the press after Angela lost her phone. On our honeymoon, she wanted to spice things up. This from a woman who penciled in our sex life. She had a local photographer do boudoir shots at our island destination. Bedroom. Beach. Dinner.

The images flash back to me.

Angela in the skimpiest thing I've ever seen a woman wear. Sheer and lacey with straps and clasps. Then the beach in her bikini and me in that damn suit. The shot that made the press was one she took with her phone after I watched her remove her teeny bikini in a private alcove off our room. God, how I wanted her like she was on that trip, but she was never like that again.

We'd been hot for each other from the start but not like the flame burning between Janessa and myself. Angela was smart, strategic, and power-hungry, and somehow, I found that attractive despite the regulated sex life. When we went on our honeymoon, I thought we were turning a corner. Instead, it was a blip. A few snapshots. Insurance, she later called it. She'd use those images to get what she wanted from me if she ever needed them.

Hard to scream scandal when it's consensual between a newly married couple just experimenting with boudoir images, but Angela was devious like that as I later learned.

When she had an affair.

When she wanted to use Lucy to her advantage for political gain.

I didn't trust her after that photo leaked. She lost her phone, she said, but when a second image was sent to me upon our divorce, I knew it was a warning.

Unwarranted. Unnecessary. But still a threat.

I toss my keys on the kitchen counter and then look up to see two heads peeking over the couch in the sitting area off the kitchen. The television pauses on a movie, and Lucy and Vega stare at me.

I take a deep breath and place my hands on the island countertop.

"Hey, Pint. Hi, Vega. Did you girls have fun at the movies?"

"It was good, Dad," Lucy says, speaking for both of them. She straightens on the couch and leans her little arms over the back cushions. "Dad, did you know Vega's dad is famous?" Her voice rises with enthusiasm, but Vega hisses Lucy's name beside her.

I stand taller and try to catch Vega's eyes, but she's glaring at Lucy. "I don't think—"

"Her dad is Richard Swank. Do you know who that is?"

My heart races with the name. Richard Swank, center fielder for Houston and recently…

"He's a baseball player, and he's been traded to Atlanta." Her little voice lifts higher, excitement filling it, but Vega continues to glare at Lucy.

"Lucy, I told you, you couldn't tell anybody," Vega mutters, her voice low but not low enough.

Lucy turns to her new friend, her eyes going innocent. "But it's my dad. He isn't going to tell anyone."

"I said no one," Vega reminds her.

"I thought you meant the kids at camp, but still, it's my dad. Who is he going to tell?" Lucy looks up at me, her eyes confident I'll keep this secret.

"I won't tell a soul," I say as Vega shifts to look over the cushions at me. I swipe a big X over my chest and then draw a line along my lips like I'm zipping them together. Then I act as if I'm throwing away the key by tossing it over my shoulder.

"My mom's still going to be mad," Vega says, shifting her gaze back to the paused television.

"You don't need to tell her," Lucy says, turning to her friend.

"But you just told your dad, and my mom will want to know. She doesn't want anyone knowing who we are."

What? My brows pinch. A million questions run through my head. Why not? What happened? Are they in danger?

"But it's so cool. He might be coming back for you," Lucy encourages, and I'm reminded of the tremble in Janessa when Jordan announced Richard Swank was being traded to Atlanta. That's only an hour away. If they don't want to be found, he's too close.

"Lucy," I softly call her name. "I think Vega has her reasons for asking you to keep a secret, and you should have honored that."

Vega looks back at me for a second and then stands from the couch.

"I'd like to go home, Mr. Harrington," she says, looking down at her feet.

"But you said you'd spend the night. I don't want you to go," Lucy whines.

"I think I should see my mom."

"Your mother is still out. I saw her in town at the pub." I just did ridiculously sexy things to your mom, who obviously has a huge secret of her own.

"Mami can take me," Vega states the nickname for her grandmother, and as if on cue, Rosa enters the room.

"Oh. Mr. Charlie. I didn't know you return," Rosa says in her faltering accent. She looks from the girls to me and back. Her brow pinches when she sees Vega, and Vega steps up to her.

"I'd like to go home," she says, looking up at her grandmother. Rosa looks at me again and then back at her grandchild. "Okay."

Glancing at me one more time, Rosa asks, "If I'm done for this evening…?" A question lingers, and I'm reminded of what Janessa said. *My parents work for you. I work for you.*

Rosa and Henri are trusted and loyal…servants. I swallow the bitterness in my throat. *It's not like that*, I tell myself. I need them. They're practically family. They've never complained. I pay them well. I've allowed them time off and include health benefits. Still, I suddenly feel guilty about their employment with me.

"Thank you, Rosa. That's all today."

Vega steps up to her grandmother, who slips an arm over her shoulder and leads her through the kitchen to the back hall where there's an exit. Where a path outside leads around the pool, along the tennis courts I converted to a batting cage and to the coach house. Where Vega and Janessa are living.

Everything feels wrong inside me, and I turn to Lucy once I hear the back door click shut. Lucy's pained face breaks my heart, but this is a teachable moment.

"Pint, when someone tells you something in confidence, you shouldn't share it unless that person is in danger of harming herself or others." I pause, inhaling a deep breath. "Do you think Vega and her mother are in danger?" Why all the mystery around Richard Swank?

"I don't know," Lucy says. "She told me once before that her dad was famous, but she had to keep it a secret. I thought she might be making it up to sound…better than me." Lucy shrugs. "Then today on the radio in the car she heard the announcer talking about Richard Swank, and she turned to me and whispered, '*That's my dad.*'" Lucy lowers her voice to imitate her friend.

"Did she say why she needed to keep it a secret?" I hate that I'm prying through a child, but my heart gallops. I'm growing concerned the reason is bigger than just being secretive.

"She just said her mom didn't want anyone to know." Lucy shrugs, and I'm skeptical it's that simple. Not that I think Janessa would namedrop or hope to get ahead by being the ballplayer's ex-wife. If anything, her reluctance to talk about him ratchets up my fearful suspicions.

"Huh," I say. "I'm going to shower quick and change." I glance at the clock over the stove. "Give me fifteen minutes, and we can watch something together."

"*What a Girl Wants?*" Lucy beams at me as she asks. She loves this 2003 movie about a girl who learns her dad is a famous Englishman in Parliament. In some ways, I worry she reverses the roles in her head, wishing the fictional political father was her real-life mother. At the end of the movie, the man gives everything up for his daughter and her mother, the woman who got away. It's rubbish, to use a British term, but I watch it to humor Lucy.

After a quick shower and a change into casual clothes of sweatpants and a T-shirt, I sit next to my daughter on the couch, who leans her head on my shoulder. Slipping my arm over her, I tug her to my chest as we start the movie we've watched a million times. My fingers twitch for my phone, eager to research Richard Swank for any clues to his ex-wife's reasons for secrets.

Maybe it's none of your damn business, my subconscious warns.

Maybe she's in trouble, my head states.

Maybe I'm not really ready to let her go like I told her earlier tonight.

One last time and then we stop.

However, I can't stop. I can't shut off the way my body craves her or the way my heart bleeds into the mix. It's more than a pull to fuck her. It's a desire to know more about her, get closer to her, and have her in my life. I understand all her reasons to hold back. Her parents. Her job. Maybe her ex-husband.

But I don't want to accept any of those excuses.

I want to know what's going on with her.

As Lucy grows heavier on my chest, I cautiously lean forward and pick up my phone resting on the ottoman. Lucy shifts but doesn't wake, and I'm reminded of her as an infant, curled up and sleeping in the crook of my arm or flat against my belly. Her little body melting into the warmth of me, knowing I'd never let anything happen to her.

That instinct to protect is ingrained in me.

I click on my phone, feeling no guilt now that Lucy sleeps against me. With one hand, I type in Richard Swank's name. The first bits of information announce his mid-season trade to Atlanta, citing a need to be closer to his family. As I continue scrolling, I see picture after picture of him with his former wife, and I wonder if I'm misinformed. *Are* they really divorced? As I dig deeper, I find other images. Him with a blonde. Him with a blue-eyed beauty. Him with glassy eyes, his lips on the temple of a redhead.

Son of a bitch.

I make a mental note to research further tomorrow. Marriage license. Divorce records. I'm exerting power I shouldn't use to my advantage, but I need to know. Clicking off my phone, I toss it back to the ottoman.

Janessa has cause to divorce him. I'm not a fan of cheaters, especially as it happened to me. But why the secrecy? What exactly is she hiding?

Chapter 14
Walking Away

[Charlie]

"Take a walk with me," I command when I finally see Janessa on Monday. Lucy sulked all weekend as Vega wouldn't speak to her, and I didn't want to pry into their family time on the weekend. Still, the temptation to race around my property and bang on the coach house door was real.

She's so close yet so distant.

"I don't think that's a good idea," Janessa says, glancing up at me from her office on the second floor of the old building. She's wearing glasses again today with her hair pulled to the base of her neck, and I want to fulfill dirty secretary fantasies with her wearing nothing more than those lenses. Of course, I don't have that fantasy about my real-life assistant. Charity just doesn't provoke this desire in me.

"I want to discuss this walkability thing you mentioned last week."

Janessa shifts from behind her desk, and I see she has on heels. *Fuck me.*

"I can't walk in these," she says, and I sigh. I won't let her avoid me. I need to speak with her, and I want to do it where it's perceived as nothing more than the mayor speaking with a community employee.

"This is business," I assure her although ulterior motives knock at my chest. Yep. I want alone time with her where I can't ravish her, and she might speak to me. Walking across town seems safe enough.

"Fine," she huffs. "I have some flats in my car that I use when I drive." *Makes sense*, I guess, so I follow her out to the street parking where her father's truck is the vehicle she references.

"Don't you have your own car?"

"My father lets me use his truck. Says it's better for the mountain roads." Her lips twist. She's lying, and I realize my question is personal.

Not going to pry, I tell myself. Just going to nudge.

Still, it's strange to consider, if her former husband is a famous baseball player, why doesn't she have her own car, her own place, or anything of value? My thoughts return to my bedroom when I caught her with my grandmother's ring on her finger. Was she trying to steal it after all?

Janessa slips on her flatter shoes, and I hold out a hand, expressing I follow her lead. Blue Ridge has a Main Street with three blocks of business—First, Second, and Third Streets. Original, I realize, but I didn't name them. The municipal offices, like the mayor's building, the courthouse, and the fire and police departments, are opposite First, which leads south and out of Blue Ridge. The church property Janessa mentioned is on the other side of Third, almost to Scenic Road, so that's the direction we head.

At first, we don't talk to one another. I wave at people from the community and pause to introduce Janessa as a new employee. I point at Wine&Dine and suggest a coffee from the diner, but Janessa shakes her head, declining my offer.

We walk onward.

We pass Pearl's, BookEnds, and the Pub.

"Explain the train to me," she finally says, and my head lifts for the blue boxcar sitting as a centerpiece to our town.

"Once upon a time, people took scenic train rides up the mountain. It was a destination, I suppose, and one not easily reached. Dolores McIntyre and her husband, Seamus, owned a farm up here, and Dolores thought a coffee shop would be a nice resting spot for visitors. She sold fried chicken and egg salad sandwiches from her poultry farm to go with the coffee, and eventually, the diner was born. More businesses popped up, and Blue Ridge become a place to visit." I pause, scratching at the back of my neck. "The community has had its ups and downs, one of which was the desire of a former mayor to increase the population. He wanted subdivisions and cookie-cutter homes, thinking he'd build his own little kingdom up here." I snort, recalling all I know of Kip Chance, Dolores Chance's father. She's the second Dolores in the McIntyre line and runs the diner of her namesake. "Anyway, when I became mayor a dozen years ago, I knew our town needed something other than population growth to sustain it. We needed to offer what people want in the mountains, respite and peace."

My eyes lower to the side of her face as her eyes squint, and she glances at the train.

"My plan has been to please the people but encourage tourism. It's a double-edged sword some days."

Janessa nods and turns to face me. "Keeping the locals happy while finding ways to attract visitors does seem daunting."

We continue walking.

"It's one reason I think a walking trail would be beneficial. It satisfies both locals and visitors, making it easy for each party to get around town and wander out of it to explore the great outdoors nearby."

"Wyatt would argue that's what the National Forest Preservation system is for," I joke.

"Wyatt is from the good old boys' club. What you need is a bridge between the two. I'll show you when we near the church."

I'm pleased she understands our destination, and we fall silent a few minutes more until we pass Hetty's Flower Shop marking the end of downtown proper and then walk along the gravel edge of the road a bit.

"I see what you mean," I mutter, taking in the lack of a sidewalk. "A bike trail would be beneficial here." People can walk or ride on a trail, and the mix of gravel and patchy grass isn't necessarily safe.

"I think you should have a train park here as well. Celebrate the train history," she adds, walking in front of me as the current path is narrow. My eyes focus on the curve of her ass under a flowy dress.

I want to touch her again. Instead, I slip my hands inside the pockets of my pants.

"You have a lot of ideas for someone with no experience," I state. Researching her a bit after plunging down the rabbit hole of Richard Swank, I learned Janessa had a short history in sports marketing for a Major League Baseball team. She graduated college back in the day when sports marketing wasn't a thing, so she has a business degree in marketing with exercise science as a minor. What I want to know is why the girl from Texas who earned a full-ride scholarship and graduated top in her class gave up a career after only a decade?

"I'm pretty certain I must have been the only person to apply for the job," she jests. "It still feels like a dream that I got it." A smile fills her voice although I can't see her face, and I want to spin her, kiss her, and assure her she's qualified for the position. I want to feel her smile against my lips.

"I don't know if you were the only one who applied, but you were certainly the best candidate."

She stops walking and turns to face me. "Was I really?"

"Of course," I say, brows pinching.

"And it wasn't because we…you know…against the fence in your batting cage?"

"What? No, of course not." Is that what she thinks? "I didn't have any say in your hiring. It just happened."

Her hip juts out, and she rests her fists on them. "Well, that's reassuring."

"Did you honestly think you got the job because we…?" I let my voice trail as she hadn't labeled it either.

"I wasn't certain, and I figured it was one reason you kept coming for me."

"Kept. Coming. For you?" Each word is a question. "I'm…attracted to you, not fucking you because you owe me."

"Again, strangely reassuring," she mutters, repeating herself. She then turns to walk away, but I'm not having this. Reaching for her upper arm, I curl my fingers around her and stop her from taking another step.

"Look," I begin, falling under her spell when those green eyes latch onto mine. The emerald color sparkles under the bright sunlight of the morning. "I'm not just fucking you, okay? I'll admit I'm a little out of control around you and definitely out of my element. Goody Two-shoes Charlie," I mock myself. "But I *like* being with you. You…you make me feel alive."

Her breath catches, and then she bites the corner of her lip.

"Please don't do that," I groan, closing my eyes.

"Why not?" she whispers.

"Because I'm trying to *be* good even though I want so badly to kiss you." The truth pours out of me as we stand on the side of the road. I slowly open my lids, peering down at her upturned face, those eyes sparkling like they do when I slip inside her. *Fuck.*

When I release her arm, the crackle between us lingers on my fingers. I step back and wave a hand for her to continue. After only a few more steps, we can walk side by side again and thank goodness because watching the sway of her hips has me hard.

As we near the church parking lot, I ask her to explain her vision to me again, and I watch her become animated in describing what she sees. She holds up her hands like it's a camera shot, and she's framing the images. A restored church but now a community center. Basketball courts and maybe a baseball diamond. A train park playground. And the walking slash bike path leading up to it and flowing beyond it to the forest.

"That's certainly a lot," I say, blowing out a breath. "I like your ideas, but there will be some resistance. We already have basketball courts and baseball diamonds near the schools."

She nods, accepting what I'm saying.

We walk closer to the church, but we can't enter. It's locked. "I can call the realtor if we want to see inside. I've already looked through the place, though. The raised chancel could be a stage for concerts. Removing the pews makes it more of an open hall for markets and other activities. Maybe a community dance or something."

She shrugs, and I smile. She has a vision.

"Why do you want to work here?" I ask, hoping it's not too personal.

"I just want to be a part of something," she says, crossing her arms and looking around the overgrown grass area and the in-need-of-repair parking lot.

"I understand the feeling. I wanted to be mayor to give back to a place I considered special to me. This is my home, but what is it to you?" *Nudge-nudge.*

"I'd like it to be my home, too," she says, lowering her voice.

"Are you in danger?" I ask, keeping my voice cool. Her head swings, and her eyes blink at me. "Tell me the truth. Give me something."

"I'm not in danger, and I'm not on the run either, if that's your next question. I just want to disappear."

"Tell me who Richard Swank is to you?" I ask, giving her one more chance to open up to me. When she doesn't answer after a silent minute, I speak for her. "He was your husband and is Vega's father. You're divorced, and he's moving to Atlanta."

Her eyes narrow. "Snooping much?"

"Lucy told me." I hold her eyes, and her shoulders fall.

"Vega mentioned she said something to Lucy." Janessa shakes her head, lowering her face once again toward the ground. My fingers lift her chin.

"Let me in," I whisper. "Let me help you."

"I don't need help. I needed to get away from him."

"Why?"

Her brow pinches. "If you looked me up, I'm sure you've seen the pictures." *Ah, yes, pictures tell a thousand tales.*

"My wife cheated on me, remember? It was public, and I was just blind."

"Well, my eyes were wide open, but I wouldn't do anything to lose my child. I wasn't worried about my reputation," she snarks, implying my Goodie Two-shoes nomenclature.

"Her affair hurt and broke the heart of my child." My voice roughens as I release her chin, but her hand reaches out for my chest.

"I'm sorry, Charlie. That was unfair of me. And I'm sorry that happened to you." Her voice softens.

"Is he why you won't open up to me? What did he do to you?"

She sighs, looking down at her feet. "Vega walked into our house and saw a woman sucking him off. *Another* woman," she emphasizes.

"Bastard," I hiss.

"He is, but my hesitation with us isn't about him, Charlie," she groans. "This is a lose-lose situation. I'm new to town and work in your office. What will people think? Not to mention, I live in your coach house, and my parents are longtime employees of yours."

"That's all about me, and I don't care. What about you? What do you lose?" Me. *Say me.* Say you don't want to lose me.

"I left a volatile, hostile marriage, and I've no interest in going from one man's bed to another."

"Then what the fuck have we been doing?" I snap, swiping a hand through my hair.

"We're attracted to each other. I can't explain it, but I can't have it become *a thing*."

"Are you still in love with him? Do you still want him?"

"Absolutely not!" she shrieks. "I want a man who respects me and who values my ideas and suggestions. Sees I have a brain and not just a body."

"Do you think I don't respect you?" I gasp. I took her up against a fence, over my desk, in a bathroom, and on a chair in the Pub, but it's not like I *disrespect* her.

"I think you don't know me, Charlie."

"I'm trying to," I blurt, exasperated by this conversation.

"And I'm trying to sort myself out before I drag someone else into my lane."

Fuck. I don't like this. I understand it, but I don't like it. When Angela was caught fucking another man at a party we were hosting to raise money for my campaign, I didn't think I could ever trust a woman again. And as I had Lucy to consider, I needed to pull myself together and move forward before I could even think of bedding someone. I've had one-night stands here and there, but nothing has made me feel like I feel with Janessa. Alive, just as I told her. For the first time in forty-five years, I feel something I've never felt before, and she does this to me.

"I get it," I mutter, crestfallen like a boy who's breaking up with his girl. I recall the feeling from being a teen. My eyes squint off in the distance, not focusing on any one thing. Turning for the church, I glance up at the steeple.

"Do you need money?" I ask, not able to face her with the question. "Is that why you were trying on my grandmother's ring that morning?"

"My God, I didn't intend to steal the ring, Charlie. Don't insult me *now*. I told you I wasn't stealing it that morning, and I later told you I was there to help out my mother, who had to take my father to the doctor."

"Why did you put it on then?" I ask, lowering my eyes to hers. Her arm flails out to her side, slapping back at her thigh before she looks me in the eye.

"I just thought it was beautiful. Richard bought me gaudy, garish things, and it was so simple yet dignified. Elegant and pretty. I wondered what it would look like on. I was just curious, and I apologized," she says, but for some reason, my irritation grows with her explanation.

"Curious? Is that what you're doing with me?" Is she using me to get herself off? Fill a void she won't admit she feels? I remember the emptiness when I discovered Angela's affair. The betrayal. The hurt. The need to feel like someone else might want me.

"Don't say that." She exhales, and her hands clasp together before her. Demure. Penitent. How appropriate we stand before a church? "I like you, Charlie, when I shouldn't."

I nod again, turning my face as if she slapped me. "I get it," I say again, and then reach for my phone in my pocket.

"I'll call someone to pick us up. We don't need to walk back."

I've had enough exercise today, and my heart aches not from the exertion but from the wasted energy of wanting someone who won't have me.

Chapter 15
Attack to the Heart

[Charlie]

"Where's Rosa?" I ask my mother when I return home from my morning run. I wake at five a.m. and take the time to clear my head before I start each day. Of course, lately, my head is filled with thoughts of Janessa. Why won't she open up to me? Why won't she let me in? I want to prove I do respect her, and I understand her need to prove herself. I just want to be there for her.

"I don't know," Mother says. I called her when Rosa was fifteen minutes late, and I needed to get out. Knowing my mother would be awake and Rosa must be running late, I just needed someone to sit in the house while Lucy slept. I don't leave Lucy in the house alone when I run so I compromise with Rosa. She comes over early, sets up for the day, and then when I return, she has an hour to go back to her place for whatever she needs. This morning, I'm wondering if I'm missing something. She's two hours late. I don't recall her telling me she couldn't be here, and while I'd like to strut over to the coach house, I'm avoiding Janessa. That's what she wants.

We agreed. One last time and then we'd stop.

Or maybe I said that, and she hammered home the idea during our discussion outside the church.

"Do you recall Rosa saying she wouldn't be here?" I ask Lucy, who is now awake and sleepily sitting at the kitchen island.

"She didn't say anything to me. You know you can leave me alone, Dad. I'm ten," she states, exasperated with me as her elbow rests on the island countertop, and she watches my mother pull out a pan for breakfast.

"I know you're ten, and that's why I'm not leaving you home alone yet, Pint." I mimic her tone back to her.

Maybe Lucy could call Vega, although I know Lucy's been walking gingerly around her new friend. She said Vega didn't get in trouble with her mother for Lucy telling me about their dad, but Vega's still upset with her.

She doesn't think she can trust me, Lucy whined when she told me what happened.

Can she? I remember asking Lucy, hinting at her betrayal in speaking of Vega's secret. Then I think of myself. Can Janessa trust me? Does she not see that she can? Our instant attraction might seem surface level, but underneath, I like what I've learned about her. Her laughter. Her intelligence. Her plans for the future of this town, a town I want her to call home. I want her to let me learn more, but the rejection is real.

I dial Rosa's number but don't get an answer. Shrugging off my concern, I decide to shower. I walk to my mother, kiss her temple, and head upstairs, but something niggles inside my chest. An unsettling feeling I dismiss as conflicting emotions over Janessa.

+ + +

"Where's Janessa?" I ask Charity after entering my office. An hour has passed since Janessa should have been present. Not that I'm keeping tabs on her, but I have a sense of when she's in the old house. I can't see the street from my office in the back of the place, so I stand inside Charity's reception area and stare out at the street where Henri's truck is distinctly missing.

"She called in sick," Charity says, and I turn to face her.

"What's wrong with her?"

Charity shrugs as though she doesn't know but more likely doesn't care. She hasn't been the same since Janessa was hired, and I don't know how to read her. The Bernards are old family friends since my father and Ford grew up together. The three daughters run roughly younger than Mati to my age, and a rumor suggests that a Bernard woman should marry one of us Harrington brothers. For me, the attraction was never present. They were just girls, who were friends, but Charity's been acting strange lately. Henhouse drama is not my thing, but I've seen it between Angela and Charity. Pecking order and who's the leader waffled between them. Charity likes to assure she's on top.

"I was wondering if I could speak with you," Charity begins, sheepishly asking and then licking her lips. She stands with a nervous expression on her face as she swipes her hands down her hips and then rounds her desk. Stepping up to me, she stops a little too close to me.

"Daddy wants you to run for Congress," she states, trying to hold my eyes in a weird non-blinking manner. "And you know I think you'd be the perfect candidate." She takes a deep breath and exhales. "You're intelligent and levelheaded. Kind and supportive. You see things. Have a vision. You know what you want and then go after it." Her voice lowers, and for some reason, I sweat a little.

"He thinks you could make a real difference for our district and the state." When her hand comes to my chest, all kinds of wrong prickles over my skin. She curls her hand around my tie and smooths it against her palm. "You could make a difference, Charlie. I believe in you."

"Thank you, Charity, that means a lot to me." I swallow as I reach for my tie and gently tug it from her grasp.

"Does it, Charlie? Do I mean something to you?"

Umm. That's not exactly what I said, but she does mean something me. Office wife, remember? She knows me and reads me better than most, and we've been doing this for ten years.

"Charity," I whisper, my voice shaky as I fear what's happening.

"We could go all the way, Charlie. I could be on top." Her eyes widen. "I mean, you could be on top of me." Her mouth pops open. "I mean...I mean, you could rise to the top."

I bite the inside of my cheek, both flabbergasted at what she's saying and trying not to laugh.

Is she seducing me? Does she hope I'll run for Congress with her at my side? She steps closer to me, running her hand along my tie again and pausing at the end, stopping too close to my waistband.

"Charity." I finally find the strength to level my voice. "What are you doing?"

"Convincing you to take me." She closes her eyes. "Take the risk." Her eyes pop open. "I mean, take the challenge and run for Congress."

Have mercy.

My hand covers hers, which still latches onto my tie. "Charity, I—"

"Did you hear what happened at the diner today?" Gretchen O'Leary calls out, bursting through the front door, which has a clear line of sight to this room. Gretchen's eagle eyes narrow on my hand covering Charity's, and it looks all kinds of wrong, especially when I forcefully drop Charity's hand, making us appear even guiltier of something that is not happening. That is never going to happen.

"What happened?" I ask nonchalantly as if I don't really care about town gossip, but I'll humor Gretchen this morning. Humor her as I try to make sense of the fact my assistant just came onto me.

"Poor Henri Cruz. Dropped down in the middle of the restaurant. They think it's his heart."

Turning away from Charity, I step up to Gretchen. "What happened?" I ask again, gripping her shoulders as I want more details.

"He was in the diner having breakfast with his daughter. I didn't realize Jan Cruz was Henri's kin." Gretchen pauses, and I circle my finger, motioning for her to speed up the situation.

"Anyway, an ambulance came, and they took him to County Regional Hospital."

"Did Janessa go with him?"

Gretchen's brows pinch. "Of course. She turned white as a ghost, muttering all kinds of things in Spanish to him, but he wasn't responding, poor man."

"Cancel my morning," I call over my shoulder to Charity, my eyes narrowing in suspicion. *Janessa called in sick.* I level my assistant with a glare but don't have time to discuss this incident. I step around her, find my keys in my desk, and then exit the office.

Fifteen minutes later, I'm rushing into the emergency room. While I'm not family, I'm recognized as the mayor, and I explain how Henri works for me. I'm sent to the telemetry unit as he's been admitted for observation. Coming into a waiting room just outside the entrance, I ask the nurse to pass along a message to the daughter.

After an excruciating ten minutes of waiting, Janessa appears through the double doors. I stand, and without thought, I step up to her and fold her into my arms. Thankfully, she doesn't press me away but melts into my chest.

"How are you?" I ask, still holding her to me.

"Shaken," she admits into my shirt, and then she tugs back to look up at me. "What are you doing here?"

"I heard what happened. Rosa didn't come in this morning, but I left my mother in charge of Lucy, and I didn't give it a thought. I should have thought." I tug her back to me.

"You had no way of knowing. We were at the diner when he gripped his chest, turned ash colored, and then collapsed. I've never been so scared."

Her arms tighten on me, and I press at her back as if to get her closer to me.

"What can I do for you?" I ask, lowering my lips for her hair. She shakes her head, pulling out of my grasp. *Dammit.* Whenever I offer her help is when she pulls away the most. I loosen my hold, feeling her slip from me. Taking a full step back, she puts distance between us. She's dressed for work, so another skirt and blouse, and I would do anything to remove it and show her how I can help her. I also want to remove the concern on her face.

"He's going to be okay," I say as if I know this for a fact. I reach for her cheeks, and thankfully, she doesn't tug out of my touch, allowing me to stroke my thumb along the corner of her mouth.

"Mami's in there with him, and I'd like to stay with her. I called the office and told Charity." My lips twist. My assistant and I need to have a serious conversation when I return to the office, but for now, I want to stay here with Janessa.

"Where's Vega?" I ask, and Janessa's eyes widen. "She had to come with my mother. I sent her down to the cafeteria with her iPad and some money for breakfast."

"I'll call my mother." I release her face and reach for my phone. Janessa's hand covers my wrist.

"You don't need to do that."

"Let me help you," I say, knowing I won't take no for an answer. "My mother can keep both the girls entertained for the day. In fact, she'll love it."

"But I don't want her to drive here for Vega, and I can't leave."

"I'll take her. Do you trust me?" I ask, feeling as if she might not trust me with her child.

"I trust you, Charlie." Her voice softens as her brows pinch as if she's questioning her own statement. For now, I'll take those words, no questions asked.

"First, what can I do for you?"

She shakes her head. "We called my younger brother, Zander, and he's coming in. We just don't know what's wrong with Papi. They're saying it wasn't a heart attack, but his heart isn't right."

"Okay. Okay, let me take Vega to my mother's. Do you need me to bring you anything? Pick up some food for you?" *Anything. Just tell me how I can help you*, I want to yell.

"I'm okay, Charlie. It was so sweet of you to come here." She tips on her toes and presses a kiss to the corner of my lips.

"There's nothing I wouldn't do for you," I tell her as she lowers back down, my fingers twitch. I want to grip her hips and pull her back to me, but I take a breath, and she steps away from me.

"Vega's in the cafeteria. I'll go get her."

"I'll come with you," I say, following her lead, realizing I'd follow her anywhere.

+ + +

The day feels endless after I take Vega to my mother who agrees to let both girls spend the night, making it a little party in hopes of taking Vega's mind off her grandfather. I'd like to do something for Janessa, but I feel helpless. Returning to the office, I plan to ignore my assistant as best I can.

"Charlie, I want to explain," Charity says, following me to my office door.

"I don't want to talk." It's the most direct I've ever been with her. Closing my door, I hole up in my office, taking calls, working on my client list, and reviewing Janessa's plans for the community center. It's a good idea, but costly, and I'm not certain the town council will pass this budget in the next budgeting meeting without more specifics.

Setting the plan aside, I realize how late it actually is and decide to head home. Mother invited me to stop over for a late supper, but I pass after checking in on the girls. I just want a shower and my bed, but like those three bears who come home, finding someone has eaten their porridge and sat in their chairs, I find someone curled up in my bed, and she's no Goldilocks but a raven-haired temptress.

Chapter 16
Into His Bed Means into My Heart

[Janessa]

Tender fingers brush back my hair, and slowly, my eyes open to find Charlie crouched next to the bed.

"Hey," I whisper hoarsely.

"Hey." He smiles with a crook to his lips. His fingers still comb through my hair and curl over my ear. "What are you doing here?"

His room holds only the glow of the side table light I left on for him.

"You told me the next time I was in your bedroom that I should be naked and willing in your bed."

His eyes widen.

"And I promise I'm not stealing anything."

"Too late," he mutters, and my forehead furrows.

"What do you mean?"

He shakes his head, dismissing the comment, and leans forward to press a kiss to my temple.

"How are you doing?" he asks.

"I'd never been so scared in my life. One minute, my father and I were eating breakfast, and he was lifting his coffee mug for his lips. The next, the mug crashed to the floor, his arm stiff. His eyes went blank, and his skin turned a smoky ash color. He tumbled from the chair as I screamed. The rest is a blur of police and ambulance. Then the emergency room where they admitted him for observation." I pause, mellowing under Charlie's touch.

"Mami sent me home because they'd only let one person stay in the room. My brother should be here tomorrow." Twisting in Charlie's sheets, I note his bed is comfortable, and it's been a while since I've been in anything bigger than the twin I sleep in across from Vega. Searching for a clock, I ask, "What time is it?"

"It's after ten."

I turn back for Charlie. "You're just getting home now?" I question, hating the hesitation in my voice and the implication. Richard would come home hours later than expected and always have an excuse when he smelled like alcohol and cheap perfume. Charlie doesn't smell like either of those things.

"I got a late start today, and I had things I wanted to wrap up."

I slowly sit, taking the sheet with me to cover my chest. "I'm sorry."

"Not your fault," Charlie says, leaning back to watch me rise. "Just stating a fact. It's been a long day." His eyes lower to the hand at my chest, holding the sheet against it.

"What are you wearing under there?" his gravelly voice asks, and I hold his eyes in response. "How willing are you?" he teases, and I slowly smile.

"It's a bit of a contradiction, but I just need this, and you offered me anything, so…" As my words drift, Charlie slowly stands. I watch as he tugs the open tie completely off his neck and then unbuttons his shirt, one torturous button at a time. He tugs the remainder of the shirt from his pants and then drags his dress shirt and undershirt over his head from the back of his neck. So sexy.

"I should shower," he says, still holding my eyes as his belt unbuckles, and I bite my lip, watching him drag it cautiously from the loops. He snaps it once free, and I flinch, but Charlie continues to stare at me as he drops the leather strap to the floor. His legs move, suggesting the removal of his shoes, and then he lowers for his socks. Finally, his pants come unzipped, and he tugs them down.

Before me stands Mayor McSteamy in his black boxer briefs and full package filling those snug shorts. He lifts a knee for the edge of the bed and then climbs up and over me, straddling my legs. His hands cup my cheeks and his head lowers, delicately taking my mouth with his. The kiss is sweet and lingering as he moves from one corner of my lips to the other, sipping at the sensitive skin and sucking at the lower curve.

"Charlie," I whisper. "Don't be gentle with me." I can't take it if he makes love to me. I can't be held responsible for how I'll react. The emotional hold will be too strong, and I need it rough. I need to forget about my dad and Richard and sleeping in a twin bed in my parents' house for just a little while.

"You still okay with the fact we haven't been using condoms?" he questions, acting responsibly for the first time. "I'll follow your lead, but I want to continue being bare inside you."

"I'm okay with that," I say, dismissing the fact I've already had an accidental pregnancy.

"I want to take care of you," Charlie says, his voice as tender as the kisses he's giving me.

"Then take care of me, Charlie, but make it burn."

"You have no idea what you're asking me."

"Show me." I pause. "Sir."

Suddenly, his mouth crashes against mine, opening to engulf my lips and surge for my tongue. The muscle tangles, twirling and sparring against mine until I almost can't breathe. With one hand, Charlie forcefully tugs at the sheet, exposing my naked breasts. He sits back only briefly and then dives for one achy globe, but cupping and massaging the other. His tongue swirls around the nipple while the fingers on his other hand pucker the nipple to a peak. Then he simultaneously nips me while pinching the other stiff nub.

I cry out, and Charlie pulls back, taking both my hands and lifting them over my head.

"Don't move." His mouth comes to mine again for one powerful kiss before drawing back, and asking, "Ever been tied up?"

I shake my head, and Charlie hops off me, reaching for the tie he tossed on the floor. Climbing back over my thighs, he wraps an arm around my middle and tugs me down the bed so I'm flat on my back. Then he wraps my wrists together and hooks a part of the tie behind the headboard of his sleigh bed.

"Charlie," I hiss.

"You take what I give," he says, and those eyes flame. I'm not certain how I feel being tied up and unable to touch him, but the second his mouth returns to a breast and two fingers plunge into my depths, I forgot all about my wrists over my head. My eyes close, and I let Charlie play my body like an instrument. His tongue on my nipple. His fingers up my channel. My hips rock, and Charlie presses kisses down my belly. I open my eyes to watch him as he watches his fingers slipping in and out of me.

"You respond to me," he mutters as if surprised at my body's reaction. What body wouldn't respond to that intense stare, those penetrating fingers, and then that tongue of his?

Good God. He's wicked as he licks and laps, and I struggle against the binding at my wrists.

"Charlie, oh God. Charlie, I want to touch you."

"You said to make it burn, sweetheart, and I plan to set you on fire." His mouth latches only onto my clit, sucking it so hard I see stars, but he isn't finished, and I'm only on edge. His tongue slips inside me, teasing me with its thickness before moving back to the sensitive hood and then delving two fingers inside me again.

I cry out his name. It's too much and not enough, and then I break apart. My knees clamp together around his head. His mouth is relentless as my hips buck, and then my legs fall open, and I feel it building again.

"Charlie," I hiss, both a question and a concern. He's going to make me immediately come a second time. Last time this happened, he stopped and slipped himself inside me, but he makes no effort to move. His tongue tangos, pressing forward to swipe at already drenched folds, and I explode once more, nearly as forcefully as the first. My head lifts off the pillows, but with my constricted hands, I can't touch him. I can't comb my fingers into his hair and hold his head to me. Instead, I rock my hips against his face, and he lets me. He takes me with that tongue of his until I'm weightless.

Pulling back, he rolls up to his knees and stretches his arms, stroking his hands up and down my front, then over my breasts but not stopping to pleasure them. As my heart rate lowers, he straddles my body and crawls over me until the apex of his legs nears my face. Shoving down his briefs, he reveals the solid length I'm all too familiar with. One hand wraps over his headboard while his other guides his stiff shaft to my lips.

"Take me," he demands. I open, closing my lips around him, and he works himself, dragging back and forth between my cheeks, then pressing a little farther with each rock forward. My eyes glance up at him, watching the beautiful man straining over me. His eyes close as he dances. His hips come forward. His dick slips farther.

"Your mouth," he chokes while he groans, then breaks off as though he can't tell me all he wants to say. My mouth performs like his tongue maneuvered over me—swiping and stroking—and I want to give this to him. I want to feel him at the back of my throat and down my esophagus, all the way to my belly as he's already filled another organ, the one that keeps the blood pumping in my body. And right now, I'm pumping. My cheeks hollow, and my tongues circles him. Then he pulls out abruptly.

Moving back down my body, he easily enters me. I didn't need a warning because I knew where he was going, but I feel unprepared for the surge. The way he fills me takes my breath away. He moves back and forth, dragging out the pleasure, and my hips reply with thrusts of their own, holding him inside me.

"I love your body," he says, coasting around the swell of my breast and lowering over my belly. He sits back, lifting my thighs so my backside rests on his knees as he continues to slide in and out of me. His hand skims lower until his thumb hooks on my clit, and he flicks the hood.

"Charlie," I hiss.

"You'll give me one more," he demands, and I don't want to disappoint him, but *three?* It's been a miracle I've had two back to back.

Charlie works at me, and I take the pleasing strokes and teasing rubs. I don't believe I'll get where he wants, and then he shifts. He taps me in a place I'm unfamiliar with, and I gasp. Charlie slowly smiles down at me.

"One more," he commands. My hands curl around the tie holding my wrists together as my body begins to hum. *How is he doing that?* I don't have time to ask before everything rushes to my center. Up my legs and down my belly, the prickles and tingles heighten until they crash at my core, holding Charlie deep within me.

I scream his name, lifting my head once again to watch him pummel into me. His mischievous smile and a twinkle to those eyes tell me there's more to come, and too quickly, he pulls out of me. My backside falls to the bed, and I jolt at the sudden drop.

"Flip." It isn't a command but a direction. His hands come to my hips, and he rotates me. I'm surprised by how easily I twist with the tie at my wrists. Awkwardly, I lie stretched out.

"Knees up," Charlie says, holding a hand on my backside. "Move higher. Kneel."

Holy…Sitting upright, I scoot on my knees until my kneecaps nearly touch the solid wood headboard as my fingers curl over the edge, still tied together.

"Up," he demands, and I lift higher, pressing my knees into the bed until Charlie's knees are under me, spreading my thighs. He guides me back down—reverse cowgirl—and slips inside me. He stills.

"Jesus," he hisses, resting his head on my shoulder a second as I'm sitting on his lap with his front pressed to my back. His hands circle my belly, and then he slides them up to my breasts, cupping each in a hand and giving them a sharp tug. I yelp, and Charlie jolts upward. I cry out again as he bucks under me, forcing me to ride his lap. One of his hands comes forward, curling over mine on the headboard. He rocks forward, his hips press upward, moving mine to dance over him.

"I'm going to lose it," he strains, bucking harder, increasing the ride of me over him. A hand comes to my hip. He lifts me as if moving me off him. Then a sharp smack fills the room, and I feel the sting on my ass. I cry out his name, and he drops me over him, plunging upward into me and stills.

"Holy fuck," he mutters as he jets off inside me, pulsing within me. We hold this position for a minute, both our breaths coming swiftly. With shaky fingers, Charlie unties my wrists, tugs my hands to my chest, and pulls us down to the bed. We lie on our side, sideways across the mattress.

"Are you okay?" he whispers into my hair, his breathing coming in heavy rasps.

"I've never been better," I say, admitting a truth to him. I'd never felt anything like what I feel when I'm with him. He pulls one of my arms up and back so his lips can kiss my wrist.

"I didn't hurt you." There's a question of concern, and I shake my head. I liked it more than I should admit. Moving back, he slips out of me and then presses me to my back. Something trickles between my thighs, but I ignore it as he looks down at me. "You'll stay, right?"

There's more in that question, asking me for a promise, but here's where the truth can't be shared.

"For a few hours," I say, and he lowers to kiss my mouth, slow and sweet once again.

Chapter 17
Caught

[Janessa]

"Dad?" The young female cry sends us both shooting upright in bed as we hear the call from the lower level. I don't need to check a clock. The bright light streaming into Charlie's room is enough to tell me it's morning, and I shouldn't be here.

"Where are your clothes?" Charlie whispers, looking off the side of the bed.

"Bathroom," I mutter, recalling how I took off my things in there and hung them on a hook on the back of the door.

"Go," he hushes, and I scramble from the sheets, racing for the bathroom. I softly close the door and then lean my back against it, my heart racing as I stand naked inside his bathroom with his daughter running up the stairs.

"Dad," Lucy says, barging into his room. My eyes close. Please tell me he was able to dress before she entered.

I don't hear the next few things as I take a moment to calm my breathing. I turn for the door, reaching for my dress when it opens. Charlie shuts it behind him and locks it.

"Shower," he whispers.

"What?" I hiss.

"I told her to give me fifteen minutes. I need to shower. I can't go downstairs without it."

"What about me?" I question.

"Shower." His lips curl, but my mouth gapes.

"Charlie, I'm serious. How am I going to get out of here? I'm too old to climb down a trellis or something."

His head tilts with his back to the door. "Have you done that kind of thing before?"

"I'll never tell," I tease.

"How about last night?" His voice lowers.

I shake my head. "I've never done anything like that before." My voice rings with surprise. It was quite a trip, and one I'd like to take again, but for now, I need to get out of here. Charlie steps forward, gives me a quick kiss, and then holds my eyes.

"Good morning," he whispers, his lips slowly curling.

"Good morning, sir," I mock.

With a hand at my hip, I'm walked backward until I'm inside the two-person shower with a partial opening. His hand doesn't leave my hip as his other reaches for the faucet. His lips crash mine as the cold water hits us, and I scream, which he catches with his mouth. Slowly, the water heats, and Charlie's kisses slow. He pulls back and reaches for the shampoo, squirting some in his hand and then holding up mine for more. We each shampoo our own hair, and I find the moment surreal. I vigorously scrub, my hands obviously on my head, but Charlie's eyes lower for my breasts, the sudsy bubbles flowing down to cover them.

"I want you again." It's a natural phenomenon that men are hard in the morning, and I've already felt the evidence of Charlie, but he speaks as if he's surprised with himself.

"Charlie, we have like thirteen minutes. We don't have time, plus I need to get out of here."

"It's either I slip into you or you watch me whack off in here because I need to get rid of this." He gestures to himself, and I cover my mouth to stifle the laugh. Then I move my hand forward, circling into a fist around his thick shaft. He's so hard, so solid, and instantly, I have lady boner needs as well.

"Charlie," I hiss, my voice hitching, letting him know what he's doing to me to be touching him, coating him with the water and a touch of his dripping shampoo.

"Turn around," he says, only I shake my head.

"You turn around."

His brows pinch, but he spins for the tile. I rub both hands down his back and then wrap one over his hip, slipping lower until I fist him again.

His breath catches. I reach for his other hand and bring it behind him, leading his fingers between my thighs.

"Dammit," he moans, reaching for me, and hooking his fingers into me. I roll forward, riding his fingers and pressing my breasts into his back while my hand works its magic over him. "This is insane." He chuckles, but I'm too lost in his touch to laugh. The things this man does to me. The desire I have for him. It's not ending even though I say it will be the last each time. Last night, I needed him on my terms. I wanted to decide when it would our last time together, and so I came here to stake my claim.

And then he took it all from me again.

And I so willingly gave it to him.

Naked and willing in my bed.

I'd been there.

"Janessa," he warns, and I tug faster. He moves into my fist, guiding himself to the place he needs. Then he stills, slapping a hand on the tile. His fingers fumble at me, but I pull back. I don't need this so much for me but to bring him to his knees. He spins to face me, cupping the back of my neck and tugging my mouth to him.

"I never want to disappoint you," he growls.

"I'm more than satisfied," I tell him, hoping to appease him, but his fingers return, working at me until my body gives in. As I claw at his shoulders and bite his nipple to lessen the moan, he mutters over my head, "That's better."

Removing his fingers, he reaches for his soap—the mountainy, manly one—and he washes off his body. Slipping around me, I follow his back, wondering what he's thinking.

"I can buy you five minutes. I'll keep Lucy in the kitchen, and you can go out the front door."

The front seems even more obvious than sneaking out the back door, but either way, I need to get out of this house. I should have returned to the hospital during the night. Instead, I'd fallen asleep against Charlie, who woke me in the middle of the night for another round of riveting sex.

He's relentless, and we're reckless, and I love every minute of it.

Once Charlie leaves, I dress quickly, tucking my hair into a tight bun to disguise the wetness. I'm dressed and fussing with my hair as I step out of Charlie's room into the upper hallway and listen for Lucy and Charlie's voices when a familiar tone questions my name.

"Nessa?"

"Mami?" My head shoots up, and I freeze, hand on my wet hair, wearing the same clothes as yesterday as I stare at my mother.

"Nessa," her voice strains as she steps closer to me, her eyes shifting to the lower level.

"What are you doing here?" I ask, instantly thinking of Papi, but her eyes narrow.

"What are *you* doing?" she hisses, her voice changing to Spanish, curses following about hell and damnation.

"Mami, let's talk about this later," I suggest, reaching for her arm and turning us both so my back is to the staircase. I need to get out of here. Shutting out her words, I spin for the stairs and race down them. Reaching for the front door, I open it and step out. I'd like to slam the door in my agitation at my mother, but I close it as softly as I can, and then break into a barefoot sprint around Charlie's house for the path leading to the coach house.

+ + +

Once at the coach house, I find Vega alone.

"How are you doing, baby?" I ask her as she sits on her twin bed while I undress and pray she doesn't recognize my clothing is the same from yesterday. Then again, she didn't just catch me coming out of Charlie's bedroom and has no reason to question my appearance.

"Is Papi going to be okay?" she asks, hugging a pillow to her chest, and I drop to my knees before her.

"He's going to be just fine," I try to assure her although I have no idea if he will. One minute, my father was telling me how happy he was I'd moved to Blue Ridge, and the next, he was on the floor of the diner.

"Is he going to die?" she questions, her lower lip trembling, and I tug her to me, not wanting to think such thoughts myself. Since we've moved here, my father has taken an immediate liking to Vega, spending more time with her than he ever did with me when I was a child. He wasn't present during those formative years. He missed out on this age with me. He's been stealing back time by investing his in Vega, and the two have grown close quickly. I'd hoped my father could replace Richard in Vega's heart. If she couldn't have her father, her grandfather was the next best substitute, and I refused to believe we'd lose him so quickly after gaining him for Vega.

"He's getting the best care, baby. Hopefully, we'll know more today. His heart just hurts, baby." I weakly smile. I can relate. Mine aches for Charlie and all that I want to have with him, and all that I can't.

"Change, baby," I tell her, patting her leg as we both need to change our clothes. Vega will go to art camp for the day, and I'm hoping it distracts her thoughts.

I find Mami in her kitchen and learn she came home to change because my brother, Zander, showed up during the night. I don't know why she was at Charlie's as he understands she needs to take care of my father. Still, Mami scowls at me, and I ignore her glare.

"Let's just get to Papi," I tell her before the call for prayers, and my soul begins again.

On the twenty-minute drive to the hospital, my mind replays the brief conversations Charlie and I had during the night.

I don't want to pressure you. I just want you to know I'd like to see you. Outside of work. Outside of these moments. I want to date you, learn more about you, Charlie told me in the late hours.

I want those things, too, Charlie, but now isn't the time, I said, and I'm thankful he thought it was because of my father and not because I have a deal with Richard, and I can't break it. I will not risk losing my child. Not even for Charlie.

I don't want Lucy to go to her mother's, but I don't have a choice. I follow the rules of the custody decree so as not to make waves with her. The frustration in his voice reminded me of what he'd said about his powerhouse ex-wife and the bitch she is. Who takes photos for future leverage over her husband? What mother uses her child like that? *Maybe during those two weeks, we could at least meet here and have dinner together.*

We know each other pretty well, I teased, but I knew what he meant. More than the physical attraction, there was something just under my skin that told me Charlie was a good man and a good fit for me. I just didn't know if I was ready to expose all my secrets or my heart to him.

Charlie shifted on the bed while I joked. *You know I want you for more than your body, right? I want your laughter and your smile. I want the tender touch you've given Lucy and the love in your eyes for Vega. I want to hear all your ideas and make you fall in love with my city.* Underlying his speech were almost the words…almost the plea for me to fall in love with him, but it seemed silly that Charlie would ask such a thing of me when I was fighting it myself. It wasn't that I didn't want to love him; it was that I couldn't yet.

I drop Mami off at the hospital entrance and find a spot in the parking lot. Entering the main lobby, I do a double take when I see the devil himself sitting in a seat in the waiting area.

"Richard," I hiss, stepping up to my ex-husband. A woman I don't recognize sits next to him. She looks more formal than Richard's typical type with a tight knot of hair at the base of her neck and subtle makeup. Richard's wearing dark track pants and a long-sleeved shirt with Atlanta across the chest while this woman wears a fitted pantsuit. My ex-husband is a Viking of sorts with sandy blond hair curling against his nape and a sculpted beard. He's tall and broad with strength in his arms from being a center fielder. He's a good-looking man, but he's lost his luster and will never be handsome to me again.

Richard rubs his hands along his thighs and then stands. Stepping up to me, he leans in to kiss my cheek, but I step back on instinct.

"Janessa," he states my name before looking over his shoulder at the woman watching us.

"What are you doing here?" I question, shifting my eyes to the woman. She looks like a lawyer. "I see you brought your latest dish with you."

The woman scowls behind a pair of glasses.

"I heard about your father. I came as soon as I could," Richard says, ignoring my comment.

I don't even want to know how he knew I was here or that my father had fallen ill, but then again…

"How did you know?" I hiss, risking a glance at the lawyer-looking lady. *Is Richard stalking me? Having me followed?*

"Janessa, you know I'll always know where you are," he says, and I hold up a hand, not interested in him telling me how I'm his, I'll always be his, like he broke down at our divorce reading.

"I signed away everything to prevent this kind of thing," I tell him.

"I'm…changing," Richard says, looking over his shoulder at the woman behind him.

"Who is she?" I snap, nodding in her direction.

"This is Ruthie Avery. She's my sports manager."

I tip my head, well aware that Richard has an agent, and it's not a woman. His agent made sure I didn't know my worth with Richard. I stare at the woman who stands and offers a hand. Shaking it in return, she clarifies who she is.

"I'm actually an image manager. I work with Imperial Sports Associates, the company that represents Mr. Swank."

"A what?" I ask

"Image manager. I work with athletes to…umm…rectify their reputation." Ruthie clears her throat, glancing up at Richard. My head swings back and forth between them. *Is she sleeping with him?* I tell myself I don't care, and I don't. However, she looks like an intelligent woman who wouldn't fall for his bullshit. I turn back to Richard.

"What happened in Houston?" I snap. Mid-season trades are not unheard of in baseball, but Richard being moved seems unprecedented. Nothing is ever simple with him.

Scratching at the back of his neck, he says, "Is there somewhere we can talk?"

My head vigorously shakes. "No. I'm here for my father, and you're leaving." My voice is rising, and Ruthie steps forward.

"Richard," Ruthie warns.

"Janessa, I need this," Richard groans, ignoring the woman's hand rising before him, a signal from his image manager to step back.

"No, *oh no*. Whatever you're thinking, no." I don't even want to know what they might be thinking, but the fact they're standing here says I'm involved somehow when I want nothing to do with anything to *rectify* Richard's reputation.

"Richard," Ms. Avery attempts a second time.

"You owe me," Richard says, his voice straining.

"I owe you nothing. You took everything." Then my eyes widen. *Vega.* "We have an agreement. A legal, binding agreement. Don't make me file a restraining order." My tone turns to ice. I've never stood up to Richard as much as I did toward the end. Thankfully, the general manager of his team liked me. He knew there was trouble between us, and he told Richard to sort himself out by giving me what I wanted.

I wanted nothing but Vega.

No automobile. No allowance. Not even alimony or child support. I just wanted him to leave us alone.

"Richard, this isn't helping," Ruthie interjects, stepping before Richard and looking up at him. "You hired me for a reason, and you need to listen to me, or there's no point."

Richard turns his head to the side and exhales. Slowly, things fall into place. When I left, Richard must have continued in his ways, and the general manager said enough. Rather than keep him for his skill, the team traded him because of his drama. One thing I had to agree to in the divorce was not to mention our divorce until the season ended.

Helping Richard save face.

With Ruthie physically between Richard and me, a familiar voice behind me crashes our unwanted reunion.

"What's going on here?"

Charlie?

A calm I didn't expect seeps under my skin, and my body prickles with relief at the sound of his voice. As much as I've refused his help, his presence strengthens my resolve.

"Richard, you need to leave."

Chapter 18
With an Ex Comes a Why?

[Charlie]

Richard?

As I entered the hospital, I paused at the scene before me. A man begging Janessa for something, telling her she owes him. A woman standing between Janessa and a man who is her ex-husband.

"What's going on here?" I ask, stepping up to the three of them.

"Charlie," Janessa whispers under her breath, her head lowering. My eyes move from her to the woman in a pantsuit.

"Richard, you need to leave," Janessa boldly states the second my hand lands on her lower back. When no one speaks after her request, Richard glares at my hand. Janessa stares at her ex, and a third person shakes her head side to side, so I decide to address her first.

"Charlie Harrington, Mayor of Blue Ridge."

The suited woman offers her hand. "Ruthie Avery. I represent this man, Richard Swank."

"Nice to meet you. I represent Janessa Cruz," I state as we shake hands.

Janessa's ex snorts. "Cruz? It's Swank."

Holding up my hand to signal he stop talking, I interject. "I'm certain this isn't a sympathy visit but being as Ms. Cruz has family in this hospital, I suggest you make an appointment with my office, and we can discuss what you're doing here at that time."

"I'm not his attorney," Ruthie clarifies. "I'm his image manager."

My brows pinch, but I know what this means. Angela has someone similar in her campaign for office. That person came up with the single-mother angle.

"Well, I *am* an attorney as well as the mayor, and I still request an appointment, but not today." Slipping my hand to her elbow, I gently nudge her to start moving.

"Nessa?" her ex-husband pleads.

"Keep moving," I mutter as we turn for the elevator. Heavy feet stomp behind me, and I release Janessa's arm, telling her to go ahead, and then I spin to face her ex-husband.

"Mr. Swank, don't make me call the sheriff."

This stops the baseball player in his tracks, and he narrows his eyes at me. The woman behind him lowers her head in defeat. "She's my wife." Richard speaks over my shoulder, and I sense Janessa has not left the hallway.

"Actually, she's not," I remind him.

His head tips. "How do you know that?" His voice has lowered, and he pauses, taking me in. He's taller than me by a few inches and broader, but I'd scrap with him if I need to. I might be considered the good one, but as the youngest of four brothers, I know how to fight.

His voice turns sinister when he leans forward and says, "Are you doing her? You tap that?"

Stepping up to him, I casually slip my hands into my pockets to conceal my fists and control the vibration of anger coming over my body. "Mr. Swank, I'd advise you to be respectful." I'm not about to explain to him attorney-client confidentiality, and then I swallow hard around the word. *Client*. Not only do Janessa and I have the employer-employee confines, but now I'm crossing other lines of attorney-client privilege.

I glance at the image manager. "I'm not certain what the goal is here, but I suggest you keep your client in control, or he'll have more than his image to repair."

"Are you threatening me?" Richard says, closing the distance between us. My eyes roam the size of his body, and his manager steps up to his back, warning him with a stern voice.

"I wouldn't dream of it," I say, crooking up my lip because believe it or not, I can play dirty if I need to. I learned from the master. *My* ex-wife.

At my side once again, Janessa's soft voice speaks. "Richard, go away."

"Are you protecting him? Why are you protecting him? Are you fucking him?" Her ex-husband's voice escalates as he leans closer to me, ready to chest bump me like boys in the schoolyard. Janessa's fingers wrap around my upper arm, and I want to sneer at him, point out she's touching me, not him, but I stop myself.

"Richard, this isn't helping," his image manager interjects while Janessa encourages me, "Charlie, walk with me."

The plea in her tone and the words themselves turn my head. I'd follow her anywhere and gladly be her knight in shining armor.

+ + +

"I'm sorry you saw that," Janessa states, keeping her head lowered before we enter the elevator. With another person inside the lift, we don't speak, and she feels miles away from me. When we silently arrive at the telemetry unit, Janessa picks up the pace when she sees a man talking on the phone outside her father's room. Rushing up to him, they collide in a hug but quickly separate. By the time I've made it to them, her arms flap, her voice angrily animated as she addresses a man who is definitely her sibling. Same jet-black hair and same brilliant green eyes although his are slightly lighter.

"How could you do this to me?" she groans, tossing her arms out to her sides while she speaks to her brother.

"He called me drunk and whining. He said he just wanted to talk to Vega. Talk."

"So you told him where we are?" Her voice rises.

"He says he doesn't have her number," he states as if that's an explanation.

"I threw her phone away."

My brows lift at this information. Janessa hangs her head, shaking it from side to side, and her brother reaches out for her shoulder.

"I'm sorry, Nessa."

His hand comes to her shoulder, but she swats it off her. "I can't believe this." She reaches forward and shoves his shoulder. His eyes widen, but then he smiles as if he recognizes something in his sister.

"Ah, there she is," he teases, and she punches his other shoulder. Within a second, she's smacking him left to right, and I step in. Slipping an arm around her waist, I tug her back.

"No," she snarls, still reaching for her sibling, and her brother chuckles.

"Zander Cruz, and you are?" He tweaks a thick brow.

"Charlie Harrington." I wait only a second for the name to register since I employ his parents.

Janessa struggles in my arms, hers still grappling like she wants to scratch her brother's eyes out.

"Well, this is interesting," Zander teases, a suggestive twist to his lips.

"You know nothing," Janessa snaps. "You're so stupid, Zander."

The words intend to hurt, and for a second, it shows on his face that they've met their mark, but then he looks away from her. "I didn't think he'd show up here."

"That's the problem, Zander. You never think." Janessa settles against me, her hands curling over my forearm at her waist. "I can't talk to you right now."

Her brother has the grace to nod once and then roll off the wall, turning in the direction of the door to her father's room. He disappears inside it, and Janessa whispers, "Charlie, let go of me."

"We need to talk," I demand, tugging her under my arm for a small solarium at the end of the hall. I shut the door behind us as I release her, and she stumbles forward. Both her hands slip into her thick dark hair, tugging it free from the knot in the back. She reaches for the hairband and loosens all her hair, and I have a flash of her last night in bed. How are we standing here like this now, breathing heavily at one another?

"Sit," I command, and her brows lift. "As your attorney, I need to know everything."

"You are not my attorney," she says.

"I am now." My eyes narrow at her, warning her not to argue with me.

"I don't need your help," she snaps.

"The fuck you don't." I exhale, swiping a hand through my hair. "I'm not leaving you to take care of him on your own or whatever noble thing you think you can handle without support. I need the truth. Now." Something in my expression warns her to follow my demand.

She lowers in a seat, but I remain standing. Slipping my hands into my pockets, I'm trying to stay calm.

What the fuck is her ex doing here, and what does he want?

"I was married to Richard for ten years." I know this fact, and I stare down at her until she looks up at me, and repeats, "Ten years."

Ah. A shotgun wedding.

"I'd fallen for his charm while I worked for Arizona's marketing team. His agent thought a marriage and a baby would be good for his reputation because he'd always been volatile. A hothead on and off the field. Eventually, he was transferred to Houston, and I gave up my career to follow him. I was arm candy," she states, turning her head in the direction of the window. "I was so stupid."

"Don't say that about yourself," I hiss, knowing we all do things when we're young and want to believe in love.

"No, really. I didn't sign a prenup. *Pregnant*," she emphasizes. "I thought he'd never do anything to ruin us. He needed me, and I loved him." Her voice strains.

"Without a prenup, you could have sued him for everything," I say, and her head hangs again, her hair curtaining her face. I lower to a crouch before her.

"Okay, keep talking." I soften my voice, desperate to touch her knee and assure her I understand.

"I didn't care about the money. I'd never had any, and I didn't know how to live the rich and famous lifestyle anyway." Her head lifts. "I'm a poor girl with immigrant parents, raised by my grandmother in a shit part of Texas. I came from nothing, so I misunderstood everything. *Just stand there and look good, Nessa*," she mocks. "He didn't respect my education, career, or opinion. I was a pretty piece of ass, and he was stuck with a baby and me."

I swallow back the bile in my throat. Richard Swank is the asshole, not her.

"Vega walking in on him was the last straw. I couldn't have her exposed to his lifestyle. I shouldn't have let so much slide." She shakes her head again. "But I knew I'd have nothing if I left before that incident. I'd burned bridges when I left Arizona. My work experience was over a decade old. And I had no money without him. Do you have any idea how hard it was to come to my parents?" Her voice lowers. "I'm forty-three and using my dad's truck like a teenager, sleeping in a twin bed across from my daughter, and borrowing money from my parents to buy clothes for my new job."

"I'll give you a raise," I say, and she bitterly chuckles.

"It isn't about the money, Charlie. It's my pride." Her fingers clasp together as she balances her arms on her knees. "I wanted so much more for myself, and then for Vega, and look where I'm at." Her eyes close.

"You're where you're supposed to be," I whisper. *Here. With me.*

"I don't know what Richard's doing here."

"I suppose, if that woman really is an image manager, they're hoping you'll serve some purpose for him. Supportive ex-husband? Man wanting to see his kid? He shows good faith by coming to your side at a time of need."

I'm missing something here. Even my explanation doesn't make sense to my ears.

"Our divorce agreement meant I gave up everything but got sole custody of Vega. No visitation. No communication. But I don't share the divorce until the day the season ends. I'm still his wife in the eyes of the public."

My forehead furrows. Is this it? Is this why she holds back?

"What does the *public*," I hiss the word, "have to do with anything? And where do people think you are?"

"Pretending I'm his wife a little longer protects Richard. No one cares about divorces after the season, but during it, it's a media shitshow.

And according to the team, I'm visiting my family." She shrugs, her voice defeated.

"So the trade to Atlanta must mean…"

"He wants to be closer to his family."

Does he think he can win her back? With the scene in the lobby, I'd say not a chance, but I can't process this yet.

"What is he doing here?" she asks, sounding exhausted.

"As your attorney, that's what I intend to find out."

Her head lifts, her eyes weary. There's no look of longing in them like she gives me when we're physically together. She wants me, or at least her body does, but emotionally, she's as distant as ever.

+ + +

"What we're asking for is Mrs. Swank to continue acting as Richard's wife until the end of the season. In return, she'll be paid one million dollars for her time."

I stare at the woman before me in her pencil skirt and tightly buttoned suit jacket. It's the day after we've met in the hospital lobby, and Ruthie Avery has honored my request to make an appointment with me.

Last night, Vega spent the night at my home with Lucy. However, Janessa did not magically appear in my bedroom as I hoped. With her family gathered to support her father, I understand, *I do*, but I missed her in my bed.

"I'll need to discuss this with my client," I state, swallowing back the bitterness of the word in my throat. She isn't my client; she's my… What? *What is she to me?* Regardless, I want to tell this woman to fuck her suggestion, Richard Swank, and herself even though I imagine she's only doing her job.

"However, I understand a legal and binding agreement exists in which Ms. Cruz"—I correct her name—"does not need to see her ex-husband, denying all assets with him in return for sole custody and no visitation from Mr. Swank."

"Vega is a must. He needs to show he's a good father," Ruthie states.

"But he's not, and we both know it." I stare at her over my desk. Her expression says she agrees. She knows he's a worthless son of a bitch who mistreated his wife and ignored his daughter, but now he needs them, if only for a short term. Atlanta is demanding he appear as a family man to right the reputation of a playboy in Houston.

"What is the timeframe again?" I hate that I've asked, but I'm trying to think like an attorney and not someone falling for the woman in question.

"The season could go as long as October if they make it to the World Series."

I glare at her. That's more than three months. *No deal*, I want to scream. None of this is even up for consideration.

"She doesn't need to have sex with him. She doesn't even need to live with him. We can continue to play it that she's staying with family. *He* came here to be near her and her family. Her father's heart condition is a bonus."

"You don't really think that, do you?" I peer at the woman before me. She can't possibly be that coldhearted, and I see as she swallows back her own words that she isn't. She's been trained to be this calculating, but this isn't who she is. At least, I hope not. How ruthless can Ruthie be? "What is the intention? They're seen in public?"

"She attends a few games. He goes to activities for Vega."

"And how does this end?"

"Irreconcilable differences as the divorce decree already states."

"Because you can't put adultery and emotional abuse as a reason," I huff, thinking of my own divorce. "It can't be this simple. He just walks away."

"He does. Only one condition during the time period. She isn't allowed to date anyone. No secret arrangements. No public displays. Devoted wife until the end." Ruthie narrows her eyes at me as if she knows something, and she isn't wrong.

"You're kidding me, right?" I snap. Leaning forward, I realize I'm no longer containing my irritation with this entire discussion or my status as an attorney and not someone emotionally attached to Janessa. I can't believe we're even going back and forth on this as if negotiating a real possibility. Janessa will never go for this. *Never.*

+ + +

"You aren't seriously considering this?" I scoff. I had Janessa on the phone ten minutes after Ruthie left my office, and silence fills the line instead of the adamant *when hell freezes over* I was expecting.

"There's just so much going on," she mutters, and I hear the resolve in her voice. However, I'm too upset that there is even a remote possibility she'll continue to play pretend for him.

"No fucking way," I blow ahead. "You aren't doing it."

"Oh, really? Speaking as my attorney, are you advising against it?" Her voice drips with sarcasm.

No, speaking as a man who worships you.

"Janessa," I hiss, lowering my voice as a hand slips into my hair and tugs at the short ends. This can't be happening. She's refused to let me help her in any manner, but she'll think about this—this farce of an arrangement—for a million dollars. "Is it about the money?"

She's quiet for a moment, and I think about what she told me. She said it was never about the money, but things change. People—and circumstances—change our minds. I go completely off the rail, making a suggestion I hadn't given two seconds to consider.

"Move in with me. I can set you up in the guest room if you wish. We can play it that we're engaged. I can help you get out of this."

"Charlie," she groans. "I'd only be trading one playact for another."

"How far of a stretch would it be? We're together."

Her silence weighs between us again.

Aren't we?

She came to my room. She told me she needed me.

"I see," I say softly, scrubbing a hand down my face.

"Charlie." Her voice softens. "How would it look if I moved in with you? I'm newly divorced, which hasn't been announced, by a man in the public eye, and then I'm engaged? It screams scandal as though I'm the one who stepped out on him and not the other way around. Then there's you. I'm new to town, my parents work for you, and I suddenly get a job, but I'm also in your bed. How does that look for you?"

Logically, she's right, but emotionally, my heart hurts. It's what she isn't addressing that causes the ache. Would it be so wrong to *act* like we are together? No, not act—just be with one another.

"You're very conscious of how things look. After being treated like arm candy, I thought you'd realize image wasn't everything. I see I'm wrong."

Her breath hitches through the phone.

"Charlie, the bottom line is, I refuse to do anything that risks my losing Vega. It's already written, sealed, and stamped that my daughter is mine, but Richard is more powerful than I am. If he can find an angle to twist things in his favor, he will, and I won't give him any cause to turn the decree around and say I didn't follow it. Nothing, Charlie. Not even you will give me a reason to lose her."

I hear what she's saying, and deep down, I understand it, but my irritation grows to anger that she thinks I'd risk her losing her child.

"I'll await your decision, but Mr. Swank's assistant suggests you decide by Monday."

Somehow, I don't think she needs the forty-eight hours. She's already decided, and it isn't a vote in my favor.

Chapter 19
Charming Charlie

[Janessa]

When I return to my father's room, I still hold my phone in my hand. I take a seat near the foot of the bed as Mami sits beside Papi. Zander is next to me, and we stare at our father in silence. In so many ways, I don't know my parents. I didn't live with them in my developing years. Then they found jobs in Texas, and we were together through middle school and high school when I was too busy to hang out with family. When I went off to college, I didn't look back on the place I grew up. My abuela died; her husband long gone. My parents found work in Georgia, and I didn't visit. I was building a career, and then I met Richard. Charming. Sexy. Richard.

And I got pregnant.

My father was disappointed, but I dismissed his judgment. He had no right. He hadn't raised me.

Then I had a child, and I understood so much better all that they sacrificed and did to give Zander and myself a better life, and we had better. Homes. Cars. Education. Only, I'd given it all up, first because I loved Richard and then because I hated him.

And now, he needs me, or so he says. I'm certain there's another way around this mess, but I can't think straight right now. Richard. My father. Charlie.

Charlie sounded so hurt, and so hard, when I tried to explain how we couldn't be together—not publicly. It isn't that I don't want to be with Charlie. I don't want to consider being without him, but I can't. Not yet. I signed an NDA on the status of my marriage until the end of the baseball season, and I intend to follow the decree, unlike Richard, who wants to bend the rules to his advantage.

I glance up at the floral arrangement sent to Papi's room. It's ostentatious and unnecessary. The card was even worse.

Thinking of you and your father. With love, Richard.

Love? Ha. Richard doesn't know what love is. He claimed he grew up without it, thus desperate to have it and give it. Even when I thought I was a good teacher, giving him my love and the beauty of a child, he didn't learn. He talked the talk but didn't toe the line to be any different than his parents.

Once again, I consider my own parents and their distance from their children for totally different reasons and in a different manner. It wasn't alcohol. It wasn't adultery. They were decent, hardworking people who wanted more for their children.

A million dollars.

How hard would it be to pretend Richard and I are still married? I *pretended* most of our marriage. Still, divorce was my freedom, and I don't want to go back to the prison of Richard.

But a million bucks?

I could give Vega so much.

I have a job, but it will take us years to regain what we'd given up. A house. A car. Her education. I sold it all to save our souls.

Sitting straighter in my seat, I take a deep breath as I glance down at my phone. I should call Charlie back. I should try to explain myself better and help him understand.

"You doing okay?" Zander asks. I still want to smack him. My brother is a punk, even at forty. He hasn't grown up in any manner. He has a good job and a nice home in Arizona, but he still behaves the same way he did as a teenager with excess women, booze, and drugs.

"I've been better," I mutter.

"I doubt it," he says under his breath. We might be in our forties, but I could hold my own trying to kick his ass. I was the sports girl while he was the computer geek. Opposites raised in the same household, he acts out now to make up for those nerd years. *Nerds rule the world*, a teacher once said, and she had Zander in mind when she mentioned it.

"What's that supposed to mean?" I hiss, keeping my eyes forward, hoping Mami isn't listening. She's hardly looked at me since she caught me coming out of Charlie's bedroom yesterday morning.

Was it only twenty-four hours ago he had me in so many ways?

"You're so much better off without him," Zander says, and I turn to face him.

"Then why would you tell him where I was?"

Zander shrugs, not dismissing me, but just not able to answer. See, here's the other thing about my brother. While he might be all computer geek smart, he has no common sense. I really think when he isn't looking at a screen, his brain just shuts off, and typically, his dick takes over.

"I don't like him being here anymore than you do," Zander says.

"Do you even know why he's here?"

Zander rolls his head on the back of the chair and peers at me. "Realized he was a fool and should have never let you go?"

"Ha. He wants to pay me a million dollars to pretend to still be married to him."

"Holy shit," Zander says, sitting forward, and Mami hisses at him, cursing him in return in Spanish. He twists in his seat and stares at me. "A *million* dollars?"

His voice drifts, the excitement not surprising, and I see the dollar signs inside those green eyes.

"You're not considering doing it, are you?"

This does surprise me, and I stare back at him.

"It's a lot of money. For Vega."

Zander falls back in his seat. He loves my girl, and in many ways, I wish he lived closer because she's going to need a father figure. Not that Zander's a role model with his womanizing ways, but he is good to his niece.

My thoughts flip to Charlie. He's so good with his own daughter, and he's been so accommodating with Vega by letting her stay at his house. She texts me with updates of the things she's been doing with Elaina Harrington and then with Charlie.

Swimming. A bonfire in their backyard. S'mores.

It sounds great.

"Even for Vega, that's blood money, Nessa. You can't take it. You've already sacrificed enough of yourself."

Again, his support surprises me.

"You like it here, right?" he asks, his forehead furrowing in question.

"I do." I don't even have to think about it. It's only been a month, and I'm in love with Blue Ridge. The town. The people. My job. Charlie.

I blink at the thought. I can't love Charlie. It's too much, too soon.

My heart races a little faster.

Do I? Can I?

Don't hop from one fire into another, I remind myself. I'm here to straighten out me. Renew. Refresh. Start over. Only, I sigh at the thought. I'm forty-three, and I'm so far behind.

+ + +

There's been no change in Papi's status, so Mami suggests I check on Vega and Charlie. She takes her job seriously, and she wants to make certain Charlie and Lucy are surviving without her.

"Janessa?" Sheepishly, I look down at my feet when Charlie opens his front door. It seems strange to enter this way, but then again, it's how I exited the other morning.

"Mami wanted me to check on you and Lucy. She thought you might not be eating well without her."

Charlie slowly grins at the statement as he steps back, allowing me into his home.

"You know, I do know my way around the kitchen."

My brow arches in question before I follow him to said kitchen and find a large pizza box on the island.

"Know your way around the kitchen, huh?"

"Yep, it's called delivery, and dinner is served."

I can't help the smile gracing my own lips. It's so good to see him after this afternoon's phone call.

"I bet you'd really like to know how Vega is?" He tips his head and calls out for the girls. Feet thunder from the second floor, and then I see Vega.

"Baby," I hiss as she leaps for me. She's too big for me to pick up, but the feel of her arms around my neck settles me. There's nothing like the hug of a child. I turn and kiss her cheek. "I've missed you."

It's only been a few days, but the whirlwind of my father and then Richard's return makes me wish we could just curl into those two twin beds in the coach house.

Vega separates from me. "How is Papi?" She calls my father by the same name as I do.

"He's doing better, I think. The doctor said he can come home tomorrow." I don't know what this means for Charlie. My father shouldn't be tending his yard and gardens until he gets the medical all clear, and even then, it might be time for my father to slow down.

"Speaking of home, we should probably get going," I say to Vega. It's late, and Charlie needs to work tomorrow.

"Did you eat?" he interjects at the same time that Lucy whines, "I thought you were spending the night again."

Lucy has really taken to Vega and vice versa. At first, I worried that Lucy's friendship was a reminder of all Vega left behind, and she'd resent her. In some ways, I think Vega likes to hang out at Charlie's for the same reason—it's a reminder of what we left behind. The pool. The large house. But the two girls have really formed a bond, and although Vega was angry that Lucy spilled her secret, she quickly forgave her. It's more fun sleeping in twin beds across from your best friend than your mother.

"I don't want to impose again," I state because Vega's already been at Charlie's mother's house and now here.

"It's not an imposition," Charlie says. "Pint enjoys the company. I'm boring." It's so sweet that he has a nickname for her, and I've been meaning to ask about it. Also, there isn't one boring thing about Charlie Harrington, but recalling his evil ex-wife, I imagine he's been told he was boring in the past.

Vega looks at me with pleading eyes, and Lucy adds to it with a pouty lip and fluttering eyelids.

"Does that work on you?" I tease, glancing up at Charlie. He can't fall for the charms of his daughter so easily, or he'll have his hands full when she's a teen. Then again, Lucy seems mature beyond her years. This becomes another connection I hadn't recognized between Vega and Lucy. They are both used to parents in the public eye.

"Most days." Charlie shrugs. "Does it work if I join in?" He pouts with his full lips and flutters his lids, exaggerating the motions of his daughter.

"Very charming, Charlie."

His lips curl again as his lids lower only a little bit. "I try to be."

Oh, he is.

He pushes the pizza box in my direction, and I sigh. "Fine." It's hardly a whisper of a word, but the girls break into cheers. Vega hugs me, and then the two of them run off again, feet thundering up the stairs.

"I grew up in a house of boys and one sister, and running in the house drove my mother crazy." Charlie smiles to himself, opening the box before me. "I always thought I'd have a house full of kids to do the same to me."

There's sadness in his voice as he turns for a cabinet and reaches for a plate. I don't really want pizza, but I should eat. Charlie places two slices on the dish and then reaches for a bottle of wine on the counter.

"Red okay?"

I nod. I could definitely use wine.

"It's really none of my business, but why don't you have a house full of children?" Charlie is extremely good-looking. There'd be no reason not to take him to bed and be impregnated continuously with the vigor of him.

"Angela didn't want children." Charlie lowers his voice as he pulls a glass from a cabinet. Turning to face me, he softly speaks. "She didn't even want Lucy."

"That's horrible," I whisper before I have time to think. There are always reasons women don't want children, and I try not to judge, but motherhood is one of the greatest gifts. "I'm sorry, that was insensitive."

"She wanted an abortion. I wouldn't let her do it."

I gasp. Aborting Vega had never even crossed my mind when I found out I was pregnant, and to my surprise, Richard asked me to marry him. For his reputation. A family gives a good impression.

"I'm sorry," I say, uncertain what else to say.

"Angela was very driven, and although we were married, she did not want a child. We'd been married only a year when she got pregnant. As soon as she told me and I convinced her to keep it, I decided to come home. I wanted to raise my child here, and the best way to convince Angela to move was to make it political, so I decided to run for mayor."

I stare up at him as I reach for my wine. I didn't know these things about him. In fact, I still don't know much about him at all, other than how me makes me physically feel and the fact he's giving me a chance to run his town's park district.

"It worked in my favor. Young couple. Baby on the way. It was meant to be a notch in my career, but when I ran for a second term, Angela was upset. She had an affair and almost ruined me. The town didn't have faith in a mayor who couldn't keep his wife under control."

I gasp. "People did not say that."

"Oh, they did. I almost lost, but my opponent wasn't from Blue Ridge, and that made all the difference to the town. Amid scandalous photographs and a public divorce, I became mayor again, and I'm obviously still here." Charlie has been serving for years. He shrugs. "I like being mayor."

"What about Congress?"

"I definitely think there could be a spot for me." He lifts his head. "I could do so much more for the community that drives tourism to Georgia if I were out there." He waves his hand in the general direction of a window. "But I don't know about Lucy."

I give a weak smile. "Decisions always feel bigger when a child is involved."

Charlie nods. "She's flexible, and she'll go where I go, but I hate to uproot her."

"Could she stay here?" I look around the grand kitchen.

"This is the mayor's house. A provision provided by a former mayor." Charlie rolls his eyes. "I suppose there's a loophole around it, and my parents might prefer that as they won't want some random person moving in every term, but I don't want to miss out with Lucy. My dad was always there for me, and I want to be there for her. I need to be there double as she hardly sees her mother."

"Vega told me Lucy isn't excited she has to visit her mother at the end of the month." If I had to lose Vega for two weeks, I'd be beside myself. Who knows what things she'd see from Richard and his posse of women?

"I'm not excited myself," Charlie mutters, and I remember him telling me this during our night together. "I don't trust Angela."

"I know the feeling," I retort, and Charlie's eyes narrow at me.

"Then why would you consider his proposal?"

"Charlie, please." I sigh, exasperated. I swipe fingers into my long hair and hold it back as my elbow rests on his island. There's been too much in the past couple of days.

"Right. Not letting me in," Charlie says as he reaches for my unfinished glass of wine. I think he's going to dump it down the sink and tell me to get out, but he surprises me by picking up his own glass and then walking over to the couch in a small sitting area off the kitchen. The elaborate house has your typical formal living room and dining room toward the front, but this kitchen area is my favorite. A large island with stools but also a sit-down dining area and then a couch and entertainment center behind the table. It's spacious but homey in this area of the house, and I follow Charlie without his instruction.

The oversized ottoman holds a tray for our wine glasses, and after setting them on the metal, Charlie falls back on the couch. I take a seat as well although not sitting as close as I'd like.

"Come closer to me," he says, his eyes focused on the television which is on.

"What about the girls?" I whisper. It's not like Charlie and I have a public relationship. I can't say we even have a private one other than enjoying each other through sex, but I wouldn't mind being closer to him. I wouldn't mind cuddling on the couch with my feet up.

"We'd definitely hear them if they came thundering down those steps," Charlie teases, so I move a little closer. His arm flips to the back of the couch, and my thigh presses against his, but I don't lean into him as I wish, and he doesn't wrap his arm around me, also like I want.

"Surprisingly, Richard was happy when I told him I was pregnant." I don't know why I mention this, but Charlie's opened up to me, so I need to do the same for him. "I stupidly thought a baby would change him." I lower my head. I was thirty-two with naïve dreams that a child would change a man. Old enough to know better myself. Innocent enough to believe differently. I'd been a picky lover over the years with only a few boyfriends as I didn't want anyone suggesting I slept my way to the top as a woman in sports marketing, a field dominated by men. Nor did I want to hook up with men who didn't respect my intelligence, thinking I was only a pretty face on athletics. I'd had a softball scholarship, full ride to college. How did a pretty face get me that? I was out to prove myself, and then I made one foolish mistake.

"He wanted to marry me. Said it would be good for his image, and I thought he meant making him a family man. He meant covering up his indiscretions." It's hard to admit how blind I'd been. How much of an enabler, perhaps? I didn't want to believe Richard would do something like take a blonde to spring training celebrations or hook up with a brunette at a fundraiser I didn't attend.

Charlie's fingers come to the edge of my hair and twirl strands around them. His eyes remain focused on the television, but his other arm leans on the armrest of the couch, bracing his temple against his propped-up hand.

"It's hard to see what's right before you when you think you're in love," Charlie says.

He might be the only one who understands. My mother did not want to hear of my unhappiness. The other wives acted as if it came with the territory. Only Richard's general manager had sympathy for me. He didn't think Richard was fair to me, but he wanted Richard's talent for his team.

Something must have happened because now Richard was let go.

"Did you love Angela?" It's an invasive question, but I'm still curious. Charlie removes his arm from the edge of the couch and slouches lower into the cushions. He tugs me along with him, bringing me closer to his side, his fingers still playing with my hair.

"I loved her ambition and her spirit, but when sex becomes something on a calendar instead of spontaneous, my interest waned. Unfortunately, I thought that's how it was even though I knew it shouldn't be that way. My sister's husband was my law partner before he died—"

"Oh, I'm sorry," I interject. His current partner is the son of his former partner and brother-in-law.

"We didn't share secrets about our marriages, but Chris would let it slip if he and Mati had a particularly good night or did something unusual. He loved to tease me to see me blush and horrify me as he was speaking of my sister. *So Mati and I broke in the new kitchen counter*, he'd say, and I'd start la-la-laing because I didn't want to hear it." Charlie chuckles to himself as he mimics their conversation. "My family thought Angela was a coldhearted bitch, and they weren't wrong. I wrote it off as them being small town before accepting she had a small heart."

"I'm sorry it was like that for you." Richard would have never lived by a calendar. However, he did prefer it in your typical places and positions, at least with me. He'd never taken me against a chain-link fence or an office desk as Charlie had. Charlie and I have been nothing but spontaneous.

"It's one reason I like you," he says, his voice lowering.

My hand comes to Charlie's thigh, tracing circles with my thumb on the firm muscle under his sweatpants. For a suit man, he wears casual just as well. My fingers seem to have a mind of their own, and the circles turn to lines stroking up and down Charlie's leg. He shifts a second, and I wonder if he's turned on. I'm getting turned on by touching him. We haven't been slow with one another. It would be too intimate, I suppose, if we were.

His fingers lower to my neck, brushing back my hair from my shoulder and tickling fine lines up and down my skin. My head tilts, leaning against his shoulder and exposing more of my neck to him.

"Whatcha doing?" The high-pitched female titter comes from the side of the couch, and Charlie and I spring forward as though we've been caught making out. Close. So close. Lucy breaks into giggles, but Vega stares back at me. She hasn't seen me with anyone other than her father. How many women has Lucy caught her father with? Have there been others here before me? He's been divorced a long time. He couldn't possibly have gone without dates, relationships even.

Charlie's sitting forward with his elbows on his knee, disguising what I'm certain is obvious in those sweatpants. I slip a hand between us, attempting to subtly slide apart from him and give us some distance. Lucy walks around the oversized ottoman, and Charlie watches her cross the room and then wedge herself into the minimal space between the couch edge and Charlie. Vega slips next to me. This couch isn't really meant to hold two full adults and two growing girls, but we fit.

Charlie sits back and lifts an arm for Lucy, who tucks her head against his chest. Vega wraps her hands around my arm and leans her head on my shoulder. I turn to kiss her hair, breathing her in, and close my eyes. What am I doing here? What am I doing with Charlie?

The four of us sit in awkward silence for what feels like an eternity. My hand still rests between Charlie and me, but it twitches, wishing to return to its place on his thigh. I want him to tug me back to him, close my eyes, and pretend we are a family, just as Charlie and I have been pretending—pretending we aren't wildly attracted to each other.

"You two are boring," Lucy eventually says, popping her head up. "We want to go swimming."

"It's almost midnight," Charlie states, and Lucy tries her pouty lip, fluttering lids thing again. "No, Pint." His voice deepens, and I'm surprised at how easily she gives up the act. Maybe he isn't such a pushover after all.

"Can Vega still spend the night?" Lucy directs her gaze to me, minus the whining. I turn to face Vega, meeting eyes that match mine.

"Can I, Mom?" I really think I should take Vega home. We haven't seen each other in days, and with her father in town, which she doesn't even know yet, we need to talk.

"I don't think tonight's—"

"Maybe one more night," Charlie interjects, and the depth in his voice sounds like the night he told me only one more time, and then we'd stop. My eyes close, and Vega squeezes my arm.

"Fine," I hiss.

Lucy squeals, and Vega tips up for my cheek, kissing me quickly. "You're the best, Mom."

Both girls leap from the couch.

"Pint, time for bed, though. No more wandering the house," Charlie warns. "Lights out in fifteen."

"Dad," she groans.

"It's almost midnight," he states.

"It's summer. We don't have school tomorrow."

"No, but I have work. Upstairs. Lights out. Fifteen," Charlie demands.

"Thirty?" Lucy questions.

"Ten," Charlie bargains.

"Okay, fifteen works." Lucy kisses Charlie's cheek and then walks around the ottoman. To my surprise, she leans down to give me a hug as well, and then she and Vega disappear through the kitchen.

"How did you get her to be so agreeable?" I state, a chuckle in my voice.

"Years of practice." He sighs, and I'm reminded again that Charlie has been a single parent for a long time while it's only been a month or so for me. Then again, I'd been a single-married-parent most of my marriage. Vega and I did everything together.

"I'll check on them in twenty," he states.

"You just said fifteen," I tease.

"Yeah, but it is summer."

"You're a softy," I joke, but Charlie surprises me by picking up my hand and tugging it over his middle, lowering it for the bulge in his sweats. "I'm hard for you, dammit. I can't seem to help myself." He drags my hand down the thick length before releasing it and returning my hand to the cushion.

"Charlie," I purr, leaning toward him.

"I don't want this tonight," he says, and I freeze, pulling back. *Oh, God.* This is embarrassing. I shift, ready to stand and excuse myself, but Charlie reaches out for my forearm. "Don't go. I just mean, we don't need to do this tonight. Besides, I'm still angry."

"Angry?" I choke.

"Yes, that you'd even consider playing along with this scheme of your ex's."

"Charlie, I haven't made any decisions."

"And that upsets me even more," he mutters, reaching for his glass of wine and downing the remainder of it. He sets the stemware back on the tray with a light tap and swipes his hands through his hair.

"I don't want to fight with you," I say because I just can't muster the energy. I want Charlie to comfort me, not shut me out. I need him, and that's when I realize I've crossed a line. I shouldn't feel this desire for him. It's more than a yearning to be physical with him. I'm enjoying this moment of closeness tonight too much.

When Charlie doesn't respond, I say, "I should go."

He turns his head to me, his eyes pinned to mine. "Don't leave." There's something in them that trickles down to my soul. He sounds like he means more.

Don't be with Richard. Don't leave Blue Ridge. Promise me you'll stay, he said the night I spent in his bed.

I lean back into the cushion, not making any promises, but admitting I want to stay on his couch for a little longer.

We stare mindlessly at the television for the next thirty minutes, not exactly returning to the position we formerly sat in or the comfort which we felt, but I don't move, and neither does Charlie. Eventually, he stands and heads upstairs, checking on the girls as he told them, giving in to thirty minutes instead of fifteen.

"They're both crashed," he said when he returns. He slumps onto the couch as he previously did and shifts me, so my head falls to his lap. I lie on my back, staring up at him.

"How do you know?" Little girls are good at faking it. I've hosted a slumber party or two.

"I have my ways, and I know how to pretend. My brothers used to sneak out and then pull the stillness necessary to pretend-sleep if either of our parents checked on them."

"Your brothers, but not you?" I tease.

"I was always the good one. The one who walked the straight line."

"Your straight line veers a bit in private," I joke, and Charlie's eyes shift down to me.

"What do you mean?"

"Us."

The soft glow of the television illuminates his brown eyes. The volume is so low he might as well mute it.

"I've never been with anyone the way I am with you."

My breath catches. *Does he mean it?* "What about other women? I mean, you must have brought dates home or had relationships or…"

"No one. I don't trust people to be close to Lucy, and I've never ever brought a woman to my home. I haven't had a relationship since my marriage."

"But—"

He holds up a hand to stop me.

But Charlie's so sexual.

"I'm not a saint, and a decade is a long time, but it's never been like this before for me," he admits, and I shift, sitting up to place my mouth against his. We kiss, slow and sweet, savoring one another's lips for a minute.

"I haven't been with anyone since Richard, and even then, we weren't together that last year. Not once."

Charlie's mouth tenderly returns to mine. His hand cups my cheek as he takes his time to kiss me thoroughly. I'm starting to melt under the delicate attention when he pulls away.

"Lie back how you were."

My brows pinch, but I return to my back, head in Charlie's lap. His fingers outline my face, stroking over my cheek and down my nose. He brushes over my forehead, circles down to my chin, and then wipes his thumb over my lips.

"Do you have any idea how beautiful you are?"

It's said with reverence and not the insult of arm candy. His brows pinch as if he can't believe it himself. I'm beautiful to him.

I'm about to thank him, but he pushes his thumb past my lips, and I suck it, taking my time to swirl my tongue against the thick pad and draw down the length of the digit. He slowly drags it from my lips and moves down my chin and along my throat before slipping his hand into my shirt. His fingers skim lower, dipping under my bra and cupping me. Squeezing at the heaviness, I press upward as my eyes roll back. Charlie massages me, teasing me and tugging the nipple taut. He removes his hand, but at this angle, he can't reach the other as easily. Instead, he slips out of my shirt and runs his hand over my belly.

Snap goes the button of my jeans.

"Push them down a little bit," he whispers, and his deep, commanding voice sets me on fire. I press at the sides, lowering my jeans just a little bit to loosen them so Charlie's hand can slip lower.

"So wet," he moans as his fingers curl and cup my ready folds.

"You do this to me," I whisper.

"I make you wet?" he questions, his voice roughens, but he's well aware of how damp I get for him.

"Yes, sir." I hiss as a finger enters me.

"Fuck," he groans, pulling back to add a second one. He takes his time, dragging his fingers back and forth to draw out the pleasure. I can't take it. With his eyes watching mine and his fingers disappearing in my jeans, I shift.

"What?" Charlie chokes, but rolling to my shoulder, I tug down his sweats.

"No, sweetheart," he says.

"Yes, baby." I move his waistband enough to get my lips over his thick shaft, lowering my mouth to draw him in. His fingers never leave my jeans, and he returns them to my channel even though we rest in this awkward position. I rise a bit to my elbow, angling better to draw him deeper into my mouth. His fingers work within me, dipping deeper and forcing faster. The movement of my mouth matches the rhythm of his fingers.

"God, I want to fuck you," he strains, and I increase my suction. My hand curls around the part of him that wouldn't fit in my mouth, and I squeeze. "Fuck that, actually," he hisses. "I want to make love to you."

I release him with a pop, looking up at his face.

"Charlie?"

"I know, the girls, but still, I want to slide into you and take my time with you. I want to feel you come around me."

Goddammit. My mouth returns to his shaft, swirling my tongue around the length as his fingers work harder within me.

"I'd slide so deep and then pull to the edge…" Charlie whispers, his other hand coming to the back of my head. His hips move the slightest bit, and I realize he's doing to my mouth what he'd do to me.

"I take my time to reach the depth of you…" He slowly thrusts upward, tickling the back of my throat. My eyes water. He's too much, but I want this for him. I want to feel him lose control—sweet, satisfying control.

"Draw you to the edge and keep you there…" he continues, moving his fingers in a slow beat. Slow enough for my hips to chase those retreating fingers, not wanting him to leave my body. We take this time to tease one another. Soft surges and rolling hips, and then it becomes too much.

"Charlie," I warn around him. His hand doesn't leave the back of my head. His fingers increase their intensity. My hips rock, working with the friction he's creating while my mouth hoovers over him. I'm out of control with rhythm dancing in my head as my channel draws him to me, and my mouth latches onto him.

"Nessa," he groans, and I know he's close. I move my hand to cup his sac, squeezing as his fingers press inward. He breaks first. A jolt and a jet as I swallow around him. The excitement of doing this to him, bringing him to this point with only my mouth, sets me off as well. My hips still, and my knees clamp. Charlie tugs my hair a bit, signaling for me to release him. Dragging myself upward, I brace on my elbow, my other hand fisting into the couch cushion as I come undone around his fingers.

Once I settle, I lower to press a final kiss to the tip of him exposed above the rim of his sweats. He chuckles, withdrawing his fingers from my pants, and I press all the way upward to face him.

"I'll never get enough of you," he says. His voice is earnest, and if I'm honest with myself on only this, I feel the same. I'll never be full of Charlie Harrington.

Chapter 20
Coming Clean

[Charlie]

Being with her like this on my couch wasn't enough, and after a round of soft kisses, I need more from her.

"We can't do this here," she mutters against my lips as if reading my mind, and I accept that the exposure of sex on my couch is a risk.

"Bedroom?" I suggest against her mouth, but she shakes her head. She doesn't want to get caught up there again and with the girls so close. "Laundry room?"

"What?" She giggles as she leans away from me, but I quickly stand, take her hand, and practically drag her to the laundry room, which is off the hallway leading to the back entrance. The pocket door slides shut, and we're submerged into darkness minus the thin shade on the window. Hands roam and grope until I have her jeans to her ankles and my sweats below my ass.

"Turn around," I tell her, and she spins, lowering her upper half against the dryer. It isn't the most romantic spot, and we certainly aren't making love like I wanted, but my need is too great. I must be inside her. My hand slips over her perfectly sculpted ass. Fingers twitching, I pull back and smack her smooth skin. Her knees bang on the metal dryer as she hisses, "What the hell?" And then I ram into her.

She tries to look at me over her shoulder, elbows on the surface of the dryer, but I'm a man on a mission. I want to imprint myself on her.

"Don't fuck Richard," I growl as I surge into her, my hips out of control as I thrust into her heat.

"I'm not fucking Richard," she snaps, pressing back to take each pulse, each push. Her pussy clenches me in that way I like, like she doesn't want me to leave her body.

"I want to be the only one you fuck," I hiss, holding her hips as my dick disappears into her. I can hardly see, but I don't need to witness what I'm doing. I feel her. The wetness coating me. The heat of her around me. The depths I can reach within. I want to mark her heart like she's marked mine.

"You're the only one, Charlie." Her voice tries to soften, but she stutters as I don't let up and continue to relentlessly hammer into her.

"Only me," I demand because she's the only one for me. The one I want by my side, in my bed, in my soul.

"Charlie," she warns, but I don't want to hear her tell me we can't see each other or be together. This is it. This is us. Too soon, I delve forward, pausing inside her as tiny sparks of white dance before my eyes, and I fill her with my seed. I'd impregnate her if I could. I'd make her mine in all manners, and I'd love her more than that dickhead ever could.

"Shit," I hiss, realizing she didn't come. My hand slides over the swell of her hip and lowers for her clit, rubbing at her until her hand on my wrist stops me.

"Charlie?" Her voice lowers, and something in it tells me she doesn't want me to continue. She doesn't want me to get her off, and I'm pissed at myself for taking advantage and at her for letting me lose control without taking her over the edge as well.

"I want you to come," I whine like a child, lowering my head for her shoulder. *I want you to have a reason to never leave.* It's irrational. Even I know sex cannot save a marriage.

My head pops up. We aren't married, and thankfully, she isn't still married to Richard, but what if…If he gets to her, could he tempt her into sex? Could he remind her how good they'd once been? Could he reassure her through touch and affection that he means it this time? He'll stick.

I don't like it. I don't like my thoughts or our position, and I quickly pull out of her. Bending at the waist, I tug up my sweats while she rights her jeans.

My mouth opens, and I'm ready to apologize when the pocket door slides open, and I'm blinded a second by the light in the hallway.

"Dad, what are you doing in here?"

Janessa's hands clutch the dryer as Lucy stares up at me. I reach for the washer lid and open it.

"I'm looking for my jeans. Tomorrow will be a casual day at the office." My voice shakes as I lie to my child, and my heart races between what I'd just done with Janessa and the knowing glare of Lucy.

"It's dark in here," she says.

"No wonder I can't find them. So what are you doing out of bed?"

"Vega's crying."

Janessa pushes past me and races for the main staircase.

"What happened, Pint?" I ask, reaching out for my daughter.

"I think her grandpa died."

Oh, my God. *No.*

+ + +

I can't forgive myself, and I'm certain Janessa won't forgive me either. If we hadn't been fucking up against my dryer, she would have gotten the call of her father's passing. Why Vega was called I still don't know, and I realize that even though Janessa claimed she threw out Vega's cell phone, she must have bought her a new one.

Still, I stand with guilt weighing on my chest as she stands at the burial ground…with Richard at her side.

Somehow, he was present at the hospital when she arrived. He was by her side at the funeral service, and he's the one with an arm around her shoulder as she cries while they lower her father's casket.

Richard.

Not me.

I don't know how he did it, other than playing on her weakness at the moment. Me, on the other hand, I haven't been able to get close to her.

After she scooped Vega to her chest in Lucy's room and then used her daughter's phone to call her brother, it was confirmed her father died during the night. Zander had been in the cafeteria getting a late-night coffee, but her mother had been in the room. Vega remained with us for the night, and Zander collected her the next day.

Not Janessa.

"Mami's taking this very hard," her brother said to me as he scooped his niece into his arms as though she weighed nothing.

It was understandable. What was not understandable was Janessa not reaching for me when I was reaching out to her. I wanted to comfort her. I wanted to bring her to me and tell her we'd work it out. Her. Us. Richard. Even her parents. This was their home, and her mother was free to stay even without Henri.

"What's wrong with you?" my brother hisses beside me at the cemetery. Giant didn't know Henri per se, so it's nice of him to show at the funeral. In fact, most of my family is here since Henri was my groundskeeper for years. He was like an extended part of my family, and I loved my own for supporting him.

"I'm coming out of my skin," I say, shaking my leg, coins rattling in my pocket. I couldn't stand watching Richard rub a hand down his ex-wife's back and then settle it near her ass. Too close.

"Is this about Jan?" Giant asks, recalling the night in the Pub a few weeks back. I'd gotten caught by my eldest brother coming down the stairs before Janessa, and the cross between pissed and pleasure was still etched in my face.

Whatcha doing up there? Giant asked, but I simply shook my head. I didn't have a clue what I was doing with this woman or how she rattled me to my core. That night, I said it would be our last night and look where we are. A funeral with her ex's arm around her.

"Shh." I hush my brother because he knows. While I stood there telling him I wasn't doing anything upstairs, Janessa came down the steps and caught us in the hallway. Without meeting my eyes, she excused herself, and my eyes didn't leave the retreat of her back.

That didn't look like nothing. Giant chuckled. He was too observant some days, but at least it hadn't been Billy. He would have been merciless had he caught me getting laid…again.

"What's that guy doing groping Jan at her father's funeral?" Billy mutters next to me, and I close my eyes. So much for silence from him.

"That's her ex," I mutter.

"He looks like Richard Swank, new center fielder for Atlanta," Billy says, his voice too loud for a funeral.

I huff.

"Damn, Charlie. How you gonna compete with that?" Billy adds, making me feel like the child who didn't make the cut. I might have played baseball in college, but I obviously didn't go pro. Giant reaches around me and taps Billy on the back of the head, just as he did when we were kids.

"I'm just saying, he's all brawny and muscly. Isn't that the shit women would say about him?" Billy chuckles softly. "I bet he can go for hours."

Sweet Jesus. "I wouldn't know," I mumble, and Billy snorts.

"That's what I mean." Billy's still picking on me. At my expense, he's assuming I know nothing about sexual stamina. "And that's her ex?"

"Okay, that's enough," I say a little too loudly, and Giant knocks my shoulder to quiet me.

As the final prayer is said and the casket lowered, Rosa sobs, stringing together words of anguish I don't understand. Zander Cruz steps forward to pull his mother to him, and Richard wraps an arm about Janessa, bringing her into his chest.

"I'm done," I say to no one in particular as I turn away from the congregation of people and cross the grass to my car. I drove separate from my brothers, leaving the office to attend the service and planning to head back there to drown my thoughts.

Chapter 21
Funeral Folly

[Janessa]

"I'm done," I mutter to my brother next to me. We've been standing for hours, accepting hugs and condolences from people we don't know. In addition to our parents working for Charlie Harrington, they knew several people in the community and were active members in their church, so the line of well-wishers seems endless. The church generously hosted the funeral luncheon in its basement, and I could use a drink despite the midafternoon timing.

I have no idea what Richard is doing here, what game he's playing, or why he felt he could touch me during the funeral. I'd been looking over my shoulder every chance I had, waiting for camera flashes to capture the doting husband at his wife's side.

Ha.

Most of the time, I'd notice Charlie hovering nearby but not close enough. I hadn't returned his calls because I didn't know what to say. Things were left unresolved the other night in his laundry room after we were caught once again by his daughter only seconds after I'd pulled up my pants.

Good God, we were playing with fire.

"How are you holding up?" Roxanne asks me, holding up a cup of tea for me.

"I could use something stronger than that," I whisper, and her head tilts.

"Want to get out of here?"

I hate to leave my mother, but I need a break. It's been three days of constant crying, calling out for my father, and wailing in broken Spanish about him leaving her. I'm not trying to be insensitive to my mother's emotions, but I'm coming out of my skin, and Zander is suspiciously absent at night. Vega's taken to covering her head with a pillow, and I allowed her to go to Charlie's for the afternoon and swim instead of suffering through this never-ending funeral luncheon.

"The Pub is only a mile away. We can sneak out and be back within twenty minutes."

It's a devious plan, but I like the way Roxanne thinks, so I mindlessly follow her lead after she sets down the teacup and guides me to a back hallway as if we were headed to the restroom. Once we exit the main hall, we both race up the stairs like teenage girls breaking free of the Catholic school I attended as a child.

We slip into her car and head only a few blocks to the Blue Ridge Microbrewery & Pub. Roxanne doesn't wait for us to be officially seated. She just tips her head at the bartender, Clyde, and pushes me into the farthest booth.

"What do we have here?" Billy asks. He was at the funeral, but I didn't notice him at the luncheon. It was nice of his family to attend. Giant and Letty. Billy and Roxanne. Mr. and Mrs. Harrington. Charlie.

"Escape. We have nineteen minutes on the clock," Roxanne says, and Billy chuckles.

"You escaping prison or something?" He leans against the booth, crossing his arms.

"Something like that," I mutter.

"I'm sorry about your father," he offers, and I weakly smile in acceptance. I've had the same frozen curve to my lips all morning. It's my look of appreciation, one I perfected while on the arm of Richard.

Just smile and don't speak, Nessa. I curse him under my clenched teeth.

"Thank you."

"Okay, two summer ales coming up."

"Quick," Roxanne snaps, and Billy chuckles again.

"Darlin', you know I like to take my time."

My cheeks heat as do Roxanne's, but she also tips her face upward, and he cups the back of her neck, leaning in for a quick kiss.

"William," she says against his mouth. "Seventeen."

"On it." Billy backs away, and Roxanne looks over at me. My swollen eyes ache from the silent tears I've shed at night. Certainly, Roxanne can read the exhaustion in the bags under my eyes as I've tried to assure my mother that Zander and I will take care of everything. There's a pain in my heart that I didn't know my father as well as I should, and he still treated me like I was Daddy's little girl.

"Your mother told me she saw you coming out of Charlie's bedroom."

"Papi, it wasn't like that," I lied and then told him he should only be thinking of getting better.

"I don't care if I work for him, I'll kill him if he hurts you like Richard did."

Aw Daddy, where had you been earlier in my life?

Tears fill my eyes at the memory. We hadn't had the chance to talk further, discuss things, or make a plan. I hadn't told my parents Richard was back. I didn't want them to worry. But Richard took it upon himself to show up late the other evening and try to talk to my dad. He wanted to assure him he'd look after me. I worry his words might have pushed my father over the edge.

A tear plops from my eyes onto the wooden tabletop.

"Ah, honey." Roxanne reaches for my hand from across the table, and my fingers shake as I return my sunglasses to my eyes despite being inside the dim pub. "My mom died when I was in high school, and my father ten years ago, so I understand. You let it all out."

I nod, lowering my head and cupping my forehead with my palm as the tears fall into the lenses of my sunglasses.

"What's this?" Charlie's sharp voice forces my eyes to close, and then he's next to me, filling in the space beside me in the booth. "Nessa, sweetheart."

His arm comes around my back, and he tugs me into his chest, pressing a kiss to my temple. How did he know I was here?

"She just needed a few minutes," Roxanne explains.

"I have her," he mumbles into my hair. My eyes remain closed behind my dark glasses. "The luncheon is almost over, but some people are headed to the coach house."

Oh, God. Why can't they leave us alone? I know they mean well, but the hovering makes my skin itch.

"Take my truck. Get her out of here." Billy's stern voice suggests he's returned to the table as well. Maybe he called Charlie. "Go out the back."

Charlie gently tugs me from the booth seat, never letting me slip from his arm.

"Just for a little bit," I whisper as I curl into him when we stand.

"For as long as you need," he assures me and leads me out a back exit and into the alley behind the Pub.

+ + +

To my surprise, Charlie takes me to his house. Billy's pickup is our only disguise as Charlie pulls into the garage of his home on the same property as my parents. There is a line of cars down the outer drive leading to the coach house. For a few seconds, I feel guilty I'm not there to hold up my mother, but Zander can handle it a little longer. He hasn't seen my mother in years, the same as me. I only wish it was under better circumstances.

With an arm still around my shoulders when we enter his house, Charlie immediately turns me for a staircase inside the back door, leading to the second floor.

"Where are Lucy and Vega?" I ask, not wanting to be caught again by our daughters.

"My mother has them. They decided against swimming, and she's entertaining them at her house."

Charlie continues to lead me up the back staircase and then down the hall to his room. Once inside, he locks the double doors to it.

"Charlie," I whisper, uncertain what he wants from me right now, and not certain I can muster my attraction to him.

"Bathroom," he says, shrugging off his suit coat and tossing it on the bed. He waves a hand forward, directing me to enter the smaller room of his, and I pause near the sink. Memories flash of him rinsing my hand, attempting to remove the ring from my finger. Then us in the two-person shower. The tub faucet comes on, stealing my thoughts. Besides a rain shower, Charlie also has a deep freestanding tub that he's filling as he tugs his tie free and rolls up his sleeves.

He steps up to me and wordlessly unzips my black dress. He holds the sides as he lowers it to the floor, and I slip out of the material. His eyes roam my body as I stand in my heels and black lace underthings. I'm waiting for him to tell me he thinks I'm beautiful or he wants to fuck me, but he doesn't say either.

"Take off your shoes," he quietly commands, and while I do, he strokes a hand down my back. When I stand, Charlie's biting his lip as though he has something to say that he's fighting, or maybe he's struggling with the hunger of desire.

He turns me around to unclasp my bra, and I help slide down my thong. Holding out his hand, he leads me to the tub, and I step in, sinking into the heavenly warmth. With my hair in a knot at the base of my neck, I don't worry about it getting wet, and I slip as low as I can. Charlie stands over the tub, watching me melt into the steamy water. It's strange to take a bath in the middle of a summer day, but I need a moment of peace.

And this is Charlie, anticipating what I need.

"I want to join you, but I'll give you a few minutes alone."

My wet arm flings over the edge of the porcelain, water dripping onto the tile floor. "I don't want to be alone."

Charlie closes his eyes. "I saw him touching you."

I don't have the strength to argue with him, but I know who he means. I know how he feels. I'd seen Richard with his hands on others, and my insides burned, but that was in the past. I'd brushed Richard off every chance I could today. The farce of his devotion was too much.

"I know. I'm sorry." I swallow, afraid Charlie's reached the end of his rope with me. "Join me." My voice cracks, my throat clogging. I don't want to lose him.

Charlie slowly reaches for the buttons of his shirt and then tugs it from the back of his head to remove it. He unbuckles his belt and kicks off his shoes at the same time. Lowering both pants and boxers, he leaves his things in a pile on the floor, and stands for another minute, allowing me to take in the grandeur of him.

Mayor McSteamy.

He's so blindingly beautiful, I can understand his ex's desire to photograph him.

My arm still dangles outside the tub, and I wiggle my fingers as my eyes focus on his growing erection.

"Scoot forward," he says, and I allow him room to slip in behind me. Once his hands are on my skin, pulling me back against his chest, I relax in a way I haven't done for days.

We stay quiet as Charlie just holds me. I'm aware of his stiffness pressing up against my backside, but my eyes close, just taking in this moment with him.

"I wasn't as close to him as I should have been," I finally say. Not that I feel the need to speak but more the words want to come out. "I should have been a better daughter."

Charlie kisses my shoulder. "I'm sure you did what you could."

Charlie doesn't know. These are the things we don't talk about. My upbringing. Where I come from.

"Zander and I went for long periods of time without seeing them, both as children and adults." My abuela comes to mind. How innocent we were as children. How we didn't know we'd gone without until we had more. "I should have come to see them."

But Richard.

He wanted me to deny them. Play up the poor girl turned scholarship superstar. The one who had a career but gave it up for family. If only he'd done the same thing and put his family first.

Charlie's arms slip from my waist, and he massages my shoulders.

"Tell me a good memory you have of your father."

"One time, he took us ice skating. In Texas, who ice skates?" I softly laugh. "But it was near the holidays, and a chill filled the air. An outdoor rink was made in downtown Houston, and he took us. It was nighttime, and lights hung over the ice." I remember thinking it was magical, and I was happy my parents had returned. We were finally going to be a family. The four of us, not two sets of two. It didn't last. I grew to be a surly teen, and my father worked long hours as did my mother. I was embarrassed by them some days and prayed they wouldn't attend a game or school function.

My eyes close. I'm a terrible daughter.

"It sounds like a nice memory," Charlie says, moving his attention to my neck, and I tip my head forward. His fingers dig into my hair, loosening the bun. "Tell me more."

For the next few minutes, I tell him snippets of memories, striving for the good ones and not the bad. Not the ones where Papi yelled at me for letting my grades slip, or told me a girl couldn't do something boys normally did, or expressed his disappointment when I told him I was pregnant out of wedlock, even if I was thirty-two years old.

Eventually, I quiet, falling into my memories as they meld together but also concentrating on the feel of Charlie's fingers digging into my skin.

"That feels so good," I whisper. His palms coast over my shoulders and down to my fingers. He works each digit, taking his time to press and stretch at them. Each hand falls back to the water after he finishes, and his hands lower beneath the water and squeeze my thighs. My knees bend, and Charlie presses at the inside of each leg, working his way to my center.

"Charlie," I groan with a slight chuckle. He just can't resist, and I'm liking it too much. His fingers coast over me—first from one hand and then the next—until finally one set settles and rubs at my clit. His other hand moves up my body for a breast, and his mouth lowers to my neck. It's sensory overload with his teeth nipping, his fingers pinching, and two fingers pushing into me.

I moan his name, and he replies, "I owe you for the other night. You didn't come, and I never want to leave you unsatisfied." It's a sweet sentiment as my ex never cared one way or the other.

"You always satisfy me, Charlie." He's quiet as his attention increases. Fingers working at both my center and my breasts while his teeth become more aggressive.

"Do I make you happy?" he asks, and I hum in response, not able to find even the simplest of words, like *yes*. "I want to please you."

"You do," I whisper, falling under his spell as his fingers move faster and others pinch harder. He sucks at my neck, breaking skin for a mark, but I don't care at the moment. I fall into him, coming long and sweet, luscious and lapping like the water in this tub.

"Hmm, sweetheart. I love it when you come like this." He knows what he's done, dragging it out of me, and I spin, forcing his fingers to release me. Rising on my knees, I straddle him. The water sloshes around us, crashing over the edge of the tub, but my eyes stay fixed on him. My mouth covers his, taking my time to draw out the kiss. My tongue seeks his as my fingers dig into his hair.

"I need you," I tell him, and he grips himself, so I balance on the tip. Sex in water is different, and I lower in shuddering halts before he's fully inside me. Once sheathed within, we still and continue to kiss until his fingers dig into my hips. Slowly, I dance over him, taking my time to feel him moving inside me. The water rushes around us, but I float into an oblivion of only Charlie. My hands curl around the back of his neck, and I hold on as I rock, rubbing my clit against his pubic bone in a way the friction is too much.

When I warn him with only his name, he sits upright and takes my mouth, swallowing my moan as I come again around him. He comes within seconds while I'm clenching at him, but he doesn't stop kissing me. As we settle into the sweetness after our lingering orgasm, our foreheads press together, and Charlie blurts, "Don't go back to Richard."

Reality slams into me. I don't want to discuss Richard.

"Charlie, not now."

"Not ever," he says, tightening his hold on me. "I don't want to see him touching you. I don't want him using you or Vega. Tell him no deal. Tell him to go away." His voice pleads with me, but my irritation grows.

"I'm not discussing him with you like this." I slip off him and stand, allowing water to cascade down my body like a waterfall. Charlie reaches forward and tugs my hips, so my center comes to his lips. His tongue comes forward, and he licks me once.

I cry out in shock and instant stimulation.

How can I want him again?

"Tell me I'm yours and you're mine, not his."

"Oh, my God." I tug free of his grasp and step out of the tub. I can't do this with him. Not after what we just did. I reach for a towel and hastily dry off.

"I'm serious about you moving in with me. We can pretend we're engaged. It will take the heat off you." Charlie stands behind me, but I refuse to look at the water display I'm certain graces his firm body. He reaches for a towel as well, then steps out of the tub and covers himself at the waist. He doesn't bother to dry off.

"You're asking me to pretend with one man compared to another?" My heart races with the thought. Doesn't he understand? I'm not pretending with Charlie. Besides, how would that look for him?

I slip into my underwear and latch my bra while Charlie watches me. Reaching for my dress, I step into it and then a shoe. Lifting my other foot, I slip into the second one.

"I'm not pretending anything," he says as I struggle to reach my zipper until Charlie grabs it and slowly zips me up.

"I'm not pretending either. *With anyone.*" I smooth down the sides of my dress, refusing to look at him. I will not play house with him. Not with Vega involved. Not with my heart on the line. "I need to get back to my mother."

Hardly able to look at him, I exit his bathroom, feeling once again like I'm the worst person. I just skipped out on my father's funeral luncheon to have sex with a man, and that man has me all tangled up inside. It's when I'm finally outside that I reflect on his words and wonder what he meant when he said he wasn't pretending.

Chapter 22
Bedtime Stories

[Janessa]

When I return to my mother's home, Richard awaits me just outside the front door.

"Where have you been?" he snaps, blocking me from entering the house. His hand comes to my upper arm.

"Don't touch me," I say through clenched teeth as I smile at someone leaving the house. Richard's grip tightens on me. Where is his image manager? Shouldn't she be here policing him? "What are you doing here, anyway?"

"I'm here to support my wife, who's been missing for an hour," he says under his breath, nodding at someone in the driveway. I tug free when he looks away from me.

"As I'm not your wife, I don't need your support, and I'm not doing this. I'm not pretending with you."

"It's a million dollars," he mutters, turning back to me.

"Richard, something you fail to remember, along with several other things like our marriage vows, is that I don't care about the money. I cared about you, us, and Vega as our daughter, but none of that mattered to you. I don't want your money, and I'm not playing this little game with you."

"Are you fucking someone?" His dark eyes narrow as he looks down at me, his sight latching onto the spot where I'm certain Charlie left a mark. Once upon a time, I fell in love with those eyes. Another time, I feared them. Today, I couldn't give a shit.

"If I was, it would never be your business." I cross my arms and glare up at him.

"You'll always be my business," he retorts, holding my gaze. "Plus, we have a deal."

"I was never your business, Richard. Not when you married me, fathered our child, or stepped out the first time, or the second, or the twentieth, and the moment our daughter walked in on you with someone else, you no longer became *our* business. We're finished." I'm not even going to address his accusation of sleeping with someone. We're divorced.

I move to step around him, but he stops me again. His fingers come to my elbow.

"I've told you once before, don't walk away from me." The words were said when Vega and I left. He warned me not to leave. Then he begged me as we sat before lawyers, but there was no going back to him.

"Excuse me." A female Southern drawl dripping with determination comes up behind me, and we both shift as if we are blocking the way into the house. Only once we move, the woman comes closer; her eyes narrowed in on Richard's hand at my elbow.

"Corabelle Conrad." She sticks out her hand, eyeing Richard so he must release me in order to shake her offered hand.

"Richard Swank." He shakes and then shakes his head to move his hair. It's a nervous tic he gets before going into professional ballplayer, full-on flirt mode. "Nessa's husband."

She smiles, but there's something too saccharine about her grin, almost sarcastic. "Nessa's neighbor." She states this like it's just as important as Richard's nonexistent label. "Bless your heart, you can't keep your hands off her." Cora leans in like she's about to impart a secret but slips her arm into mine. "But I'm going to kindly suggest you take your hands off the missus. Inappropriate and all as she's grieving her daddy."

My eyes widen as my lips roll inward, fighting a startled laugh.

"The missus belongs to me." He grins largely although his eyes slowly narrow.

"The missus has a name," I mutter. "And it's no longer missus."

"That's what I've heard, so you'll be leaving unless you want me to get June on the line." Cora stands tall, facing off to my ex-husband although she and I have not officially met. She lives on the other side of the bushes lining the outer drive to the coach house. She's divorced and owns a nearby lodge.

"Who's June?" Richard's smile turns smarmy as though he's prepared to charm the next woman.

"She's the sheriff, and she does not take to men manhandling their exes." Cora's face stays sweet, but her voice turns to vitriol. "Now, I believe you were saying your sweet goodbye, and Nessa and I are going inside to sit with her mother since her father died." Her emphasis on the final word brings back all my guilt of leaving Mami alone, but it's mixed with sass to remind Richard he's being disrespectful.

"Daddy?" Vega's strangled cry turns my head, and my heart breaks with the shock on her face. She runs to him, and I hold my breath with anticipation of his reception. If I have grand ideas, he'll swoop her in his arms and hold her to him like Charlie did that day by the pool with Lucy, but I'm wrong. Vega runs to her father and then collides with his body like a brick wall. His large hand comes to her shoulder blade, and he awkwardly pats her.

"Hey, kiddo."

She looks up at him, stars in her eyes, but there are clouds covering them as well. She doesn't see him like she should despite walking in on him with someone else.

"Daddy, are you staying here, too?"

"No, I'm staying at the Conrad Lodge."

"Seeing as I own that…" Cora interjects, clearing her throat. "I look forward to seeing you there." It's another hint for Richard to leave, and he seethes as he turns back to Cora, his hand still on Vega's back. His mouth opens as though he's ready to speak—more likely to spew insults—when his image manager stumbles out of the house.

"There you are," she says, her voice tight. "We need to get going. You need to be back in Atlanta by this evening." Her eyes travel from me to him and back. She looks out of breath, but maybe she's holding hers, waiting on him to lose it. Instead, he nods at her, pats Vega one more time, and steps out of her arms. No hug. No kiss.

"I'll be calling you," he mutters under his breath to me as Ruthie holds out a hand, prompting him to walk away. Vega stares after him.

"I'll be in contact," Ruthie says to me, dipping her head, and my gut tells me that's worse. Before I can think too much more, Cora, who has her arm looped with mine, leads me into the house. My head turns back for Vega, but she remains on the walk, watching her dad leave her behind. Just as I'm ready to turn back for her, Zander comes into view and picks her up. My heart settles a little bit. He's a great uncle.

"Your father was a sweet man. I lost my daddy a long time ago, and Henri was good to me." Cora speaks under her breath. "I'm not asking for any details about that man outside. You forget about him on your front step." She tightens her arm in mine.

"Thank you." I pause and tip my head toward the door, implying her intervention with Richard. "For that."

"I know all about scandalous, adultering men like him, and I'm no longer afraid to stand up to the likes of them." She turns to face me, slowly releasing my arm. "And you shouldn't be either. There are people around here who will support you."

Again, I don't know who she means, but my thoughts jump to Charlie.

Move in with him. Pretend we're engaged. It's too much, and I can't do it to him or me. I'm too emotionally wrapped up in him to pretend, unlike how I faked my love for Richard and turned my head at his multitude of indiscretions.

"Seeing as my best friend is on the road trip of a lifetime this summer, I think you and I should become friends."

"Who's your best friend?" I ask, finding it funny that a woman over forty is asking me to be her friend like we're in first grade.

"Matilda Harrington."

I almost groan. I can't seem to get away from those Harringtons.

+ + +

That night, Vega remains quiet as we fall into our matching twin beds. Zander has gone out again, and my mother finally settled down. I'm praying the exhaustion of the day keeps her from wailing for one night.

"You okay, baby?" The past few days have been a rush of emotion and activity. I've been more focused on Mami than Vega, and I don't know what she's feeling over there.

"Why was Dad here?" Vega didn't attend the wake for my father. I didn't want her to see him like that—in the coffin—so it was a surprise when Richard showed up at the church.

"Dad's here," she whispered at my side before the funeral mass began. We were already seated, and my hand on her thigh told her not to leave the pew.

Vega also didn't go to the burial. I worried it was too much for her, and thankfully, Elaina Harrington took charge of my child once again. So, Vega hadn't had the chance to really see Richard until she found him standing before the coach house.

And he paid her all of three seconds' worth of attention and no affection.

I sigh, staring up at the ceiling, uncertain of how to answer her.

"He wants me to pretend we are still married until the season ends." I've never lied to my child, just tried to hold back the truth as best I could. She wasn't aware of his adulterous ways until she witnessed it herself. It was difficult to explain why her father was in bed with another woman, and why she was doing what she was doing to him.

"But you aren't married anymore," Vega says, and I roll to my side, seeking her face across the room.

"I'm not, baby, and I won't ever go back to him."

"Why does he want you to pretend?"

"Remember we talked about image and how important it can be for others to see someone a certain way. Your dad needs people to see him as a family man, at least while baseball is the sport of the season." In the off-season, no one will care as much about his personal life.

"He isn't a family man," she whispers, and I hear the tears in her voice. "Papi loved me more than Dad does."

I quickly flip my covers and crawl into bed with her, tucking her into my chest.

"Papi loved you very much, and he was so excited for you to live here with him." We'd only been here a little over a month, but my father was trying to fill a void in both himself and my daughter by taking Vega to places with him and asking her to help in small ways around the yard.

"I wish Dad had died instead," she whispers into my chest, and I tug her tighter.

"No, Vega. No. Daddy was a bad husband and a not-so-great man, but we don't wish him to die. We don't hate like that, baby, or it will eat us up."

She nods into my sternum, but the tears fall on my pajama shirt. Her hands slip between us so she can cover her face, and my lips come to her hair.

"We're going to be okay, baby. We're going to be okay," I say, not certain if I'm reassuring her or myself. Perhaps both.

Chapter 23
A Swing and a Miss

[Janessa]

The following Monday, I return to work. Charlie and I haven't had much interaction the remainder of the week as I refused to let Vega sleep at Lucy's again. I need her close to me, and I used my mother as an excuse.

"Mami wants you here."

My mother returned to work as well, saying she needed to busy her hands to ease her mind.

The person who doesn't go anywhere is Zander.

"I think I'm going to stick around for a little bit longer."

I don't question him although I'm surprised he's taking two weeks off in a row. Like me, he was given bereavement time, but he's added a week of vacation. Knowing Zander, he has time piled up as he works hard and hasn't taken any vacations that I know of in the past few years.

The budget proposal for the walking trail and church purchase is on the agenda for the town council meeting on my first night back, and I've tried to collect my own thoughts over the past few days despite being home with my mother. I have a sound presentation with the financial reports from three other cities matching the population of Blue Ridge that did what I'm proposing as well as a general town plan which doesn't involve destruction but more renovation of the church and creation of the walking path.

When it nears five o'clock, I come down from my office on the second floor and hear voices in the dining room turned conference room. I planned to avoid Charlie most of the day, but it wasn't necessary as I hadn't seen him. His voice stops me outside the pocket doors, which stand slightly ajar.

"I'm glad you see the light, Charlie." The voice of Wyatt Hubner makes me pause, and although I shouldn't be listening, I can't help myself.

"It's still a good proposal," Charlie says.

"But a million dollars for a sidewalk?" Wyatt scoffs.

"She's ambitious. I'll give her that," Charlie retorts, but it isn't praise. He isn't exactly defending me. "She doesn't understand the ways of small towns, but she'll get there."

"This is why outsiders shouldn't be hired," Wyatt adds.

"It isn't that," Charlie says. "She just doesn't have experience." His voice lowers, and I strain to hear what he says next. "But she's a good egg, and she'll eventually be an asset to Parks and Recreation."

A good egg? What am I, a fucking chicken? And *eventually*, but not now?

"She's a pain in the ass is more like it." Wyatt laughs, and to my dismay, so does Charlie. "Her presentation will be a waste of time as you're only going to veto it."

What?

I push open the double pocket doors, and Charlie freezes, his eyes locking on mine. Wyatt's chuckle slowly dies to a cough, and I turn on him first.

"Mr. Hubner, I look forward to wasting your time this evening." At least, Wyatt has the chagrin to blush before he stands, and mutters, "Well, I never," and I bite my lip from retorting how I imagine that's his problem.

After Wyatt exits, I glare at Charlie.

"Won't you sit?" He gestures to the conference table and all the chairs opposite him.

"No, I won't sit. Although I suppose that's how good eggs hatch," I snap. "Or is it that a good egg gets laid?" I pause. "Maybe a good egg gives a good lay."

"That's enough," Charlie barks back at me as he stands on the other side of the large oval table.

"You just dismissed me as though I'm a kid asking for candy."

Charlie sighs. "It's more complicated than that, and you know it. A million dollars isn't just lying around in our town budget, and while your proposal is a good one, it's just not doable."

"And who decides?" I cross my arms and glare at him because the purpose of the town council meeting is to let the town decide if it's in the budget. Then I recall what Wyatt said. "You're not going to approve the proposal. You're going to let me make the presentation and then make me look like a fool by rejecting it."

I stare at him, my stomach feeling like he socked me.

"It's also not that simple," he says, swiping a hand through his hair.

"But you're the mayor. You have the final say."

Charlie doesn't look at me. His knuckles brace his hands on the large conference table.

"Maybe I'll need to find a million dollars another way," I say, my voice full of the venom I feel at his rejection of my idea. His head snaps upward. I have his attention now.

"You wouldn't." His eyes narrow as he knows exactly what I'm implying. Three months with Richard and I could have the church for a community center and a train park plus the city walk.

"You never believed in this proposal, did you? You don't believe in me." Maybe I'm making more of this than it is, but I feel personally attacked. I've spoken with him about this plan, seeing him here and there in this office.

"I don't want you anywhere near him," Charlie says, rounding the table to near me, but I step back.

"Well, you don't have to worry about me when you don't believe in me."

"I didn't say that I didn't believe in you."

"You laughed when Wyatt said I was a pain in the ass."

"That was to throw him off, and you are a pain in the ass sometimes." He slowly smiles, but I don't find any humor in this conversation.

"But you still think it's true. You don't think the plan should be approved. *You* won't approve the budget for it."

"That's not it."

"Then what is *it*?" My voice rises, and my fingers curl into fists at my side. Charlie stands feet from me, and he needs to keep his distance.

"I can't just give you the money, especially since…" His voice falters, and his eyes drift away.

"You're worried someone will find out about us. If someone knows you fucked me, and then I get this project, it makes *you* look bad." My voice rises higher.

"Would you keep your voice down?" he suggests, stepping up to me and reaching for my arms, but I step back again, kicking at one of the chairs.

"It makes it look like sleeping with you for town favors works."

Charlie's eyes narrow. "It makes it look like *you* slept with me for a favor."

I gasp. *How dare he?*

"Is that what you think I did?" My voice lowers to more like a growl.

"I didn't say that."

"Then what are you saying, Charlie?"

"I'm saying I'm not going to approve the proposal, *and* I don't want people to look at you and think you slept with me to get it."

My hip juts out, and I cross my arms.

"Well, I guess we won't have to worry about that, as no one will find out, especially since it won't happen again."

I glare at him a second and then lower my arms. "Why did you give me this job, Mayor, if you aren't going to let me do it? Was it a pity position?" We had sex the night before the interview, and then the first day I got the job. Am I paying him back for hiring me without knowing it?

"It isn't pity."

"What is it then?"

Charlie doesn't answer, and the only logical thing I can think of is he hired me to get in my pants.

It worked. I fell for it. I let myself think he believed in me and my new mission, and it was all for naught.

Brushing past Charlie, I bump into his arm, acting childish as I exit. The double doors remain open, and I stalk to the chair where I left my things before barging into the conference room. From the front parlor, I see Charity watching me, standing in the middle of the reception area before the offices of Harrington & Rathstone. I meet her eyes. She smooths her hands down her skirt and comes closer to me.

"This is what you get," she whispers, holding my attention. Her eyes shift to the conference room, but Charlie has already left the room for his office. He isn't chasing me. "You can't sleep with Charlie without getting fucked, and fucking him will not get you anywhere."

I glare back at her in her uptight suit and drab brown hair pulled tightly into a bun. "My, what language you have? Is that what happened to you? Did you sleep with him, hoping to be his girl? The woman on his arm as he runs for Congress one day. Did Daddy put you up to it, or are you pining over a man who has no interest in you? He's your boss."

I could be wrong. Maybe Charlie does want someone like Charity—arm candy in a different manner. Not bosomy, curvy, or sassy like me, but demure, petite, and refined written all over her. Maybe that's what Charlie wants to match his good ole boy image and his public persona as a potential congressman.

"He's your boss, too, and you'd be wise to remember that. No one wants rumors to get around that the new girl tried to sleep her way to the top. And you're crazy if you think *you're* what Charlie wants. I'm the woman who's stood by him for ten years. I'm the one who's been here for him, and I'm the better match for him."

Her eyes roam over my body, and my heart races. I'd like to slap her. I did no such thing as sleep my way to the top, but from the argument Charlie and I just had—which I'm certain this busybody just heard—there's no doubt she thinks that's what I've done. And she looks all too happy to be the one to start the gossip.

She slept with Charlie to get what she wanted.

That type of lie was my biggest fear when I worked a decade ago in sports marketing. Oh, the irony. I could defend that Charlie is all I want, but not if he has no faith in me. Not if he's pushing our reputations to the side because he doesn't want a scandal. I've already been in this position with Richard. Sleeping with the enemy is what I call when a man wants your body but has no interest in your opinion.

Fuck him. Fuck both of them.

A good egg?

My egg is gold, and I'll be laying it elsewhere.

"You might not be wrong that you're the better match for Charlie, but Charity, there's a name for women like you. Sad comes to mind. Pathetic is next. None of the rest is Christian and charitable like your namesake, so I'll leave it at this. Maybe you're the one fucked by Charlie because he's not going to pick you as his partner. If he hasn't already, it's never going to happen. And in case you haven't noticed, he's a single man, and it seems to suit him."

I hike my bag higher on my shoulder and dismiss myself without saying goodbye.

+ + +

As if the day hasn't been bad enough, Ruthie Avery calls me as she promised. I've been ignoring Richard's text, but her call gets through to me in a moment of weakness.

"We'd like to ask you to attend Richard's first game in Atlanta on Thursday evening. Bring Vega, please. We'll set you up at a hotel and provide seats in the area reserved for wives and girlfriends."

I balk at the suggestion. How many times did Vega and I not attend a game, and another woman took my place unbeknownst to me?

"That's not doable for me."

Ruthie sighs through the phone. "Ms. Cruz, I understand he isn't a great man. That's what I've been hired for, but there's a return on this investment for you. A million dollars is nothing to scoff at as a single mother."

I'd like to smack her through the phone. I don't need the reminder of my status, let alone my financial circumstances.

"Some things are worth more than money, Ms. Avery. Like my pride."

"I understand. I do." She sighs, and I wonder if she's ever been caught up in one of her clients, knowing he's a bad man at heart but still falling for his charm. "I lost my husband. He was in the military, and I had nowhere to go but to stick with my in-laws. I work for them in this business."

If she's looking for kindred connections, I'm not making them although I feel for her plight.

"I'm sorry about your husband."

"I know what it's like to feel desperate."

"I'm not desperate," I snap. I was…*before*…when I stayed, and I accepted Richard as he is. I turned a blind eye but not anymore. I'm free now, and there's a world of difference.

"Of course not. Seeing as Mr. Swank attended the funeral, we just thought you might be willing to attend the game."

"I fail to see how the two relate."

Silence fills the line. She can't possibly think she's right. The death of my father and pretending to be a spouse at a baseball game do not equate, especially since we *are* divorced.

"You're right. I'll still leave tickets at will call, and a hotel reservation in your name if you change your mind. That's always a woman's prerogative."

Chapter 24
New Friends

[Janessa]

The presentation goes well, and the projected cityscape plans are beautiful, but I can see from the townspeople's reaction to the question of money that they aren't on board with a city walk and converting a church into a community center doesn't sit well with some.

Well-trained at keeping my brave face on, I smile while the questions fly, and then Wyatt leads the discussion to a vote. Charlie is the deciding factor in vetoing the idea, but he suggests we reconsider it in the following spring. In my opinion, next spring is too late. We need construction this year to benefit the next year's tourism cycle, but what do I know. According to him, I don't understand small-town ways.

As I pack my things, I ignore his attempts to speak with me. I have nothing to say. As I mentioned to him earlier, I don't understand why he hired me. I thought I was here to market the town through their recreational appeal and improve that interest, but I see I'm wrong. The same old programs will remain, catering only to the locals, and that's that.

Unfortunately, I can't brush off the fact I actually have a job after ten years without work, plus Vega wants to stay in Blue Ridge, and then there's my mother.

I'm upset Zander disappears every night. He let it slip he hangs at Ridged Edge, a biker bar on the outskirts of town. It isn't hard-core, just not as nice as Blue Ridge Microbrewery & Pub from what I've heard, but I'm about to learn for myself. Dismissing polite invitations for a drink at the Pub, I head to the other bar to commiserate with my brother.

"Janessa," my brother slurs upon seeing me, and I take a seat next to him on a stool. "How was the meeting?"

I hang my bag over the edge of my chair and turn for Zander. "Charlie shot it down."

A snort sounds two seats over from mine, and I turn to find a silver-haired male nursing something dark in a low glass. I turn back to my brother.

"He rejected the project. Said the town doesn't have the money, but he did it more for personal reasons."

Zander glances over at me. "Personal?"

My lips roll together as I realize my brother doesn't know about Charlie and me. He might have his suspicions, but I haven't mentioned anything outright.

"Would this be because you're banging the mayor?"

"Shh," I hiss. "Keep your voice down." I turn my head left to right and notice the man sitting two seats away stills as if he heard what Zander said. His glass pauses in midair. His lips open for a sip of his drink that isn't getting there. I spin back to my brother.

"It isn't like that." I don't know what it's like. We did have sex. A lot. We opened up to one another. A little. We clearly are not more, and tonight proved it.

"Not my business," Zander says, lifting his own drink for his lips, and I call out to a man behind the bar.

"Can I get what he's having?" Another silver-haired man glares back at me. A bandana graces his head, and the thick scruff on his jaw gives him a menacing look, but I stare back at him. Maybe this place isn't the safest to get a drink. After a second, the bartender moves, slaps a glass before me, and pours whiskey into it. Then he sets the entire bottle on the bar before us.

"Anything else, princess?" It's demeaning as though I've offended him by asking him to do his job and pour me a drink.

"Nope, I'm all set." I smile, giving him my practiced fake grin.

"Actually, she needs a million dollars for a sidewalk," Zander interjects.

"It's not a sidewalk," I snap, turning on my brother.

"No concern of mine, seeing as this town's done nothing for me," the bartender states, spreading his hands against the edge of the bar and leaning in as though he's staying for the conversation.

"Yeah, well, I'm the new girl and can't say it's done much for me either."

"Except give you a home, a job, and Charlie," Zander mutters, swallowing the last of his drink and helping himself to the bottle on the bar.

"Got something against good ole Charlie?" the man asks, and Zander snorts. If my brother dare says *my body* was against the mayor's, I'll slap him right in front of these witnesses.

"Besides the fact he has no respect for my ideas, I guess not," I say.

The man to my side snorts again, and I turn on him. "You got something against good ole Charlie?" I ask as he's clearly listening to this conversation.

"Nothing against him." He tips back his drink before adding, "But he has no sense with women."

My mouth falls open. He *was* listening, and now he's implying Charlie's bad taste runs with me. His head swivels, and he faces me.

"Not implying you, though, darlin'. Just mean Goody Two-shoes Charlie has his head up his ass when it comes to women. He doesn't know how to pick the good ones when he sees them." His eyes roam my seated body.

"Who says I'm good?" I tease, and a slow grin crooks his lips.

"That's Charlie's problem. He needs a little bad."

"And you know this about Charlie because…?" My suggestive tone lingers.

"He's my kid brother."

My brows shoot upward, and I stare. There's no way this leather vest-clad man with a white tee and jeans is related to the fitted suit civil servant of Charlie Harrington.

"Name's Ranger." He eyes the man behind the bar. "Not surprised you haven't heard of me." He softly chuckles, and I stare back at him. All the Harringtons have eyes like Charlie. It confirms they are brothers, but this man has sad blue eyes, and he looks nothing like the clean-cut of his younger sibling.

"We didn't exactly share personal stories." It's true and pathetic to admit. I don't know much about Charlie's family as a whole. Ranger was not mentioned.

"Share other things?" His eyes skim down my body again, and I'd shiver if I didn't think he was merely assessing me, not hitting on me.

"That's none of your business," I say, which seems an admission that I *have* shared other things with Charlie. Otherwise, I should have just said no.

"Charlie ain't my concern anyway." He stands from his seat and raps his knuckles on the edge of the bar. "Put their drinks on my tab."

"You don't have a damn tab," the bartender huffs, shaking his head. Ranger stalks off toward the pool tables, and another man comes behind the bar, quickly walking up to the man serving drinks.

"Sorry, boss. Thanks for that." He tips his head toward something, but I don't look.

"You're not the bartender?" I ask, slightly embarrassed at the way I assumed he was.

"Nope. I'm Justice, and I own this place." If I expected him to hold out a hand and shake mine as a means of introduction, I'm mistaken. Somehow, I feel as if I've made a terrible error but survived it anyway.

"Sorry about your sidewalk, pretty lady." He presses back from the bar as the other man removes the bottle from the wooden top.

"It was going to be a nice walk." I sigh. "With a community center and a train park. I even found someone I thought the town might dedicate the place to, making it meaningful, but they don't want to hear it."

Justice's brows pinch. "Who you gonna name it after?"

"A boy named Michael Harrington. I heard he was a town favorite."

Justice stills behind the bar. In fact, it feels like the entire place stops moving. Voices lower. Pool balls don't roll. Even the music seems to quiet.

"Michael, you say?" Justice stares back at me. His menacing look softens just a bit. "Would have been a nice memorial to the kid."

"Would have been," I state. If only Charlie hadn't disapproved of it.

+ + +

Two days later, Cora Conrad comes to the mayor's office requesting to see me, and I'm surprised by the impromptu visit. Perhaps this is more of her wanting us to be new friends.

"Let's head to the diner for lunch," she suggests, and I cringe, knowing it's the place where my father collapsed.

Cora doesn't miss a beat, clearly knowing my history. "We no longer cower to the things we fear, remember?"

Somehow, I think that's what Cora says about herself, but I like the suggestion. I need to face what I fear. I was afraid to be alone, afraid to leave Richard, but I did it. I crossed the country and accepted my station, sleeping in a twin bed across from my child.

With Cora's advice, I decide to follow her to the diner. I could use the break from the stifling silence within the office.

"I heard about your plan," she says as we walk down Main Street, the municipal portion of town divided from the business district by First Avenue. "It sounds like a good one."

I don't recall Cora being at the town council meeting, but it's a small town, and I suppose news travels fast of the new woman who wants a walkway and the rejection of her idea.

"I also heard Charlie vetoed it."

Even though I should defend him as my boss and explain the reasons given regarding finances and allocations of funds to various divisions within the town budget, I don't. I'm taking it all personally when maybe I shouldn't. Didn't Charlie turn it personal when he said he wasn't going to let people think I slept with him for this project?

"Yeah. He did," I say with an exhale.

"You know, there's another way to get things done."

Turning to Cora, I'm not certain what she means. "You could form your own community committee to support the cause. Raise the funds yourself, and then you only need the town council to approve the plan, not the financial aspect."

"I don't think I sold many on converting a church into a community center."

"Oh, pish. Let the old fogies not go there then." Cora waves her hand and pauses before the diner. "I'm just suggesting there's another way, and I'm willing to help you."

I stare at this woman who wants to be my friend. Her hair is blond and done to perfection. Her makeup flawless. Her dress designer. She's the epitome of a Southern belle in modern times, and I don't know why she'd want to be my friend.

"I'm not good at accepting help, so I'm going to decline your offer, but thank you, Cora. I appreciate you willing to stick your neck out for me."

"Do you have another solution?"

I shrug. "Quit, I guess. Let the town have its way, and I'll just sit in my office typing up schedules of events like rock painting and flower potting."

Cora chuckles. "You don't seem like a quitter to me."

"I'm not, not really, but I'll figure it out." Did I quit my marriage? I tell myself often enough it wasn't me but Richard who ruined everything. "I suppose there might be another way to get the money."

It isn't as if my job is contingent on the walkway; it's just that I wanted to make a difference somewhere, and with Charlie's rejection comes my determination to prove myself. Maybe I'll dedicate the city walk to my father. He loved gardening and landscape. He'd love a park for children and a church as a place to gather people.

With the suggestion of finding another way, the Thursday night baseball game invitation comes to mind. Would it be that difficult to pretend with Richard? Hadn't I done it for years?

"Really? Do tell," Cora says, keeping us outside the diner.

"I can't yet, but when I do, you'll be the first to know."

This somehow appeases her, as I sense she thrives on knowing things first. After accepting my answer with a nod, she opens the door to the diner where we have lunch and become new friends.

Chapter 25
Passions and Petitions

[Charlie]

I've made a terrible mistake. I've let my personal emotions get in the way of professional decisions, and I panicked. I didn't think the council had even the slightest hint that Janessa and I had been together, but when Scarlett Nugent suggested she saw Janessa under my arm exiting the back of the Pub, I froze.

You seem rather close with Ms. Cruz. I wasn't aware you were friends.

Her father worked for me, I reminded her. *He died, remember?* It had only been a week ago, and so many people turned out for Henri's funeral, she couldn't possibly forget even if she is older.

Yes, Scarlett said, still holding her gaze on me, but I looked away, leading us to other concerns of the council before the fateful moment Janessa overheard me with Wyatt.

And I didn't defend her.

I wasn't totally in the wrong. The town doesn't have a million dollars lying around for a special interest project. However, I could have supported the idea, encouraged others to be on board, and suggested ways to obtain the funds, but I didn't. I let it falter because I didn't want others to see my connection to this woman. If she wanted to plant dead trees along the median, I'd give it to her. I'd do anything for her, but I couldn't let people see that about me.

I'd already had to prove my dedication to the town over a woman when my wife was caught having her affair, and people doubted my ability. Reason suggests the two should be unrelated, but small-town people are funny like that, equating personal relationships to the community as a whole. *If I couldn't keep my wife in line, how did I expect to run a town?* The old generation said those things. Damn righteous without examining the skeletons in their own closets.

Then there was the leaked image of me in that bathing suit.

Mayor McSteamy.

Again, I had to prove myself over a freaking photograph.

It's one reason I've held back from taking up Ford Bernard's pressure to run for Congress. I've already proven myself to this town. I don't need to prove anything else.

Except you do, don't you, Charlie?

I need to prove to the woman I've been involved with that it's more than sex for me. I'm falling for her, and I don't want to lose her over a city park and an old church.

Bracing my elbow on my desk, I prop my forehead on my hand and inhale in frustration. I miss her like crazy.

A soft knock comes on my door, and for the millionth time, I hope she's come to me, that she'll let me explain, only it's not her feminine voice I hear following the opening of the door.

"Charlie, can I speak with you a moment?" Charity sheepishly looks around the wood barrier. We've had a strained relationship since her attempt at seduction on the day of Janessa's father's collapse.

"Sure," I say. Sitting back in my chair, I point at the seat opposite my desk.

"I just wanted to apologize." Does she mean when she asked me to make her the woman at my side, or maybe she means when I heard her and Janessa going off about me the other day? "I shouldn't have suggested that we…" Her eyes lower, and she wrings her fingers together. She's nervous, and I don't blame her. I'm embarrassed for her, but she's been a good friend and office companion, so I don't want to lose her.

"I'm sorry if I embarrassed you, but we've had a professional relationship for so long. I don't understand where any of that came from," I say.

Her father must have put her up to it because it seems so out of character for her. Yet as she stares back at me, wide-eyed and confused, I feel as if I've misread something.

"Charlie, you must know how I feel about you, and with Janessa present, I just didn't—"

Sitting straighter in my seat, I lean forward over my desk, which pauses her speech. "What about Janessa?"

"I didn't know you were open to office romance."

I stare at her. I blink. I stare again. "What?"

"You've always been so upstanding, and I thought it was a sense of propriety being a single father and all, but when Janessa arrived, you changed. I didn't realize you were open to people who work together to seeing one another. You must know how I feel. We'd make a great team, Charlie. We've been a great team." Her voice lowers as her head lifts higher. "I could make you happy."

I can't believe this is happening. My assistant isn't apologizing as much as coming on to me again.

"Charity, what makes you think you and I would make a good team?" I'm not trying to hurt her feelings, but she must know I'm not attracted to her.

"We have history. We're both from here and grew up together. We know one another." For some reason, I don't think she knows me as well as she thinks, and in her buttoned-up blouse, perhaps I've misjudged her, but I'm not about to throw her over my desk and discover if she can take it like Janessa.

There's no comparison.

Janessa is it for me.

"As I value our friendship and our long-standing history, as you just mentioned, I'd personally like to forget this conversation." I hold her gaze before she looks away. "I don't know what you think is happening between Ms. Cruz and myself, but—"

"You're sleeping with her." Charity's head snaps back to face me. "I heard you arguing the other day. She slept with you."

This is exactly the thing I didn't want people thinking—Janessa slept with me—without accepting that I slept with her in return. It takes two, and I realize that; however, I don't know how to respond to my assistant.

"I don't see how what I do with my personal life affects you."

"I care about you, Charlie," she emphasizes, standing to step up to the desk. "I care about this town, and your future, *our* future."

"There is no future for *us*." My meaning is clear. There will not be a Charlie and Charity.

"Are you saying you aren't running for Congress?"

"Are you suggesting the only way I can is if I have you by my side?" It's a low blow, but I'm growing agitated by this questioning, and I'm wondering when I lost focus on my assistant's intentions.

"I'm not suggesting anything, Charlie." Her eyes lower. "I just thought we'd be good together."

"You mean *together*-together if I became a congressman?" I finally question, and Charity turns bright pink. I exhale, finding the strength to say what comes out next. "Again, I'd like to suggest you walk out of my office, and we try to forget this conversation happened."

Charity closes her eyes for a moment, but when she opens them, determination fills them. "I suppose it's come to a decision, Charlie. Her or me?"

"You aren't really giving me an ultimatum, are you?" Is she threatening me? I don't even blink. "Her."

Charity's mouth falls slightly open, and she nods. "I see. I'll leave my resignation on your desk in the morning."

"Charity," I say, standing for the first time, circling my desk but then stopping before I reach for her.

"It's better this way, Charlie. I messed up. I thought we had something we'd been denying, and when Janessa came along, I misunderstood your position, but I see I was wrong. I've always valued you, sir. I…"

My eyes close. *Please don't say you love me.*

"I think I'll be going."

+ + +

Sitting on the couch, I mindlessly watch the baseball game. My feet rest on the ottoman, beer in my hand, and Lucy tucked into my side.

"Vega's so lucky. She got to go to the game."

"What?" I choke, my thoughts not on the screen as much as the interchange between my assistant and me. How could Charity think I'd fall for her, be open to her, just because someone new entered the office? When did she develop feelings for me, and how did I miss them? Still, all thoughts of Charity Bernard screech to a halt when Lucy mentions Vega's at the game, which means…

"Did her mother take her?"

"Vega said her dad wanted to see her and her mother, so he invited them to the game. She's surprised her mom said yes as her mom's angry with her dad, but Vega thinks it's a good thing. They need to talk." She speaks like a therapist.

"What do they need to talk about?" I say aloud, realizing it isn't my daughter's place to inform me, nor should I be asking her as if she knows the answer.

"Getting back together."

Leaning forward, I drink the rest of my beer in one gulp before setting the bottle on the tray on the ottoman.

This isn't happening. But as fate would have it, the camera pans over the wives' section, and there sit Janessa and Vega. They wave at the camera, and shortly afterward, Lucy's phone pings.

"It's a text from Vega, asking me if I saw her."

Lucy quickly types a response while I stare at the screen. With only a flash of thirty seconds, the image of Janessa in the stadium seat etches into my head. She looked happy and beautiful and very far away from me.

Lucy's phone pings again. "Vega says they're staying the night in some fancy hotel and seeing her dad later." My daughter's excitement rises for her friend, and I realize they share a common bond—parents who led public lives and live very separate from their child. It reminds me Lucy leaves for her mother's on Sunday. I'm still against the two-week visit, but I can't go against the custody agreement.

"That sounds…" I can't muster the words. *Awful*. Terrible. Like a bad idea.

"You know, Dad, I thought you might ask Vega's mom out on a date." Lucy pauses, and I turn my head to look at her, but she's still reading her phone. "Vega and I thought it would be cool to be sisters, but you haven't asked her mom out. Don't you think Ms. Cruz is pretty?"

"Very pretty," I mutter as the commercial break does a recap of people in the crowd before exiting to the true commercials. There's Janessa's face again. I swallow the lump in my throat. When did things get so messed up?

"You should ask her out then."

"I can't, honey. It's complicated."

"Adults always say that. It's easy. *Ms. Cruz, can I take you to dinner?*" Lucy lowers her voice to mimic someone masculine. "See? Easy. One question."

"I'm afraid she might be mad at me at the moment. Like when Vega was mad at you because you told me about her dad being famous."

"Then you should say you're sorry. I told Vega I was sorry and then promised never to betray her trust again unless I thought she was hurting herself." Lucy pauses, reminding me of what I said to her. "You don't think Ms. Cruz is hurting herself, right?"

I stare at the television, which plays a laundry detergent commercial.

Is she hurting herself? Is she hurting because we haven't spoken? Is she still mad at me? Is she going back to him?

I'm hurting, I want to tell my child, but that would just be silly.

"No, Pint. I don't think she's hurting herself. She's one tough lady, and that makes Vega strong, too."

"Yeah, but she's not tough like Mom. I mean, she's nicer and all, and doesn't get angry like Mom does."

I turn to face my child, curled into the couch. "What do you mean?"

"Mom can get mad at me when I speak or when I don't. Sometimes, I say the wrong thing or sit where I'm not supposed to."

This is the first I've heard of this, and my brows pinch. "But Mom's never hurt you, right?"

Lucy shakes her head, but sadness fills her expression. Angela better never lay a hand on our child, but Lucy's been hurt in other ways. The lack of calls. The mandated visits. And obviously, this strict behavior toward her.

"I don't want to go," she whispers, and I fall back on the couch, returning her under my arm.

"I know, sweetheart, but I can't go against the rules."

"Why not? You make them. Can't you rewrite them?"

I huff. "Not for this, Pint. Not for your visits."

"But other rules, you could break, right?"

"Like what, Pint?" My forehead furrows as I glance down at her under my arm.

"Like your dating rules. You could ask Ms. Cruz out."

"I don't have dating rules," I argue with laughter in my voice.

"You don't date," she says to me. I wonder where all this is coming from, or why we're even having this discussion.

"I don't date because you're my best girl." I squeeze her to my side.

"Dad," she drones. "I'm your only girl and your daughter, but you need someone your own age."

"Are you saying I'm old?" I laugh.

"I'm saying you must be lonely."

"Lucy." I drag out her name, still wondering why she's saying this.

"It's okay, Dad. I'm lonely sometimes, too, but now I have Vega living on the other side of the pool. It's awesome having a best friend so close. Don't you want a best friend? Isn't that what dating's like?"

Oh, God. Dating is so not like finding a best friend, but then I reconsider. Dating is the right mix between companion and lover. Could I have that with Janessa? We've been physical more than we've been friends, but we've still opened up to one another on occasion.

"I think I've burned my bridge," I mutter, glancing back at the television. Whatever Janessa and I had won't continue if she's sitting at a baseball game watching her ex-husband play.

"Then it's time to rebuild it, Dad. You're the mayor. You make all the decisions."

I'm stumped, schooled by my ten-year-old because she isn't wrong.

I make the decisions for this town, and that's why Janessa's sitting where she is. Which leaves me sitting where I am, wondering when I will make a decision for myself and not worry about what the town thinks.

+ + +

The next morning, Charity sits at her desk while her resignation rests on mine. She's given us her two weeks' notice—us because she technically works for Jordan, my partner, and me.

"What happened?" Jordan says, holding out his copy of her resignation and closing the door behind him as he enters my office.

"It's such a long story." I'm embarrassed to tell it, but I need to tell someone. Leaving out all the heavy details, I give Jordan the gist. Charity's crush. Her unrequited attention from me. And Janessa.

"You're sleeping with the hottie upstairs?" His brows lift as his smile curls. "I'm so proud of you, Uncle Charlie."

It's rare he reminds me he's my nephew as he became a full partner after his father's death almost two years ago.

"Oh, God, I shouldn't be telling you all this." I swipe two hands down my face and scrub.

"Why? It was obviously on your mind, and I'm a big boy. I'm actually proud of you. I thought you were a monk, and I didn't know how you did it."

I chuckle as I look at him, looking so much like his father, Chris. "I'm definitely no saint."

"But I've never seen you interested in anyone."

I shrug. "I guess I haven't been before. Not like this, anyway, but I've let something personal cloud my professional judgment."

Jordan tips his head. "Sounds to me like you let your professional position get in the way of your personal life."

"I…" I didn't do that, did I? "I can't have the town thinking she slept with me to get her the money she wanted."

"Is that what she did?"

"No."

"Then I don't understand. You slept together." Jordan holds up one hand. "She proposed money for a city walk." Jordan holds up his other hand. He looks between them and back at me. "The two are not together."

"But what will people think?"

Jordan tips his head. "You know, Charlie, sometimes that Goody Two-shoes reputation suits you, and other times, it just doesn't. I'm not the risk-taker between Jax and myself, but I still know when there's no other choice but to take a dare or lose out on the one thing that could make your life better. And Uncle Charlie…" he says as he stands. "There's more to life than pleasing this town."

When he nears the door, he turns back to me. "I'm sorry to lose Charity, but she can be replaced. Can you say the same for Janessa?"

Jordan gives me a weak smile and steps into the outer office, closing the door behind him and leaving me with lots to ponder.

+ + +

Monday morning, I find a petition on my desk.

"What's this?" I say to no one as we agreed to let Charity go early, still honoring her two weeks' notice. It was just too awkward between us, and I felt it was best to relieve the tension by releasing her on Friday. As I can't buzz my assistant and demand an explanation, and the petition clearly states who it's from, I march myself up the stairs to the second floor and knock on the Parks and Recreation door.

Entering, I find Corabelle Conrad sitting across from Janessa, and this situation has all kinds of bad news written on it. Corabelle is the neighbor at the end of the lane. Younger than my sister, Mati, they were not friends as children. Cora was spoiled and bratty. As a tattletale and a know-it-all, the traits carried into adulthood as a town gossip until she and her husband divorced. Then something happened, and Cora and Mati became friends.

"What's this?" I repeat, holding up the paper before me.

"It's a petition," Janessa states.

"We formed our own committee," Cora adds, a cheer in her voice.

"What committee?"

"Walk the Ridge," Cora proudly says, twisting in her seat to have a better look at me over her shoulder.

"Two people do not make a committee," I state although my voice rises.

"Oh, we have more than two on the committee. We have an entire team on our side, and we plan to raise the money for the city walk, park, and community center."

"You still need town approval," I remind both ladies.

Cora waves a dismissive hand. "You let me worry about that, Charlie Harrington. I can be very persuasive when I want something."

"And since when did you want a walkway, park, or community center?" I question. My eyes leap to Janessa, who keeps hers lowered to her hands folded on her desk.

"Since I heard about the proposal. It's an excellent proposition for our town and a nice nod to the locals while addressing the needs of tourists."

I glare at Cora. "And what about the money necessary for this project?"

"Done," Janessa says, lifting her head, and I stare at her. Her bright green eyes hold mine, determination in them, but there's something else, and my heart breaks. She did it. She went to Richard for the money.

"You should use that money for yourself," I whisper although I'm still loud enough for both women to hear me. Cora turns to Janessa, and their eyes meet for a conversation I can't interpret. Janessa shakes her head once and then turns back to me.

"Is there anything else you need, sir?"

You, I want to scream. I need you bent over this desk and to be buried in you to bring us back to right with one another. Then I think of what Lucy said. I should apologize. I should ask her out. With Cora as my witness, I blurt out my next thoughts.

"I'd like to suggest we have dinner and discuss this further."

"I don't see how din—" Janessa begins.

"That sounds like a wonderful suggestion. Let's say The Patio at six," Cora interjects, standing from her seat. Only she doesn't make to leave.

"Janessa, could I please—"

"Nope," Cora mutters again. "Perhaps your secretary could make an appointment with us. Oh wait, where is Charity?" Cora's eyes narrow at me, warning me she already knows, which is the last thing I need.

"Charity resigned," I offer, meeting Janessa's eyes around Cora. Her brows lift but then quickly lower.

"Such a shame. She's a good woman. She'll find someone else, I mean, something else," Cora corrects.

"Corabelle, don't you have somewhere to be?"

"Nope," she says again. "Committee meeting. We have business to discuss. Nice to see you, Charlie." Cora waves her hand, dismissing me while I look back at Janessa, who fights a smile. *Well, at least someone's having fun with this.* Excusing myself, I tug the door behind me, slamming it a little harder than necessary, but I'm pissed.

Just what are those two up to?

Chapter 26
Stealing Hearts

[Janessa]

Thankfully, Charlie cancels the dinner meeting, and Cora and I meet with *our team* as she calls the collection of people she's recruited to help us. I don't know how she did it, but as Cora said, she can be very persuasive. We have a new proposal for the August town council meeting in which we will present the plans again with the financials spelled out—no debt to the city. It's hard to believe it's really going to happen. We only have to hope Charlie won't find a new reason to disapprove the construction.

I'm coming home late, having spent another evening with my brother and his new friends at Ridged Edge. It's a questionable place, but it's growing on me. As I park my dad's old truck, I notice the lights on for Charlie's batting cage. I hesitate for a second, debating if I should ignore the familiar crack of a bat or finally face Charlie. Cora really flustered him this morning.

Deciding I'll only take a peek at the man I miss, I slink down the path to the old tennis courts. Standing in the shadows, I watch the power of Charlie's swing, the grace in his stance, and the concentration on his etched face. He's such a beautiful man. The ball shoots out of the machine, aiming for him. Charlie swings and misses.

"Dammit," he curses aloud.

"You need to choke up a bit."

At the sound of my voice, he spins, finding me pressed against the chain-link fence. He stills for only a second and then returns his attention to the batting machine. Another ball flies at him. He hits it head-on, and the thud reverberates against the metal opposite him. He continues to ignore me with another pitch, and then he stops. Lowering the bat for the court, he leans against the end of it. His head hangs, and my heart breaks.

"I thought you'd understand I was doing it to protect you." His low voice travels to me, and I almost miss all the words.

From outside the cage, I reply. "I thought you'd understand I need to do this to prove to myself I can."

Charlie picks up the bat and takes a few steps closer to my position. Leaning forward once again with both hands on the end of the wooden stick, Charlie looks up at me.

"How would I know that? I feel like I hardly know anything about you."

"When I gave up my career to be Richard's wife, I was happy to be the mother to our child. But as Vega grew and Richard separated from me, I needed something more. I missed my job. This is my second chance, and by some miracle, you hired me. I want to make a mark." My forehead lowers for the metal links. "Maybe I dreamed too big?" My fingers curl into the fencing. Maybe it was too ambitious. What do I care about this town? I'm new here. But like I said, I'm hoping for a fresh start.

"I don't think any dream is too big." Charlie's voice surprises me. He's standing closer, just on the other side of the fence, but I feel like we stand miles apart.

"I miss you," I blurt, looking up at him, and Charlie's lips twist.

"I miss you. Everything is falling apart."

This reminds me I didn't know about Charity. "What happened with Charity?"

"She hit on me, and I didn't reciprocate, so she quit."

"Oh, my God." I laugh.

"It isn't funny," Charlie says, looking up at me, his eyes serious.

I swallow back more laughter. "It's a little funny."

"How's that?" He cocks his head to the side.

"Because look at you, Charlie, and look at her. You're all masculine and intense and amazing in the bedroom, and she seems mousy and meek and just wanting to be on the arm of a congressman."

Charlie's brows lift. "You think I'm amazing in bed?"

I chuckle softly. "Come on, Charlie. You know you are."

He steps closer to the fence, linking his fingers through the metal, similar to mine only higher. "Actually, I don't know that. I suddenly feel like I don't know anything about myself. Who am I? What do I want?"

"Who do you think you are, Charlie?"

"I'm the town's mayor and work hard for my city. I love my daughter, and it almost killed me to put her on the plane yesterday for her mandated two-week visit with her mother."

"Charlie," I hiss. "I'm so sorry." Instead of going to him, I press myself against the cage between us, needing to be closer but not trusting myself.

He shrugs.

"What do you want?" My voice lowers, and my eyes shift, afraid to look at him and hear the truth. How he wants someone like Charity Bernard and a congressman position. A life where he'll have a safe girl on his arm and a high-profile job.

"You," he whispers. His forehead leans against the chain links. "I only want you."

I release the fencing and circle around the opening to him. He hasn't moved; his forehead still presses to the metal. My arms wrap around his back, and my forehead leans into his spine. His hand covers my forearm, but he doesn't move.

"You went to him," he mutters.

"It was plan A, but I was quickly reminded it was a mistake. I'm going with plan B instead."

Charlie spins in my arms, loosely slipping his arms up my back as mine fall to his warm chest. "What happened?"

"Vega and I went to see Richard as asked, but when the game ended and we entered the field, a woman got to him first, making a scene about our presence. Poor Ruthie. As much as she tried to have the woman removed, it was obvious she was there for him. He brought her there, and it was another reminder of why I can't even pretend with him."

"But you still went to him."

"I can't be with a man who doesn't believe in me." My hands smooth down Charlie's chest, and I expect him to release me, but he tightens his hold.

"I believe in you. I just doubt myself."

"What do you doubt, Charlie?"

"My decision-making." He snorts. "How you might feel about me."

"All you have to do is ask me," I say, toying with the fabric stretched over his firm chest.

"How do you feel?" He jiggles me in his arms.

"You make me feel alive in a way I don't think I ever have. I crave you, and it scares me. I don't want to feel I need you to survive."

"What if I need you? What if I feel like I can't go on without you?"

"Charlie," I whisper, the honesty too much. "What about your reputation or mine?"

"I owe this town so much, but at the same time, it owes me. I don't know why I feel the need to defend myself, but I'm more worried about you."

"Let me worry about me," I say, patting his chest.

"That's just it. You're all I think about." He lifts a hand and swipes it over the baseball cap on his head, taking it off and then placing it back on again.

"I think about you all the time, too."

"Then what do we do?" Charlie asks, and his voice is so earnest and uncertain.

"I guess, I remain your dirty little secret," I tease.

"Don't say that. Don't think that." He tightens his hold on me.

"Well, we can't be public, right? Not while I work for you, and I want this project."

Will he ask me to quit? Will he tell me to give up the city walk?

Charlie's head falls to mine. "What's plan B?"

"For us?"

"For the park and such?"

"Forgive me, but I can't tell you." I want to tell him. I want to share all the wonderful things Cora came up with, and the support we have in place. He's the first person I thought to tell when things came together, but at the same time, he can't know our strategy. I don't trust that he won't shoot me down again.

"You don't trust me?" His head pops up, and his eyes meet mine. The typical gray-brown shines like whiskey with the glow of the lights.

"I don't want you to sabotage my plan."

Charlie releases me, pressing himself back into the fence, and I step away from him. The distance returns between us.

"I need to look out for Vega and me, Charlie. I need to make a new home for us. She wants to stay here. *I* want to stay here."

Maybe it's the wrong thing to say. Maybe I got too caught up in him, and I'm mixing up my reasons to remain in Blue Ridge.

"I didn't sabotage you," he says, crossing his arms and turning his gaze away from me.

"You didn't support me, either."

Charlie's jaw clenches, his cheek moving in frustration. I've upset him, but he doesn't see the bigger picture for me. I need this job. I want this project, and I want to be here with him. Maybe I'm too late for the last one.

Charlie doesn't look back at me, and I sense I've been dismissed. A pit in my stomach grows.

"Good night, Charlie." I reach out for his chest again and caress my hand down his shirt before releasing him and turning for the exit. I'm almost to the opening in the fence when his arms circle my waist.

"Why can't I let you walk away?" he breathes into my hair. "I'm so pissed off, yet I want to take you up against this fence."

My body comes to life, everything racing—my heart, my blood, my sex.

"One last time," I whisper like he has said to me on a few occasions. Suddenly, I'm face-first against the fence. Charlie reaches for the light box and flips the switch, submerging us in darkness. His hands roughly lift my skirt and tug down my underwear. My fingers curl into the chain links, holding my cheek away from the cool metal. Without foreplay or warning, Charlie lines himself up with me and slams into me. I cry out, lifting on my toes for a second as we both still, adjusting to the rush. His fingers find mine clutching the metal fencing and curl over the back of them as his lips near my ear.

"You lied to me." He pulls his hips back and then surges forward again. I whimper in pleasure. He feels so good. I've missed him, but I didn't realize how much until just now with him inside me again. He draws back and then thrusts forward, both of us catching our breaths.

"How did I lie?" I choke on the words as he rams into me, sliding so deep and then teasing me at the edge as if he'll leave my body.

"When you came to my bed, naked and willing, you promised not to steal anything from me." His voice is rough, stuttering from his fierce pace. His fingers pinch over mine. He's using the fence as leverage to fill me. *Deliciously* fill me.

"I didn't steal anything from you, Charlie," I remind him, my own voice stammering as I force myself backward, clenching in fear he'll escape my body.

He doesn't reply but moves faster, pressing harder. I'm on the edge, and he hears it in the hitch of my breath. A hand lowers for my clit, roughly stroking until I fall apart around him, and then he stills, filling me with his release as he whispers, "You stole my heart."

Abruptly, he pulls out of me. My dress lowers, but I don't release my grip on the fence, afraid my legs won't hold me up, and then I see Charlie. He's left the batting pen and disappears in the darkness of the yard without a glance back at me.

Chapter 27
Plan B

[Charlie]

Fuck!

I can't believe what we did, and thinking about it, I'm hard again before I enter my shower. My hand slams against the tile while I take matters into my palm, reliving the feel of her around me. The racing of her heart. The hammering of my dick into her wet depths.

My God, what is she doing to me?

And what did I admit to her?

She stole my heart.

My forehead presses against my forearm, leaning against the steamy tile as the water pelts my bare skin. I'm losing my mind over her, and I'm spinning out of control.

She doesn't trust me. She didn't have to say it for me to know, and we both know you can't have a relationship without trust.

Slamming my hand against the tile again, I curse repeatedly as I don't know what to do.

I just want her back in my house and in my bed. I want back in her good graces.

Spent from the physical exertion of batting and then the lusty actions against the fence, I finish in the shower and then wrap a towel around my waist.

Between Janessa's appearance and Lucy's earlier phone call, I'm suddenly exhausted, and I climb into my bed after tugging on boxer briefs; only my thoughts don't rest.

"Daddy, Mom said she's doubling down her efforts for senator." Without knowing what she means, Lucy's fear matches mine. Her campaign is holding on by a thread. How will she use our daughter? Angela still possesses those boudoir images from our wedding, including a series of me in and out of that damn bathing suit. Thankfully, she didn't

release the naked ones, but there is no telling how far she'll go to get what she wants. She can try to destroy me, but I won't let her use our daughter.

I have such poor taste in women, I think, and then I turn toward the pillow next to me and realize that's incorrect. Janessa is everything I've never had before, and she's made all the difference. Over time, I might have given in to Charity Bernard had I known her feelings before Janessa's arrival. I might have chosen a safe woman, but I'd been down that misleading path. Despite Angela's drive to be something more, life with her was passionless. Unlike with Janessa. Janessa's determined to get what she wants as well, but she only wants to make a mark on this community, not the entire universe.

My hand smooths over the pillow. I miss her. I told her as much, but then I had to turn into a crazed man and take her up against the fence.

I spin for my phone on the nightstand and scroll for her number.

Tell her you're sorry, Lucy said. I still hadn't done it.

I'm sorry it doesn't seem like I support you. I only want the best for you. I let the phone fall to my chest, hardly feeling better.

I don't want to be in your way either.

You could never be in the way. I'm the one who cockblocked myself, yet she still gave in to me along the fence line. *One last time*, she said, but it can't end. **Don't say we're over**.

My phone rings in my hand, and I answer it, breathless with the anticipation of hearing her voice.

"Charlie, you're the one who walked away tonight."

"I know, and I'm sorry. I'm sorry for everything. I'm sorry I can't keep my hands off you, and I want you so much. I'm sorry I thought I was protecting your reputation and got in the way of something I didn't know you wanted so badly. I'm sorry I—"

"Please stop," she says, her voice quiet as she interjects. "You don't need to apologize for doing your job."

"But am I doing my job? Am I doing it well?"

"Can I ask you something? Do you want to be in Congress?"

"Would you go with me if I did?"

"That isn't a part of the question." Her voice remains quiet and soft, and I want her in this bed next to me. I want to see her face when we talk.

"Say it was. Say I do run. Would you come with me?"

"Charlie, take me out of the equation."

I consider Angela and how upset Lucy is that her mother is running for re-election. Could she handle two parents working on a grander scale for the government?

"I don't want to run," I whisper.

"Ever or now?"

"Ever." I'm happy where I am. Some people strive for more in politics, but I'm good right where I'm planted.

"Was that so difficult, Charlie? You're good at being mayor, and you like it. That's a bonus."

"Sometimes, I need to make tough decisions."

"We all do, Charlie. Even the little people." She laughs, and I want to see her smile.

"I wish you were here," I say, opening myself up even more to her.

"Me too. The twin bed and Vega's snoring are getting old."

"You could still move in as I said the other day. I'll give you a guest room." And then I'll sneak in every night and have my way with her.

She chuckles. "And how would that look to the town?"

She's right, but I'm starting not to care what the community thinks of me.

"Tell me plan B."

"Charlie," she groans.

"I want you to trust me."

"I do, but not with this. You'll find out in due time." She pauses. "It's not bad, Charlie."

"I'm tired of being good," I whisper.

She purrs, and instantly, I'm hard again. I scrub a hand down my face. I'm like a teenager and just as giddy.

"Where are you?" I ask if she isn't in the bed across from her daughter yet.

"I'm outside. There's a dock back here."

"You're still on my property," I tease, wanting to jump out of bed and rush to the dock jutting into the river on the edge of my land.

"In many ways, I'm already living with you." Because she lives in the coach house with her mother, brother, and daughter.

"It's not close enough."

+ + +

When I see Janessa the next morning, she smiles shyly at me as she says good morning and climbs the stairs for her office. I watch the sway of her hips and the flex of her legs as she climbs upward, disappearing at the landing.

A throat clears next to me. "Enjoying the view?" my law partner asks.

"I'm in love with her," I admit to Jordan, and he slowly smiles, lifting his coffee mug in salute.

"Here's to risk-taking." With that, he turns on his heels and heads to his office like it's any other ordinary day.

Only the days turn into a week, and I don't even have a hint to the Walk the Ridge committee and its plan. Our next council meeting is a week after Lucy returns, and the days have been long. Janessa has refused my dinner invitations, stating it's best not to be seen in public together, but she's come to the house in the late evenings, and we've been together everywhere. The kitchen counter. The floor in front of the television. Even on the back staircase.

We rush one another when we're alone in the dark and keep our distance during the daylight hours, but I want more. I want to give her small moments like lunchtime at the diner and shared coffee breaks. I want dinner dates with a movie or even bowling. I want the town to know how I feel about her, but for now, she's my little secret, and I don't like it.

All hell breaks loose right before Lucy is scheduled to come home.

"Mom wants me to stay. Please say I don't have to stay," Lucy's whine breaks my heart when she calls me. While she's perfected her pouty face and working on her future-teenage angst, she's not a complainer.

"What's going on?" I question over the tears in my daughter's voice.

"She says she needs me by her side. She's playing up the single-mother role again." It's sad my daughter knows this gimmick at ten years old. It's only a ploy as Angela wants to portray an image of a hardworking woman, single mother, and doting parent, which she isn't. She only follows the decree of the custody agreement, just like she used to schedule sex in her planner.

"Lucy, I will not let that happen. You will come home Saturday as we planned."

"She's so…different. She's talking more and more about running for president in the future and how she needs me to be a good girl and comply with her. How she has plans for us. *Her and me*. But I don't want to stay with her, Dad. Please don't make me."

"Absolutely not, Pint. I will not let you stay there." My heart races in my chest. This is the type of bullshit I worried would happen. Angela can't be trusted not to pull some kind of crap.

"Dad, can I leave early? Can't you come get me and bring me home now?"

I don't want to go against the decree myself, but my insides roil and my skin itches. I don't want Lucy there another minute.

"I know the rules, Dad, but can't you break them just once? Please, Daddy." Her voice cracks, and my heart rips in half.

"I'll be there, Pint. Just give me time to find a flight, and I'll be there. Don't tell Mom, okay? It's our secret."

If Angela wants to ambush me, I have my own strategy of attack.

+ + +

"Charlie, is everything okay?" It's so great to hear Janessa's voice as I sit in a hotel room in Philadelphia, waiting for Jordan to contact me. While I know all the regulations for divorce, I did not represent myself when Angela and I separated. Chris, Mati's late husband, was my attorney, but he's gone, and I need answers. Legally, Angela cannot keep Lucy, and I don't think she wants the battle I'll cause in court to prevent her from additional visitations. What she wants is a show of goodwill toward her as Lucy's mother, and I don't have it in me to give it to her. There's no reason to act as if I trust her or will allow her to use our daughter.

Then comes the threat to expose images of me.

Naked. Risqué. Private.

Photographs that were taken while we were married, and I thought I loved her. I was so wrong.

"There's a lot going on," I say, my voice straining as I stare at the curtained window. Angela certainly wasn't expecting me when I showed up at the restaurant, crashing her little dinner party. Knowing Angela wouldn't want a scene, she watched as I held out my hand for our daughter, who stood and followed me. We waited for Angela at her condo, where she took an additional hour to show, and then we gathered Lucy's things. I would have left them all, even the new iPad I bought her at Christmas, but she couldn't part without Mr. Bear, a ratty stuffed animal she still sleeps with when she is stressed.

"Where are you?" Janessa asks.

"In Philadelphia."

"Jordan told me, but I mean, where are you exactly?"

Glancing over my shoulder, I check on Lucy, who's watching something on her iPad. She's wearing her headphones, but her eyes have begun drooping. I tell Janessa the name of my hotel and glance down at the floor beneath my feet. I explain what happened and why I'm here and how I'm waiting on Jordan's call.

"Okay, I won't keep you. Just let me know if I can do anything. Exes suck." She chuckles, and the sound travels into my chest, but I'm too tired to laugh.

As soon as we hang up, Jordan calls.

"We can't block her threat. You can only call her bluff. If she releases the images, we find a way to pull them down. We can charge her with defamation of character or slander. Same with whoever shares them.”

“Jordan, you know once something’s on the internet, it’s there forever, no matter what.”

“Not necessarily. Plus, who wants to see your junk? You’ll be old news once the next political scandal breaks. Angela will be the next political scandal.” He chuckles, but he doesn’t find the humor in the situation any more than I do. When his guffawing subsides, and I don’t respond to it, he offers another solution. “I suggest a counterattack. If she sends out nudes of you, you need something that will be more attractive than gawking at your privates.”

“And what would that be?”

“Something extreme. Your own announcement. Do something that takes the focus off the images and onto you in a positive light.”

“I don’t suppose a run for Congress will look favorable amid nude photos.” Not that I want to run or even hint that I might. I’ve already told Janessa I’m not interested in that kind of battle.

Trying to break the tension, I joke, “You don’t think seeing me naked is going to be seen favorably?” Is he saying I’m not fit to look at? I swipe a hand through my hair. It certainly won’t be flattering, but some people like that stuff.

“Dick pics are old news,” Jordan counters, and this time, I do laugh. A little bit. “But if you give them somewhere else to focus their attention, people will grab on to it.”

“Like what?”

“I don’t know, but you’re a smart man, Charlie. You’ll think of something grander than nude images. Think opposite, but big.”

“And what’s opposite of dick pictures?” I ask, hardly believing we are having such a conversation.

“Don’t know. I guess something opposite sleazy images.”

Only they weren’t sleazy at the time. Angela and I were on our honeymoon. A couple in love. We’d just celebrated our wed—

I sit straighter, pressing a hand into my thigh as I stare at the sheer material over the window.

"I might have an idea."

It's the most ridiculous thing, and I have no idea if it will work or backfire, but I must do something.

Time for me to call in a plan B of my own.

Chapter 28
Proposals

[Janessa]

Nerves riddle me as we near the next town council meeting. Charlie has returned, but he's been conspicuously absent over the past week.

I've told him his daughter is his first priority, and I expect nothing less from him.

"Don't say it like that," he said to me.

"I don't mean anything other than you're a great father, and I know you'll always put Lucy first."

Charlie sounds like a broken man. He's told me about Angela's threats to reveal the naked images and make a scandal of things if he doesn't comply with her wishes for more visitation. Personally, I don't see how the photographs won't reflect negatively on her. She took the pictures. She's the one who plans to use them. Of course, she'll do things anonymously, just as anonymous tips exposed Richard and his many flames over the course of our marriage.

With Lucy back in the house, there are no more late-night shenanigans between Charlie and me at his place. I've already had a public relationship, one visible because of my marriage to Richard, so I've relished the privacy of us being together for almost two weeks. It's as if I was getting away with something, as if I have a secret.

The *dirty little* part are the words slowly eating at me. Not that sex with Charlie isn't amazing, and it's not that sex is all we have because we've spent plenty of time chatting in his bed, on his living room carpet, or at his kitchen island. However, in public, the distance is becoming daunting as if we're doing something *wrong*. As though we're the ones having an affair when we are consensual, *unmarried* adults.

In some ways, it's been a relief to no longer sneak out of the house in the middle of the night like a rebellious teen off to meet the forbidden boyfriend. I've worried that Vega would wake and find me missing. She sleeps like the dead, though, and I might need to get her snoring checked out. Most nights, I wouldn't leave until after I was certain my mother's tears had washed her into a restless abyss for the evening, and Zander had returned from the bar.

It turns out, my brother is staying in town a bit longer than his initial two weeks.

"I think I'll take over Dad's position for a little bit." Surprised by the suggestion, Zander explains how his company, which he dedicated years to through his programming skills, sold out to a larger corporation who downsized the former employees despite seniority. As a kid, Zander hated being outdoors. He begrudgingly worked with my father and a crew of landscapers during his high school years and then spent every remaining minute in his room gaming.

"I like it here," he told me, shrugging as if he couldn't explain it any more than I can. When I asked about his house, he told me it's already on the market. "I never needed such a big place for only me." My brother's tone rang with sadness as if he's realized the role of an eternal bachelor isn't all it's cracked up to be. I'm not certain if he's had any hookups in Blue Ridge. The Ridged Edge would certainly provide him with opportunity, but I don't doubt I'd hear of it. The ladies at the diner have noticed Zander, and he was a source of discussion at the first book club I attended at Roxanne's bookstore. Her Friday First Chapter Reads are a good way to mingle with adults and giggle over books. However, it's all fun and games until your brother is the hot topic among the single women in the crowd.

Originally, I thought Cora Conrad was one of those single women available to lust after my brother, but it turns out, she's *not quite* on the market, and partially explains her connection to our team who surprisingly shows up to the town council meeting.

When our presentation begins, I see Charlie slip into the back of the high school auditorium. He doesn't come forward like I expect, choosing to linger behind a few of the taller bodies on the edge of the room. The pull I feel to him is ever-present as if my body knew he was near, and my eyes sought him out. I'm also grateful he's giving us this time to shine without interfering.

I explain the layout of the walk, the design of the park, and the plans for the church again. Cora has been persuasive. Duncan Construction has committed to renovating the church as long as Milton Duncan can film it for *Rehab Dad*, his home renovation show. Not to mention it will be a tax write-off as a donation. High schoolers have been recruited to clean up the ground area and assemble the playground equipment, including Alyce Wright's girls' volleyball team, working as a way to pay it back to the community for their unending support of the most winning team in the high school's history. We also plan to host a local fundraising walk. Milestone bricks will be inlaid in the ground commemorating the town's part in raising funds for the project. And finally, Rebel's Edge, the local motorcycle club, has decided to host a charity ride in the name of Michael Harrington, as the community center and baseball diamond behind the center will be named for him.

The townspeople go wild at this final suggestion. People stir, and voices rise, and the line of men in the back of the room stands firm and grim in their leathers and tats. Only one man is missing from the line-up, and that's Ranger. The man who did not tell me his real name was James Harrington. The same man who I've learned is the father of the young man we plan to name the center after.

"I don't see what we need another baseball diamond for. We have two here at the high school," one townsperson asks, and I see Wyatt nodding his head in agreement.

"The high school diamonds are too large for smaller children, not to mention Michael's favorite sport was baseball." I didn't know the child, but my subtle interviewing skills have given me this information. I didn't want to ask any of the family outright as no one speaks of him. "The smaller fields will cater to introductory-level baseball and softball."

"Why do we need a playground near the town center?" another person interjects. "We're surrounded by the woods and have various play areas nearby."

I address this question. "Because every town should have updated, environmentally safe play equipment, and many of the other parks don't. Building on Blue Ridge's sense of community, it's nice to have a central park, and the train theme for the future park blends with the large locomotive sitting in the middle of town."

"Having a church as a community center seems sacrilegious," another shouts, and people join the bandwagon there with agreeing jeers.

"We've been assured by the former congregation they'd be proud for their former house of God to be used as a temple of community activity." Cora adds her religious euphemisms in hopes of bringing the people down a notch.

As the crowd continues to grumble, Wyatt bangs a gavel against the podium like a judge, and a deep, rugged voice speaks above the unsettled audience.

"Giant Beer Company would like to match what the Rebels raise." Giant's voice bellows over everyone, his tone matching his stature despite his general quiet as a man. The brewery is the largest company in the area and employs a good percentage of people from the town and county proper. I watch as Justice, president of the club, turns his head in Giant's direction, and Giant nods once.

Slowly, things make sense as Michael Harrington was Giant and Charlie's nephew. My heart breaks for James, a man I don't know, and his son's story, which is just tragic. My eyes leap to Charlie, realizing the shock of plan B might be more personal in nature than I intended. This is a gesture of goodwill to the community, not a hurtful reminder of what their family lost.

Giant's support causes people to grow quieter. Cora turns her attention to Wyatt.

"Well?" She lifts a brow, expecting him to set it to a vote. Wyatt huffs.

"We'll need the mayor before we can vote."

"The mayor is present," Charlie states, stepping forward, "and I fully support this plan. The research is there. The money decided. Minus the actual construction of the walk, the donations of time and material won't cost the town a penny. The entire project is outside of the town's funds, and overall, it's a great idea."

The crowd quiets as Charlie makes his way down the center aisle, his eyes holding on to me. My heart races for some reason as he continues walking right up to me.

"In fact, I support it so much that I want the town to witness my faith in Janessa Cruz."

"Charlie," I mutter as Charlie nears the low stage, and I slowly step to the side away from Cora. We stood during the presentation and have remained upright during the questions.

Charlie climbs the short set of stairs and pauses before me. "I want them all to see how much I believe in you."

Then he lowers to one knee and takes my hand. "Janessa Cruz, will you marry me?"

Before I can answer, the crowd breaks into a rambunctious outcry once again.

Chapter 29
Failure Makes the Heart Grow Fonder

[Charlie]

As Janessa stares at me, I realize I've made a grave mistake. I hold out a gorgeous and garish ring, expectantly awaiting a response that is being drowned out by the crowd's gasps and accelerating excitement.

A smile I'm certain Janessa has perfected over the years graces her lips while her typically darker skin turns pale.

"What are you doing?" she grits through clenched teeth, her eyes shifting to the crowd for a second.

"I'm showing my faith in you by professing it to the entire town."

She cups my face and lowers for my cheek, putting her face out of sight of the general audience, as she whispers, "You have some explaining to do."

She pulls back, and I see the error of my ways. *She doesn't love me.*

I thought this would show her how I felt about her, among other things.

It's the *among other things* part which niggles at my chest, but I ignore the pressure against my ribs. Still on my knee, holding out the diamond ring, my eyes beg her to accept.

"This isn't real, is it? You're asking me to pretend, aren't you?" Her lips hardly move as she speaks through her gritted teeth. Her plastic smile freezes in place. "Stand like I've accepted and slip it on me."

This isn't how I saw things happening. This isn't how I'd hoped it would be. And I see too late, it's all going to backfire.

I stand as she suggests, put the ring on her finger, and find it looks out of place among the slenderness of her fingers. Not to mention, it's brash and overstated, which isn't how I view her. She's outside the norm—elegant and refined—and she needs a ring that expresses her simplistic beauty.

Dammit, I really messed this up.

I seek her eyes, but she avoids mine, looking down at the sparkling band of silver and glaring stone.

"Let me see," Cora says behind her, and woodenly Janessa turns, holding out her hand in another practiced move, pretending she accepted my proposal.

Pretending.

I'm no better than Richard, and the thought hits me in the gut like a sucker punch. I need air. Rubbing a hand up her back, I press a kiss to her cheek, and then step off to the side, hoping to make my way outside. It takes a while to make it through the crowd as I struggle to press forward and keep my composure. *She doesn't love me.*

I shake hands with those congratulating me.

She doesn't love me.

I smile falsely to those surprised but offering words of best wishes. *She doesn't love me.*

Rushing into the hallway, I break free of the auditorium and then hastily move forward to the first exit I find. Pressing the door open, I gulp in the night air as I bend at the waist and grip my knees once outside.

What did I just do?

"What the fuck do you think you're doing?" The gruffness of the male voice coming from my left surprises me despite its familiarity. Leaning against the exterior wall stands a man, one leg hitched up so his foot presses into the brick at his back. His arms cross, but it's the glare in those eyes that should frighten me. However, I'm not afraid of my older brother.

"James? What are you doing here?" James. My brother, who left the family after tragedy struck his, stares back at me, eyes full of ice and ire.

"Just what the fuck were you thinking?" His voice fills with rage, and his jaw clenches with anger.

"What do you mean?"

He steps up to me so quickly, I take a step back, like the kid I used to be when he approached in a bad mood.

"Don't play dumb, Charlie. We all know you're the smartest of the bunch, but this is the stupidest thing you've ever done."

"Asking her to marry me?"

His brows pinch, forming a deep crease between them. "Asking who to marry you?"

"Weren't you just in the room?" I'm growing confused, but James's agitation grows.

"You proposed to someone?" he questions.

"Were you in the meeting?" I counter. His head turns away briefly before those cold eyes return to my face.

"Yeah, I was in the meeting. Heard about the presentation as somehow my club got roped into providing a ride for funds, only one small detail someone forgot to tell me." James leans toward me, his index finger and thumb held less than an inch apart.

Michael.

"You didn't know about—?"

"Don't say his name," James hisses, and for a second, I see the menacing man he's become. Not that James wasn't always a little scary, a little aloof, and a whole lot of trouble, but he's always been my brother, and I've viewed him no other way than being my kin and loving him unconditionally because of it. I've looked into his club, and while not the most respectable, they also are not the nefarious one-percenters like people think every club is. The *Sons of Anarchy* do not live outside my town. Rebel's Edge like to party hard and get out of hand occasionally, but in general, they're decent people—a collective bunch of broken souls living on the edge. *Rebel's* Edge.

"You didn't know?" I question. If the club agreed to donate finances, how did James not know the future community center would be dedicated to his son? He's the second in command.

"No, I didn't know, and that stunt in there." His arm flails out, pointing back at the exterior double doors. "That was just bullshit. Who approved the name that woman proposed?"

"It isn't formally approved yet," I state, but if I had to guess, I'd say Cora Conrad offered the suggestion.

"Well, it wasn't Cora who said it. It was that other *bi*—"

"Don't you dare finish that word," I command, pointing a finger in my brother's face. Menacing or not, he will not disrespect Janessa. He can be however he wants with his own woman, but not mine.

"Ah, still Goodie Two-shoes Charlie. Don't drink, don't smoke, what do you do?" He mocks me with old song lyrics, and then slowly, his face hardens, even harder than it already is. "Wait a minute."

His eyes narrow, and there isn't a word to describe how he's looking at me.

"She the one you proposed to?" His brows lift, his eyes widening. As if his face is at war with itself, he fights mocking laughter while still being angry.

"Yes," I whisper, feeling unsettled about…everything.

"You in love with her?"

"Yes," I repeat myself.

"She know that?"

Does she? Have I shown her enough how attracted I am to her? Then again, the attraction is what prompted me to propose to Angela— attraction to her mind and determination—but Janessa is different, and because of that, I realize too late I have not done enough, not done this correctly.

"I…I don't know," I whisper, swallowing back the bile in my throat.

"You're a damn fool, Charlie. Got it up here"—he points at his temple, tapping a finger at the side— "but not here." He flattens a palm over his chest.

"Like you should talk," I snap, defending myself like when I was a child.

How can you be so smart and stupid at the same time?

Am not.

Are too.

We're both older, both wiser, only there's one area I think my brother has made the biggest mistake of his life, and I seem to be following in his footsteps.

"Don't you say her name either," he warns, the hiss so deep he sounds like a rattlesnake ready to strike. I wouldn't put it past him to do as much. Despite his threat, I stand taller.

"I need to get back inside," I say, looking away from him, knowing I have larger issues than my estranged brother.

Chapter 30
Ambush is Not Shrubbery

[Janessa]

Instead of celebrating an engagement, Charlie and I go our separate ways. Lucy is waiting for him at his home as Vega is for me, and I need time to process what happened.

We got the vote for Walk the Ridge.

Charlie proposed to me.

He stole our thunder.

Instead of *victory is mine*, I feel deflated. Cora worked so hard alongside me, and I'm forever grateful as I don't have the connections she does. *History*, that's what she called it. She's been here her entire life, and I am still an outsider. She has more pull than me—persuasion, she says—and instead of Charlie letting us have our moment, he had to ruin it with a proposal. A fake one.

He couldn't possibly mean we marry for real, and I wonder what he's up to. *What is his motive?*

He claimed he wanted to show the city how much he approved of me, but this isn't approval. I don't know what to call this.

I slip the ring off once inside my dad's truck and drop it in my purse. Wearing that god-awful jewelry, reminding me of the audacious engagement ring Richard had given me, was not happening. A ring like that does not quietly whisper love, but screams *look at me, I'm taken*. Owned. Possessed. Property.

I want Charlie to love me. At least, I thought I did.

I'd love to call in sick the next morning, but I pull on my big girl panties and plaster on the brave face I'd mastered over the years with Richard.

Only, I don't expect to find Charlie waiting for me the second I enter the mayor's building and then nearly dragging me into his office.

"How are you?" he asks, eyes searching my face but not settling on my eyes as his hands curl over my shoulders. His fingers clutch at me as though he's holding on for dear life.

"I think we should talk," I sass, and he nods, his lips puckering as if he wholeheartedly agrees.

"I want this," he blurts, but there's a tremble in his tenor. For a second, I look at him, really take him in. His etched cheeks that could make a model jealous. His slightly graying temples. His beautifully brown eyes like the strength of an oak. Only, that's the thing. His eyes look wild and dull, and a thin sheen of sweat graces his brow.

"What's going on?" I softly wonder aloud.

"Nothing. I just want you to know I want you. You and Vega. I'll take care of everything."

"Everything," I whisper, still questioning his tone. Not to mention, what does *everything* mean?

"Aren't you happy about the proposal?" he asks, still holding my shoulders, keeping me at arm's length and speaking to me with such aloofness.

"It's not exactly how I envisioned a second proposal," I reply. Sadly, I always hoped if it ever happened again, there would be more meaning behind the invitation to marry someone. Perhaps love would be a part of the equation, not obligation or whatever is the premise of Charlie's proposition.

"Oh. Not that. I meant the walk."

We're discussing the walk? We need to talk about us. We need to talk about what he did and why the hell he did it.

"What's wrong with you this morning?" I ask, truly concerned by his behavior. "I don't care about the walk. I want to know why you did it. Why did you ask me to marry you?"

"As I said last night, I want everyone to see I approve of you." He releases my shoulders and slips his hands into the pockets of his slacks.

I snort. "There are other ways to prove that, Charlie. A gold star or a salute would have done it. Hell, even a *congratulations* and *I'm proud of you* would have sufficed." My fingers air-quote the relevancy of the simple words he could have used instead of *will you marry me?*

"You're not wearing the ring," he says, noticing my bare finger for the first time. His voice softens like he's actually hurt.

"I…" I can't wear that thing. It's not only too much in the way of a diamond; it's too much period. Nothing makes sense.

"Charlie, we have a problem," Jordan says, barging into Charlie's office while looking down at the phone in his hand. When his head pops up, he notices me, startled and pausing at my presence. "Good morning, Janessa. Are you ready for this?"

Without warning, he spins the phone and holds it up for both Charlie and me to view, only Charlie quickly smacks it out of Jordan's hand and the phone goes flying to the floor.

"Charlie," I shriek, and scramble to the floor for the device. What the hell is wrong with him this morning? I've never seen him like this, and all my hackles rise, reminiscent of the fear Richard could put in me with a hitch of his tone or the threat of a hand that never made contact.

My eyes narrow in on the screen, which remained open and upright despite the fall. My mouth drops, and I stare at the image before me. Slowly, I stand, gaping at the photo before me. Eventually glancing from Jordan to his uncle.

"You didn't tell her, did you?" Jordan addresses Charlie, his eyes narrowed

"I was just about to." The lowness of Charlie's voice is almost as frightening as the swat of his hand at Jordan's phone.

Jordan gazes over at me, but his words address Charlie while his eyes focus on me. "I told you to tell her first."

"First?" I question. "Tell me what? And what the hell is this?" I turn the screen to the men, still uncertain I'm seeing what I'm seeing.

"That's Charlie, in all his glory," Jordan mocks, the sarcastic tone curls his lips.

Turning the phone back to me, I glance down once again at the headline.

Small town mayor bares it all as he proposes to the new woman in his life.

One picture shows Charlie on his knees before me. The other shows a full-body image of him against a wall. Similar to the swimsuit photo for Mayor McSteamy, this one reveals it all. He's naked, erect, and posing. His hands nearly cup his impressive length but rest just off-center, keeping him fully exposed. His head tilts to the side, a sheepish grin on his lips like he knows he's being watched, and he is. He isn't looking back at the camera, though. His lids lower like he has a secret.

"Who did this?" I choke, my head lifting to Charlie. Jordan dismisses himself, stepping back out of the office and closing the door behind him. Charlie has returned his hands to his pockets and remains silent with his head and eyes lowered.

"Angela," he eventually whispers.

"Did you know about this?"

His head pops up, and his eyes glare back at me. "I was there, obviously."

"I don't mean *taking* the picture. I mean the exposure of it, exposing you with it. Did you know she was going to do this?"

Puzzle pieces are falling on the table but not clicking into place yet.

Reaching for the bridge of his nose, Charlie explains, "She threatened to share them if I didn't allow her to keep Lucy for the length of her campaign. She wanted Pint to stay in Philadelphia and run the trail with her until the November election, playing up her single-mother image."

Charlie's already told me how Angela twisted the truth before. She might be considered a mother and single, but the two do not coincide as she does neither together. She hardly sees her child other than the court-mandated timeline.

I lower Jordan's phone to my side. "You said no, and she shared the photos." I'm simply restating what he told me, a niggling in my gut that I'm still missing something.

"I tried to call her bluff," he whispers.

My heart races while I grow clammy and feel nauseous. "I'm so sorry this happened to you, Charlie." And I am. This is so much more than invading someone's privacy or posting about an affair. This is an intrusion. Invasion of privacy. Defamation of character. "But what I don't understand is where I fit into this?"

I told you to tell her first, Jordan said. I glance back at the phone. An engagement photo, although pretend, and a naked image of Charlie.

How did whoever wrote this article get a copy of the pictures so quickly?

"Jordan and I thought a counterattack would work. Strike before struck. Something positive to negate the negative."

"So you asked me to marry you?" My voice roughens as it lowers, and that nausea crawls up my middle. The puzzle pieces click into place, but the sound is the clanking of a lock.

"Man in love versus naked man," he states dryly.

"Who was naked with his first love and not in love with the woman he proposed to," I clarify, sarcasm dripping from the words.

"I didn't love her."

"You don't love me either," I snap, my head pulling back.

"I…"

I hold up a hand to stop him. I don't want to hear any more lies.

"You need to make a retraction." I hold up the phone, shaking it. "Of *everything*." I toss the word back to him. Then I toss the phone on his desk. Staring at Charlie, I'm torn in two. My heart breaks for the man literally naked and exposed on such a personal level, but I'm also angry that he used something that should have been precious, like a marriage proposal, as a counterattack to his vindictive ex-wife. When Charlie doesn't look up at me, I see myself out of his office. I don't bother closing his door, but I make sure to slam the front one as I exit the building.

I'm not pretending to marry Charlie any more than I'm pretending to stay married to Richard. Then fear hits me hard in the chest.

Richard.

If he sees this, I've gone against the agreement not to speak of the divorce until after the season. If people see this article, they'll know we are separated. Even worse, they'll think I left him for another man, not that he's the one who has been sleeping around. People forgive that kind of thing in a man in the public eye, but they'll crucify me without researching all the facts.

True, I might have slept with Charlie, but that was *after* officially divorcing Richard, *after* years of an unhappy and unhealthy marriage.

People will never look at my situation for what it was and what it now is.

I will not marry Charlie Harrington.

I'm not marrying anyone ever again.

+ + +

Because I don't know where else to hide at nine in the morning, I head to Ridged Edge, the biker bar, thinking it might be open despite the fact it might also have closed a few hours ago.

It was a foolish thought, and I head back to my vehicle when I find the front door locked. Opening my truck door, I see two motorcycles pass the parking lot. I slip into the driver's seat and lower my head to the steering wheel for a second.

What am I doing here, and what have I gotten myself into with these men?

A sharp rap comes to the window, and I find Justice standing outside my father's truck. Rolling down the window, I smile although I don't have the energy to fake one more thing.

"You okay, pretty lady?" Over the past month, I've gotten to know him a little bit, and there's three things I've learned. He's scary as hell, but his eyes can go soft. His voice rumbles like his bike. There's a compassionate heart behind the leather vest. I'd never tell Justice I've noticed these things about him. He'd never admit to any of them anyway.

"Having a rough morning," I confess.

"Bar ain't open this early," he tells me.

"A girl could only wish." I turn my false smile up a notch, but it all feels wrong. Suddenly, the truck door opens, and he holds out a hand.

"How about a coffee?"

My vision shifts to the second bike, parked next to the first, both of which are directly behind the truck. With his arms crossed, looking off in the distance sits James.

"Maybe you have other plans this morning." I tip my head to Justice's biker brother, and he chuckles.

"A man can always change his plans for a woman desperate for a drink." There's some truth to his statement. I know about him and his lady friend.

"What about him?" I whisper, feeling an unpleasant vibe rippling off James.

"He'll live."

With my hand in Justice's, he tugs me out of the truck and then drops my fingers. I follow him to the front door of the bar, which he opens with a key hanging off a set on a chain he pulled from the pocket of his jeans. He flips one light switch to illuminate the place. Keeping the space dim is probably best. Bars always look better at night. Daylight exposes the truth of ones like this—dank and dingy even if scrubbed clean.

"How do you take it?" he questions as I help myself to a stool. James enters the place, sitting a few stools away from me, holding his phone in his hand.

"Americano," I reply, and Justice turns back to me.

"She means just black," James mutters.

"Thank you, Einstein, I think I know this one," Justice says before disappearing into the small kitchen area off the bar.

James drops his phone on the bar top, and I flinch while I draw in the hard wood with my thumbnail.

"What I want to know is how did you pull it off? How did you get him to do this?"

"Do what?" I ask, turning my gaze to him and meeting icy blue daggers aimed at me.

"Did you just spread those thighs and let Charlie fall between them? Tempt the good guy with those emerald eyes of yours?"

"I did no such thing," I say, turning my entire body in the direction of James. "I did not ask for this."

"Didn't ask him for a community center? Didn't decide to name it after—" He cuts himself off. "Didn't trick him into asking you to marry him?"

"I didn't trick Charlie into anything. He disapproved of the community center and walk, so I took matters into my own hands. I thought naming it after your son was a nice gesture, and as for Charlie asking me to marry him, that was his plan, not mine, and he did it to cover up the picture scandal."

"Mayor McSteamy?" he scoffs. "That's old news, sweetheart."

"No, the new ones from today."

"What the fuck are you talking about, woman?"

"Hey," Justice snaps, entering the main bar with two mugs of coffee in his hand. He sets one down before me.

"The naked pictures of Charlie," I clarify for James.

"You took naked pictures of Charlie?" Justice asks. His forehead furrows, but his tone suggests he's impressed.

"I didn't take naked pictures of Charlie. His ex-wife did on their honeymoon, and she's been hanging onto them, waiting for any excuse to expose him." My thoughts immediately drift to how Charlie told me of Angela's vindictiveness and the threat of those images over the years.

"She has some balls," Justice mutters.

"So does Charlie," James states, staring at his phone, and then he laughs, turning the device face down on the counter. "Where's my mug?" He tips his head to the coffees before Justice and me.

"Get your own. I'm not a barista, and in case you don't know this one, Einstein, it means a wench who serves coffee."

James huffs and pulls himself off his stool, flipping the middle finger at his friend before disappearing into the kitchen.

"This your rough morning, darlin'?" Justice asks.

"Yeah, this is it…in all its glory." I begin to laugh at the joke I made, laughing until tears come to my eyes. Then the salty liquid shifts, and it's no longer laughter gracing my lids.

"Hey now, settle down," Justice says, standing taller behind the bar. Both hands cover my face as the sobs take over. I haven't cried like this since the first time Richard stepped out on me. Only the first time did I allow such tears to fall. I was as heartbroken then as I am now.

I trusted Charlie. Now, I fear I've mistaken what we were doing for something it never was.

Ah, lust and love, you devilish twins.

"What's this?" James snaps, coming up beside me, but I can't face him either. He's Charlie's brother, and he's accused me of exactly what I feared would happen. Exactly what Charlie didn't want to happen. He didn't want people thinking I received any special treatment if we were together. Then he went ahead and showed the whole town we were together, giving them cause to judge me.

I lower my head for my arms, crossed over the bar top, still shuddering with the aftereffects of the tears but no longer sobbing so hard.

"I'm sorry," I mutter, finally lifting my head and swiping at my face. I try to sit straighter and curl both hands around my mug. "I'm sorry all this is happening." I turn my head to James. "And I'm sorry about your son."

His mouth falls open ready to speak when Justice snaps a sharp finger, and James closes his jaw. James looks away from me for a second.

"I love him," I whisper, and James's attention draws back to me. "The damn foolish part of all this wasn't opening my legs to him but opening my heart."

"I shouldn't've…" James begins, but I shake my head to stop him.

"For the first time in years, I felt desired and wanted and just a little bit reckless when I'd been so good for so long, pretended for so long that everything was okay when it wasn't. I just wanted a fresh start," I say, lowering my voice. "Can you imagine what it's like to want to begin again?"

Those icy eyes of James melt a little from glacial to smooth ice on a lake. "Yeah, I can get that."

"He only asked me to marry him to counter her threat. He did it for nothing."

"He did it to protect himself," Justice says.

"He did it because he loves you," James counters.

"He doesn't," I reply, my voice ringed in sadness.

"He does. He told me outside the school. He loves you."

"Funny way of showing it then," I whisper.

"A marriage proposal doesn't say *I love you?*" Justice questions.

"You can't tell me you don't know this one," James mocks, and a sad chuckle escapes me. "People marry all the time without love."

"Not me," Justice clarifies.

"You ain't ever been married," James retorts.

"Ain't ever been in love enough, and as if you're an expert," Justice retorts, tweaking up a brow, and I'm sensing we are way off topic here.

"It doesn't matter. I'm not marrying him," I interject.

"Why not?" both men say at once.

"Because I don't want anyone thinking he crawled between my thighs, and that's how I got what I wanted," I state, glaring at James.

"I shouldn't't've—"

I hold up a hand to stop him. "And I don't want anyone else mistaking that proposal as genuine. I'm not marrying him. I'm getting the walking trail started, the community center built, and the park established, and then…I guess I'll move on." My stomach turns at the thought of walking away after all that hard work, but I've made a promise to this town, and I don't want to lose more face by walking away too soon. Plus, Mami's here, and Zander plans to stay. Not to mention, I've made my first genuine female friends in Cora and Roxanne.

"Cora will be disappointed," Justice snorts. "Charlie put Cora up to this, but she really got into it." His lips clamp shut, rolling inward as if he realized too late that he'd said too much.

"What?" The interrogative on my lips squeaks within the large empty room.

"Charlie went to Cora and told her about the committee as a possible way to get around the town council. Think Cora came up with that on her own?"

"Sonofabitch," I mutter, slapping my hand on the bar. He manipulated things. *Everything*. He'd foiled me again, and again, *and again*. Despite my irritation at this information, my desire to complete the task I set for this town doubles down.

Screw Charlie.

"You sure know a lot about Corabelle Conrad," James mutters.

"Yeah, how is that?" I question, finding Cora a bit tight-lipped as well how the president of a motorcycle club and the town socialite have a friendship.

"It's called none of y'all's business," he huffs, picking up all three of our mugs between his thick fingers. "Teatime is over." He turns for the kitchen, disappearing behind the swing door, and James turns to me.

"Think I should tell him it was coffee?" he asks, and I laugh again, this time keeping the tears at bay.

Chapter 31
Don't Put a Ring on It

[Janessa]

Near ten o'clock that night, a soft knock comes on the front door of the coach house. I've been ignoring my phone all day, too upset with Charlie and Cora to make sense of anything.

Why didn't she tell me?

Why did he do it?

Before I open the door, I see him out the window. His head dipped forward, a ball cap on backward. He stands with his hands shoved in his jean pockets. He already looks defeated.

When I open the door, what I don't expect is how young he looks while older at the same time. Youth comes in the form of his attire. The jeans, which I haven't seen him wear. He's either been in a suit or sweats or shorts. The backward ball cap and the light gray tee with Atlanta on it give him the appearance of a teenage boy come to pick up a date or break up with her.

"Can we talk?" he questions, his voice without hope but still determined to ask me.

I should tell him no. I should tell him to go to hell. I should tell him where to shove his talk, but I break.

"Sure." I step out to him and pull the door behind me. "What do you want, Charlie?" I softly question, wrapping my arms around myself, tugging at the sweater I have on because of the air-conditioning in the house. The August night is still hot as blazes, but I shiver against a chill rippling up my spine.

"I just want fifteen minutes."

"Fine," I huff, turning back for the house to let Zander know I'm going for a walk. My brother was sitting in the living room with me, watching the ball game and listening to me explain what happened with Charlie. He gives me a wave, and I return to Charlie.

"Before you begin, I want you to know that Zander contacted Jordan and pulled those images from the web and erased them from the internet. He has a friend who can go deeper, removing screenshots that might appear. He'll tag the images so if they pop up anywhere, they'll disappear."

Charlie's brows lift as we stand on the front step. "That's amazing. I'll thank him for doing that. I've spent the day sending out cease and desist letters, and applying for a lawsuit against the publication, the social media journalist, and I use the term loosely, and Angela, as she's the unnamed source. I don't care who says otherwise."

I nod, glad he's able to resolve this invasion of privacy and violation of his person.

"My mother saw those images. She hates Angela."

"Well, I don't know Angela, and I hate her as well."

Charlie weakly smiles and tips his head for me to follow him, keeping his hands in his pockets. He leads us down the drive a bit and around the large bushes that block the view of the tennis court slash batting cage. My chest aches as we pass the fencing, and I remember it's the place he took me the first time and the last.

One last time. No truer words had been spoken.

We walk the path around the court and then cut across the grass, heading for the river that runs along the edge of the properties on Mountain Spring Lane. There's a dock behind Charlie's yard, and we walk in that direction.

Pausing at the end of the decking, Charlie stares into the dark, shallow water. The soft ripple should be calming, but I don't like how Charlie focuses on the river's movement.

"When I married Angela, I loved her ambition, as I told you. But I also loved how attracted I thought she was to me, pushing us to this limit I thought would carry into our marriage."

He exhales, hands still in his pockets.

"When she became pregnant, we moved here so I could run for mayor. The stepping-stone she wanted for us. *Us*, collectively. When I decided to run again, she had an affair, publicly hoping to destroy me, and I never understood how she thought that would force me to follow her. I later learned she thought I was weak and that I'd beg her to take me back—not the other way around—when she should have been begging me to keep her."

He sighs.

"The affair was embarrassing and plastered all over town; thus, the doubt I told you about when I ran for my second term. And then the images were leaked. Another ploy in hopes to discredit me. Not for her gain but because I didn't come crawling after her. Then her new game with Lucy and these current images." He exhales.

"You don't know how many times I've felt like a failure in such a spectacular way." He turns to look at me, his face shadowed by the darkness of the night. "But no failure compares to how I've reacted to you."

My breath catches, knowing he's about to tell me it's all been a mistake. Why bother even bringing me out here if he's only going to tell me we should have never been together in the first place? We both know we shouldn't have started anything, but it's hard to deny chemistry, and even now, I want to reach over and pull him to me. I want to assure him I'd never hurt him like her. I'd never be so cruel or devious, and I don't think he's a failure at all. He's successful, smart, and sexy as hell even if I'm mad at him.

"I panicked," he says.

I continue to stare up at him, still not certain where he's leading.

"I didn't want to lose you, so I thought I'd ask you to marry me. You didn't want to pretend to be engaged and move in with me, so I'd be able to kill two birds with one stone. I'd make it real. I'd save face with the community by having you as a fiancée, and I would sabotage Angela's ploy to ambush me. Only, you got hurt in the crossfire of both. I didn't prove anything to the town other than I'm an idiot, and I look good naked."

I bark out a nervous laugh, but he isn't smiling. I'm reminded his mother saw those pictures.

"How are you an idiot, Charlie?" I can think of a few ways, but I want to hear his thoughts as he hasn't been thinking about the decisions he's made lately.

"I didn't support the woman I love the way I should have, by simply holding her hand and letting her have her moment."

I ignore he said *woman he loves* and address another issue.

"I heard what you did with Cora, putting her up to asking me to form a committee."

Charlie releases a long breath of air, and his chest deflates. His head lowers. "Look, you're new to city government, and I didn't think you'd know that forming a private committee and presenting your case again could get you what you might want. I figured it would go one of two ways. You'd either tell Cora to go to hell for offering help or listen to someone other than me for advice."

"Why didn't you just tell me about committee work yourself?"

"Again, you'd either tell me to go to hell or not listen to my advice. I felt sick about turning down your passion project, and I wanted to help how I could. Mostly, I didn't tell you directly so I could save face. I didn't want anyone to know I supplied you with a way to get what you wanted. Then I wouldn't have to lie if anyone ever asked. The answer was an equivocal no…I had not instructed you that a private committee could potentially get the job done."

"You didn't trust me, Charlie. Trust that I could do this on my own."

"Did you know about private committees?" he asks, reaching behind his neck and holding his hand there as he looks over at me.

"Well, no…"

"I was trying to help."

He could have just approved the damn thing in the first place, but as time passed, I learned he couldn't just hand over the money. Cora and I investigated the town's financials, and Charlie wasn't wrong. I was overly ambitious.

"Were you attracted to my ambition? Is that why we did what we did?"

He turns completely to face me.

"I was attracted to you because you seemed attracted to me, and not because I'm the mayor, or for some other agenda, or even because I'm a Harrington. Raw chemistry. Just us." He turns his attention for the river almost embarrassed by his admission, but almost immediately twists back to me. "Let me love you. Let me show you I can be good to you. I can be good *for* you. I won't make any more schemes or plans or panic without talking to you about everything first."

He stills and takes a step closer to me. I step back, but he reaches out for me. "Careful."

Looking over my shoulder, I see I'm precariously close to the edge of the dock and at risk of falling in. My position feels prophetic.

"I don't really know what to say, Charlie. A lot has happened for both of us today, and I still have Richard to deal with."

"What happened with Richard?"

"I'm just waiting for the call that says I'm in breach of contract. Not that it reverses the divorce or retracts full custody of Vega, but I'm certain Richard's little friend Ruthie has more in store for me. If I'm not allowed to mention the divorce, a marriage proposal certainly puts a wrench in things."

"Fuck that. Fuck him. He can't have you," Charlie says, tugging me closer to him, and my hands come to his chest. "I'm sorry I messed up. I'm sorry for all of it. Thinking…well, not thinking…and then acting without more thought. I've just…" His voice drifts as my body remains stiff in his arms. Releasing me, he faces the water once again and takes a deep breath.

"I just want to love you, Janessa," he softly states over his shoulder. "I haven't ever felt this way, and I don't want to give it up."

Conflicting emotions swirl through me. I want to love him, too, but I'm hurt. He didn't believe in me, and I'm not certain I can trust him.

"I need time to process everything, Charlie." There's been so much. My father's death. Zander's arrival. The committee. The betrayal. The proposal.

"I'd like you to—" Charlie's voice cuts off as I hold out the engagement ring, the ridiculous large diamond that just isn't me.

"I think you should take this back."

His eyes leap up to mine. "You don't like the ring, hock it. But I'm not retracting the proposal. I messed up, but I meant it. I want to be with you. I want you to marry me."

I tug the sweater closer to my middle, body trembling with the desire to say yes, and the struggle with how things are happening. I shove the ring closer to him.

"I can't marry you, Charlie. Not like this."

Still trying to hold my eyes, he searches my face, but I look away. Without reaching for the ring, he huffs a final time and turns away. The thud of his footsteps over the planks does nothing to settle the pit in my stomach that I might be making a mistake in letting him go.

+ + +

"I thought you were my friend," I say to Cora the next day when she arrives at my office ready to organize. As I glance up, the chagrin on her face tells me she knew this was coming. *Justice.*

"It shouldn't matter how it started. The work began, and we accomplished it together," Cora states, holding my glare.

"It happened under false pretense," I remind her.

"Want to give it back? Turn away the money and give up what you fought for?" Cora gives as good as she gets with her stare. It sounds as if she means more than just the walk.

Without a word, I shake my head. I'm still upset about everything, but the fact is, we did find a way to raise the money, and we have a plan in place to complete the walkway. We want to host both the ride and the community walk this fall when the temperature is a little less extreme, and the colors begin to change on the trees.

We worked well together, even if I feel like she didn't want to participate.

"How did he do it?" I question, implying Charlie.

241

"He simply asked. His sister is my best friend. Charlie was my divorce attorney. We grew up next to one another on the Lane. We go way back."

That simple. He asked, and she gave in. I don't know how to ask for help, which is one reason I don't accept it when offered. I also don't want to feel beholden to anyone, especially not after my marriage to Richard, where his proposal was presented as if he was doing me a favor. The woman who became his wife, who bore his child, was obligated to him because he married me when I was pregnant.

"I don't really know what to think of our friendship," I say, glancing down at my desk.

"I'm still your friend, and we still have this committee to run *together*." Admittedly, I haven't had many girlfriends. Not like the ones I had way back when I was on a softball team, working toward a common goal of winning. That was over twenty years ago. Since then, it's been one catfight after another, working my way through a male-populated industry and coming out at the bottom. As the wife of a professional ballplayer, there was even less comradery when we should have been sticking together.

Jealousy, one of the older wives once warned me. Her husband had been on the team for years, nearing his retirement. *Fresh meat gets eaten alive by the young wives as each of them wants to believe she's better than the others, her man is better than the others, and his sins are less.*

It was a lesson I didn't understand until too late.

"Dishonesty is not a trait of friendship," I tell Cora, holding my head higher.

"I didn't lie. I omitted. There's a difference." We stare at one another, and on the tip of my tongue is a slew of questions. Is omitting what she called it when her husband took his secretary with him on a trip and did not tell her? How about when he bought that home in another state, and he didn't mention it? Was that omission? Cora and I have an understanding about cheating husbands, so I can't believe she's slinging the word *omission* at me when we both know a lie is a lie.

My chest heaves, the aggravation building until Cora looks away.

"This isn't the same thing," she whispers as if she can read my thoughts. "I didn't mean to hurt you." Taking a deep breath, she turns back to me. "I only wanted to feel useful."

Cora runs a thriving resort. How could she possibly *not* feel useful?

Then I consider myself. Didn't I want the same thing? Didn't I hope I could start fresh and make an immediate impact on this new-to-me place?

"I understand that," I admit.

"So, you forgive me?" Cora's sheepish expression surprises me. She's normally a bit more tyrannical, and she's acquiescing too easily.

"You really want to work on this committee?" I question, and she steps forward, my desk still between us.

"More than anything." She's breathless, and I don't understand why she's so committed.

"Tell me about you and Justice, and I'll consider your apology."

Cora's mouth pops open, and then her lip curls. "Girl, you know how to bargain," she teases. "But we're going to need some coffee and a donut for this tale."

She isn't off the hook with me, but she's smiling as though she got her way. She tips her head for me to follow her, and I sigh, giving in because I actually do consider her a friend, and I don't want to lose her. Plus, I really want to know her story with Justice.

+ + +

Just as I predicted, Richard is ready to retaliate, and I find him sitting on the coach house stoop three days later.

"I flew here as early as I could." He'd had a three-game series up in St. Louis.

"What do you want?" I ask, hiking my bag over my shoulder as he blocks my way from entering the house. His body takes up the entire front stoop.

"I wanted to know if you were okay."

My head flinches to the right, brows creasing to the point a headache begins. "Why?" I don't trust Richard on a good day, so this is really surprising.

"I heard about the photos, although thankfully didn't see them. I thought he was your boss." Richard swipes through his longish curls, tipping back his head. "Then again, I saw how he looked at you. I figured he just wanted in your pants, and that's why he was all protective." His large hands come back together, folding between his spread thighs and bent knees.

"He asked you to marry him." Was there a question in that statement? *Here it comes.* He's going to slap me with some suit of defamation or adultery against *him*. Always about him.

"You going to marry him?" I've known every expression of this man over the past decade. The grit. The anger. The lies. But the look in his eyes as he peers up at me, I cannot dissect. Regret perhaps? *Impossible.*

"What do you want, Richard?" My arm crosses my body like a shield, reaching for my bag strap and curling my fingers around the leather. Richard's eyes flick to my fingers. Slowly, he smiles, and he's back to the man I hate.

"He didn't buy you a ring?"

"I'm not discussing Charlie with you." I make to move, hoping the step forward will encourage him to get out of my way, but he doesn't budge. Instead, he reaches for my right hand, holds my fingers between his thick ones and rubs over them like piano keys.

"Broke my heart the day you gave back my rings," he says, his voice melancholy. Dumbass, he's looking at the wrong hand.

"Have you been drinking?" Richard stripped me of everything. Every possession. Every gift. I'd settled on all of it because I only wanted Vega.

His eyes remain focused on my fingers. "Should have been better." The comment comes out so low I'm certain I don't hear him correctly. I tug at my fingers, but he holds firm, lifting my knuckles for his forehead.

"I don't know why I did it," he whispers, and I don't even know what he's referencing.

"Then get help, Richard." My voice is harsh, but I have no pity for him. Whatever he's feeling is too late. Five blondes, two redheads, and one busty brunette going down on him before our daughter too late.

"Come back to me." His voice cracks. "Don't marry him."

I tug at my hand again, desperate to free my fingers from his thick, clammy ones. However, Richard is stronger than me. He holds just as tightly as I fight against his touch.

"You're breaching our contract," he states, looking up at me, and I realize I'm seeing something I never thought I'd see. He's desperate and panicked, and it reminds me of Charlie's proposal.

"So are you. You aren't allowed to be within ten miles of Vega, yet you keep appearing."

"I need you," he begs, and I break.

"Need me? You never needed me, Richard. I don't even know why you married me other than to save yourself. And what about me? What about what I need? When I needed you, and you were never home?"

"I was playing ball."

"You were playing the field all right, but not the kind you're paid to play." His fingers continue to hold my hand as he stares up at me like I've told him something he doesn't know.

"I didn't want you to go," he says.

"You didn't want me to stay either. I was there to cover for you."

"Why are you being so selfish?" His voice cracks like he truly believes this is on me.

"Selfish?" I snap. "Me? This is all about you," I state as I wave my free fingers at him, circling the air around him. "You need something from me, and it's the only reason you're here. You don't care about your daughter or me. You don't love us. So, I'm asking again, what do you want?" Because there's an ulterior motive here, I just don't know his angle. "And let go of my hand."

I'm almost screaming as I struggle against his hold. With his quick release, I stumble backward, catching myself before I fall on my backside. It hits me that this is Richard. I falter, but he doesn't help me. He's waiting, watching for my downfall. He thinks I'm in that position, and I'll want him to rescue me. I'll ask him to take me back.

"I'm not coming back to you, and you have—"

"Until the count of ten to get off her porch before I call the sheriff." Charlie's rugged voice interrupts us, and I spin to face him. He stands a foot behind me, calm and collected as he glares at my ex-husband. Suit versus sweats as Charlie's still dressed from court, and Richard wears his typical track pants and T-shirt.

"Ten. *Nine.*" Charlie begins, and I almost laugh. Is he really counting down?

"What the fuck?" Richard snarls, looking from Charlie to me. Charlie casually pulls his phone from his suit jacket and looks at the screen.

"Eight. *Seven.*"

"Is he serious?" Richard looks up at me, still seated on the stoop like he can't believe this is happening.

I laugh for some reason, finding this entire scene unreal. "When he starts counting, look out," I warn and then glance back at Charlie. His eyes meet mine, the brown sparking in the early evening light.

"Five. *Four.*" He presses something on his phone and then lifts it for his ear. "Hello, 911. I have a situation here."

Richard immediately stands, swiping his hands down his pants. He towers over me, but I don't cower. His eyes hit mine, and all the melancholy and sorrow is gone if it even ever was present. I misread him as I had most of our marriage, and now I want to close the book.

"Three," Charlie calls out, tipping his phone and then returning to the call. "Intruder at my coach house. Male. Six-six name of—"

"I'm going," Richard calls out, holding up both hands, palms out to stop Charlie.

"But you're still standing here," Charlie retorts. "Two and—"

"I loved you," Richard mutters. "In the beginning, I really did." He says nothing of Vega before crossing the small lawn and entering a rental car. The door slams, and the vehicle rolls backward, kicking up gravel as Richard reverses. Charlie still holds his phone to his ear, watching Richard's retreat, and my eyes drift from one man to another.

What just happened here?

Chapter 32

A Knight in Dented Armor

[Charlie]

I heard their voices as I approached the coach house and saw them despite the thickness of the hedge. He held her hand, pressing it to his forehead. Their voices had turned low, and I prepared to round the shrubbery when he spoke.

Come back to me. Don't marry him. The desperation in another man's voice. The desire to regain his former wife. It was too much for me. I couldn't fight this, and when she didn't respond, I thought I'd lost her again to her ex. I turned away from the bushes just before I made an ass of myself, revealing my presence and defending her honor. My steps were quick while I tried to disguise the tap of my hard-soled shoes on the concrete walk

Then I heard her voice. *Let go of my hand.* Her cry turned me back around, and I rounded those hedges like I was stealing second base.

It took a moment for the comedy of my demand to catch up to her. He had until the count of ten to leave, and thankfully, her eyes were on me, not him. She teased that I was serious with my countdowns, and I almost lost the charade, Giant swearing in my ear as I called him. I couldn't make a 911 call unless I knew we were in a real emergency.

To my surprise, Richard left, and I was confused.

His bowed head. His quiet voice. He confessed he loved her.

I had once loved Angela, but I recognized love could end. Somewhere along their path, Richard lost the emotion for his wife, either by choice or effort or who knows what, but it didn't last. The moment he looked at another woman and then acted on that glance, he broke everything they could have had together. For the blink of an eye, I feel sorry for the man. He lost a good woman and a beautiful child, but I don't condone idiocy. My concern is for Janessa who stares after Richard's car, tearing up the lane as he leaves.

"Are you okay?" I ask, stepping up to her.

"That's the same question he asked me." Slowly, she turns to me, eyes soft, face puzzled. "I don't know what he was doing here."

"Giving it his last-ditch effort. Game's almost over. Down two to one, and he was hoping for a big hit."

The baseball euphemism isn't lost on her.

"He struck out," she whispers.

"Seems like it hasn't been his game." I smile as she plays along.

"It hasn't been his year," she states.

Standing before her, hands tucked in my pockets, so I don't reach for her, I focus on her beautiful green eyes. "And what about me? Have I struck out?"

"Seems the home team has last at bat," she says, looking at me. "Last up. Full count. Three balls. Two strikes. But if you swing and miss again, you're out, and the game is over."

My head tilts. "I want to be clear. You're giving me another chance." No more baseball puns.

Her lips twist. "You're taking me to dinner. The Patio on Friday."

I stare at her, brows lifting. "You're kind of assertive," I tease.

"I heard you love ambitious women."

Stepping up to her, I can't fight back the desire anymore. I reach for her loose hair and curl it over her ear. "There's only one ambitious woman I love." My voice drops, and I want to lower my head for hers. I want her to read my thoughts and feel my heart and know that I mean it. I love her.

"Friday," she whispers.

"Friday," I repeat, lowering to press a kiss just off her lips and then step back before I reach for more. I can handle a strike, but you only get three at bat, and I'm not risking a strikeout.

+ + +

"Okay, food, check. Clothes, check." I rub my hands down my outfit. Casual pants and dress shirt. Not jeans, so not understated. Not a suit, so not overboard.

"Flowers?" Lucy questions, sitting on an island stool and watching me pace my kitchen frantically.

"Fuck, I forgot to get flowers."

"We should get a swear jar. I'd make a fortune." I stop walking and glare down at my daughter.

"I'm not that bad," I state.

Lucy shakes her head. "But you forgot flowers."

Right. And I don't have time to get to Hetty's Florist. I'm minutes away from picking up Janessa and surprising her with a dinner I hope won't disappoint although it isn't exactly what she asked for.

The back door opens, and I'm hoping it's her mother who is helping me orchestrate tonight. Instead, it's Vega.

"Mr. Harrington," she addresses me.

"Please, I told you, you can call me Charlie."

"My mother says I have to call you Mr. Harrington."

I shake my head. "Okay, is she almost ready?" Both girls know about tonight but have been sworn to secrecy. After all that happened, I had to have a talk with my daughter and be honest without being too open. Her mother had pictures of me that were not appropriate to share, although taken at a time when I thought we were a couple, and there were things couples did when they were much older.

Pint had glared at me. "I know about the birds and the bees, Dad."
"Oh, how?"

"Sadie." My brother Billy's sixteen-year-old daughter. I was going to need to give her a talking-to although with her father's promiscuous background, maybe he needs the lecture.

I'd then gone on to explain how I had feelings for Vega's mother and wanted her to marry me.

"Yeah, Mom's ready," Vega says, sheepishly looking up at me. I don't know how much she knows about what's already happened, but both girls know I proposed and failed. Vega told Lucy who told me, that she'd heard about the proposal. Rumors flew around summer art camp, and the girls wondered if they were going to be sisters or not. At the moment, they were in the *not* category, but I wasn't willing to give up.

"She likes yellow roses," Vega adds, and Lucy rolls her eyes and then tips her head to her best friend.

"He forgot the flowers," Pint says, her voice droning.

Vega shakes her head in disappointment. These girls are tough critics, and I feel like I'm staring at the future Elaina Harrington and Gretchen O'Leary. Southern belles. Gossip queens.

"Got a ring this time?" Vega asks, and I'm assuming she never saw the first one I gave her mother.

"I do," I say, hoping her mother will one day say those words to me.

"Mom's big on apologies, so I think if you mean what you say when you ask for forgiveness, she'll say yes."

"I've already told your mother I was sorry."

"Yeah, but was it about you or her?" I stare down at this ten-year-old, wondering about her wisdom, but then again, I know how Lucy earned hers, and I realize once again the connection between these two has to do with public-eye parents and their public sins.

I reflect on what Vega said. "It was about her. I hurt her."

Vega slowly smiles and then gives me a thumbs-up. Lucy gives her own thumbs-up, and I wish it were so easy to get that kind of review from Janessa.

"Okay, you two, off to Gran's." My mother awaits them for another pizza-movie night, and I head out to the garage.

Arriving at the coach house for Janessa, I feel like a teenage boy picking up his first date. I want tonight to be special as she's giving me a second chance to prove myself.

"You make me breathless," I say as she steps out on the stoop. Her dress is a deep green color that accentuates her eyes. When she slowly smiles, I shiver. I want to press her up against the house and take her with everything I have, tell her I love her, and let her know again I'll be good to her. Instead, I take a deep breath, hold out my arm, and escort her to the car.

We drive no more than a few yards and pull into my drive.

"Charlie, this isn't The Patio."

I turn my head from her to my yard and back. "It's not." My head tilts, and then I smile. Ignoring the scowl on her face, I exit the driver's side and walk around to her, helping her out of the car. Her fingers curl into mine, and I don't let them go as I escort her to the side gate to my backyard. Stepping to the side, I lead Janessa forward, and then she stops.

"Oh, my God," she mutters.

"I thought we'd have more privacy on this patio."

Chapter 33
Last at Bat

[Janessa]

He isn't wrong. His patio is private and absolutely stunning. The lights in the pool are on, and the patio is covered in a crisscross of outdoor bulbs. A small firepit has been placed near the dining table, and a tall bucket with a bottle of wine rests in ice. It's beautiful and romantic.

"When did you do all this?" I ask, wondering if he really did do it himself.

"This afternoon. I had some help, though."

I don't ask. I don't like to be reminded that my mother and soon, my brother work for Charlie.

"Come," Charlie directs, still holding my hand and leading me to the table. He opens the chilled wine and pours each of us a glass.

"Do you like seabass?"

"I love it," I say, a little surprised at the question, and he smiles.

"Good."

He's up to something, and I should question him, but I don't. I just take in the atmosphere he's created. He holds up his wineglass. "To you," he toasts and then sips the wine.

His phone buzzes, and he reaches for it in his pocket. "Just give me a minute." It seems rude, and I scowl, but then he places the phone on the table, upside down, and excuses himself. I expect him to enter the house, but he stops near a grill just outside his back door. Opening the lid, I watch him pull something from it and then plate the items. He returns to me and nods to the table.

"Should we sit?"

"Did you cook for me?"

"I told you I know my way around the kitchen," he teases.

"You know your way around a pizza box and how to get one delivered."

He laughs, and I stare at him. He seems nervous, and I don't want him to be. I want my Charlie. The easygoing, sexy-confident one who wants me with a passion I can't deny.

"Charlie," I say, laying my hand on his once we sit. "Relax."

His shoulders fall. "I am." But he's not. I ignore the edge to him as we eat a delicious grilled fish with wild rice and mixed summer veggies.

"When did you learn to cook this?" I hum as I set another bite on my tongue.

"Earlier today," he answers honestly, and I realize what he's done.

"Did my mother make this?" Mami knows this is my favorite dish.

Charlie adamantly shakes his head. "She only gave me pointers." Sheepishly, he reaches for his wine. It's kind of sweet to think he asked my mother for my favorite dish and then tried to cook it for us, but these are things he'd learn if we dated, not rushed into marriage.

"Charlie, you know marriage doesn't save anything. It doesn't replace something."

He sets his glass down at he looks at me. "Going right to the jugular," he teases, but his tone tells me it hurt to jump to the topic still hanging over our head.

"I've already been in that position. I know these things."

"I've been there, too," he reminds me.

"Marrying me would not be good for you, Charlie."

"I want to be bad," he states with such sincerity and seriousness that I laugh. "I mean it. If the town can't handle what's between us, then I'll quit. I'll run for Congress after all, or better yet, return to being just a lawyer."

"I'd never ask you to give anything up for me."

"You aren't." His hand lands softly on the table, but it still rattles the dishes. "The only thing I don't want to give up is you."

"Charlie."

"I want to marry you. Not for pretend, for real."

I sigh, sorry I've taken us to the heaviest subject first. I shake my head and lower my eyes for my dinner.

"Tell me about the walkway," he suggests, and I glance up to see him begging me with his eyes for something normal. So I begin with the plans Cora and I have created, and tell him everything, hoping he won't block us on anything. To my surprise, he makes a few recommendations of his own and offers a few avenues if we get roadblocked on construction. For the most part, he just listens, smiling back at me and my enthusiasm.

"I really feel like this will do something good. Like I'm making a mark." I exhale, a real sigh of contentment.

"I'm really proud of you."

"Charlie," I drone, thinking he's patronizing me.

"You knew what you wanted, and you went after it. That's admirable, and on top of it, you didn't let anything get in your way, not even me."

"You helped me get around your getting in my way."

"Yeah, but you still made the decision to keep going."

I stare at him a minute, really soaking up what he's saying and drinking in the spark of his eyes.

"Do you mean it, Charlie? Are you really proud of me?" I don't need his approval. I set out to do all this for myself, but I want it. I want him to find pride in what I've accomplished.

"There's nothing you'd do that I wouldn't be proud of. Look at Vega."

"What about Vega?"

Charlie swallows and looks away again, his wine glass dangling from his hand. "She helped me set this up. Told me your favorite dish and suggested your mother help me. She and Lucy suggested the lights, saw it in a movie, I guess, but I liked the idea." He looks at the mini-light strings over us. "I wanted to make tonight special, but I couldn't have done it alone. Your daughter knows you best. I want to be the same."

"So you cheated on this with my ten-year-old," I tease, but Charlie sits back, and his lips twist.

"You're tough to please."

My shoulders fall. He's right, but I'm also not being appreciative that he did put forth all this effort.

"Where did you see this night going, Charlie?"

His head tilts. "I just wanted to spend time with you. Have a real date and talk."

"What if I don't want to talk?" My voice drops, and Charlie stares at me.

"What do you want to do instead?" He isn't smiling, but the corner of his lip curls.

"Let's swim." Taking a final drink of my wine, I stand, pushing back my seat. I kick off my heels and walk to the edge of the pool. Taking my hair out of the clip holding it up, I let it fall and then slowly slip from my dress. Looking over my shoulder, I watch Charlie watching me peel myself free of my wrapping. In a thin thong and my bra, I dive into the pool.

Coming up for air on the opposite side, I see Charlie standing across from me on the edge. His shoes are removed, and he's working on his dress shirt. His eyes latch onto me, and we focus on one another as he tugs his shirt over his head and then forces his pants down. He steps out of them, leaving on his dark boxer briefs. The material does nothing to disguise the thickness bulging in his shorts, and the length I know fills me so well.

I've missed his body.

Gracefully, Charlie prepares to dive in, and then at the last minute, he switches it up to cannonball into his pool. I scream as a wave of water hits me and laugh when he pops up, whipping his head to the side, making his hair stand up. A boyish grin graces his face as he swims to me and then sets his hands on either side of my body, pressing up against the side of the pool.

"Are you expecting me to behave myself with you nearly naked and now covered in wet lingerie plastered to your body?"

"Yes," I tease, and Charlie's brow arches.

"Dammit." He pushes back from the poolside and backstrokes to the opposite side of the pool. Lifting his arms, he stretches them to keep his body afloat. His wingspan is impressive, just like the rest of his body. The dim pool lights under the dark sky accentuate the athleticism of his physique. I look away from him, so I'm not tempted to cross the pool and go for him.

Above us are a million stars in the clear black night. It's so peaceful here. "It's lovely," I whisper, but the sound travels over the slight waves of water, and Charlie replies.

"Yes, she is."

My gaze falls back to him, intently watching me. The attraction ripples across the water, and I don't know how I'll hold out knowing *he's* nearly naked, with wet cotton accentuating the stiffness in his briefs. The hunger in his eyes calls out to me.

"Charlie," I whisper as if warning him to stop being so sexy when he can't help it.

"Why do we need to deny it?" he asks.

"I don't know." What's wrong with having this kind of animal attraction, this crazy chemistry? "I don't want lust to be confused for love."

"It's not. At least, not for me."

Can he really mean what he says? How can he love me so quickly? I promised myself I'd never fall so fast again, if it ever happened again. I'd recognize the difference between the two L-words, but I'm blinded by how I feel about Charlie and how he feels against me. The two emotions feel one and the same.

I'm not certain who moves first, but suddenly, we're in the middle of the pool, our mouths crashing into one another. My wet body slaps against Charlie's as his hands cover my ass, and my legs lift for his hips. Instantly, my center meets his thickness, and I cry out into his mouth.

"You can't deny this," he tells me, lips still attached to mine.

He's right. *He's so right.*

"I'm so confused," I say, still kissing him.

"Then let me work it out for you."

We continue to kiss, his fingers digging into my backside while mine claw at his shoulders. My body rocks against his while the water laps around us.

There's no denying my body wants his, but what about my heart?

My heart wants him as well.

"Oh, Charlie," I groan as he walks me to the stairs, lifting me to the edge of the pool. He sets me down and tells me to lie back. The concrete isn't ideal, but I want his touch, and he gives it to me, sliding my soaked panties to the side and entering me with two long fingers. I cry out at the welcome intrusion as my back arches, and I look at the heavens over me.

His fingers move as he would, and I realize how much I've missed him, missed this connection to him. He's relentless at drawing out a quick, sharp orgasm that has me sitting up and spreading my legs wider.

"Fuck, I want to take you right here."

"Do it," I whisper, and his sticky, wet briefs lower, allowing enough space for him to release. I lie back on my elbows, digging into the concrete, and watch him position himself at my entrance. He's balancing in a half-kneel, half-stand on the stairs exiting his pool, but neither of us wants to move, other than to join as one. On a rush, he enters me, and I whimper at the sensation. He works fast, repeatedly filling me, tapping at a spot deep in my depths.

"I'm not going to last," he warns, and this is what I want. I want him to lose control over me, which makes me realize he already has. He's admitted over and over again how out of control he feels, and he's acted accordingly with the rushed proposal and the continued appeals for me. He's really…in love with me. Head over heels in love. Out of control in love.

He stills rather quickly, and the heat of him rushes inside me. He feels so good buried that deep, giving everything of him to me. I reach up, balancing on one elbow, and cup his cheek.

"I love you, Charlie."

His body stiffens.

"What?"

"I love you. I'm sorry I didn't say it before, and it's taken me this moment to realize. I love you, Charlie. I want to be with you."

"What are you saying?"

"I—"

"Wait, don't answer that." Charlie pulls out of me, and I whimper at the loss. Leaning forward, he kisses me quickly and then stands over me. "Come with me." His hands come under my armpits, and he lifts me to stand without waiting for an answer. I'm still stunned at how briskly he left my body and how he's leading me into his house. Dripping wet, we enter the back door and take the back stairs to the second level. Shivering in my soaked underthings and hearing the plop of water from Charlie's briefs, we enter his room, and he stands near the dresser, the same one he caught me near on that first morning.

"I once told you not to enter this room without being naked and willing and not to steal anything from me again..." His voice drifts. We've already had this conversation. "But you did steal something that first morning; you stole my heart."

Reaching around me, he pulls his grandmother's ring from the dish on his dresser.

"I should have just let you keep it that morning because it looked right on your finger. I'm asking you to marry me. Accept all my flaws and my desire to be good while wanting to be bad. But only bad with you." His voice drops. "I love you, Janessa. It's that simple."

"Okay, Charlie. I'll marry you."

"Just okay?" he says, bending at the knees to look up at me as he holds out the ring, and I stare down at it.

"Yes, Charlie. Yes. I love you."

I look up to meet his eyes, and he slips the ring on my finger. Lifting my knuckles, he kisses over the ring. "I am not taking that back from you."

"What about the other one?"

"We'll return it and use the money for a wedding."

Jeez. "Did it cost that much?"

"I don't care how much it cost. This ring"—he taps on the one on my finger—"this one is the one as priceless to me as you are. And I'm keeping you both." He kisses me quickly. "And Vega."

"Oh my God, what am I going to tell Vega?"

Charlie shrugs. "She already knows."

"My daughter knows I'm marrying you before I do."

"She knew you liked me." He winks. "And I couldn't ask your father for your hand, but I figured your daughter is the one who really needs to give me permission." Papi wasn't here to see that I was finally happy, and my heart hurts a little with the thought, but it's quickly replaced with the sweetness of this man asking my daughter for my hand instead.

"And Vega said yes, just like that?" I tease.

"She couldn't resist the Harrington charm," he jokes, wrapping his arms around me, and we both shiver as the wet material of our underthings touch cool skin.

"Is it time for us to do the naked part of your demands?" I ask.

Charlie nods.

"Okay, then yes to that part, too…sir."

And with the use of that word, Charlie growls and tosses me to the bed, then follows me to meet all *our* commands together.

Chapter 34
My Vow to You

[Janessa]

It's a beautiful early September day, and I stand inside a guest room of Charlie's home. Checking myself in the mirror one more time, I hardly recognize the woman reflected back at me. Who knew happiness could be as visible as a white dress? But it's not the dress covering me. It's the changes inside me that radiate back at me.

Vega and I are safely removed from Richard although there will be a time to digest what the separation from Richard will mean for my daughter. He'd already given me sole custody and had all rights for visitation removed. The loss of communication with him makes him a name on Vega's birth certificate but not her father. He's never truly been one, but I smile to myself when I think of Charlie.

Since the time of his official proposal, the genuine one in his room when he gave me his grandmother's ring to wear forever and ever, he's added Vega to his fatherly duties as if she's always been present. Pool time and attending the summer camp's final art show. Hikes as a family and dinners together. The inclusion of our children has curtailed our wild, reckless sex time, but when we sneak in things like bathroom breaks and shared laundry, we find a way to be just as reckless and wild with two ten-year-olds somewhere in our home. The girls can't wait to celebrate their joint birthday soon.

My thoughts flip to Lucy and how she and Vega have an even better understanding of one another. While her mother has been distant for years, only seeing her daughter when it suits her, Lucy accepts this reserved relationship, but an adjustment period will come for her as well. Charlie is demanding full custody from Angela with restrictions to the visitation if they even continue. For now, Angela is giving in to Charlie's demands, but he's not confident she's gone forever.

Thinking of Lucy, I take a final look at myself in the mirror, smooth over my hips at the beautiful but simple dress, and smile when a light tap comes to the door.

"Hi," Lucy softly says to me, entering the room in a yellow dress. Vega wears the same style in pink. We let the girls pick the dresses within reason. The coloring doesn't match the season, but they are only ten, and it's better than the mint green they first selected. "You wanted to see me."

"Come here, baby," I state, walking myself to the bed and then patting the space next to me. With dark hair and blue eyes, Lucy doesn't really look like a typical Harrington until she smiles and opens her mouth to speak, then she's all Charlie and not a trace of her mother.

"I wanted to give you something." I hold out a small box for her, wrapped in yellow paper. "But first, I want to tell you something."

When we told the girls we were getting married, Lucy cheered, and Vega cried. Charlie was concerned until Vega clarified she was just so happy.

"I am not your mother." It sounds stern and almost heartless, but I keep my tone soft. "I can't replace her, Lucy. She's still your mother, but what I'd like to be is your friend. Your confidant, meaning you can tell me anything. Your playmate and teacher, which means I'll try to keep up with you active girls but also know that I have things to teach you, and at times, that might mean I have to be a disciplinarian."

"That was one of my vocabulary words last year."

I smile at her interruption.

"But it also means that when it comes to you, I do what I do because I care about you. Honestly, Lucy, I already love you and not just because I love your father and you've been the best friend to Vega, but because you're a great girl who's going to be a wonderful woman someday…but hopefully not too soon." I cup her jaw and wink at her. Her little lip trembles, and I can honestly say I've not seen her cry. She's a strong child, and I credit her strength of character to her father and his family.

"Do you understand what I'm saying? I want you to let me love you as a mother should, but you don't have to call me mom, and you don't have to love me in return. Just know that *I'm* here for you. Every day."

A single tear slips from her eye, and she quickly wipes it away. Her nod tells me she understands me, but only time will really prove my words to her.

"So open this," I say, handing her the gift. Inside is a puzzle piece charm on a necklace. There are four pieces—one for each of us. Lucy stares at it until I explain the meaning.

"Your dad and I thought we'd give each of you two halves to a heart, you know like those friendship bracelets or sister charms, but we wanted to be included so we had puzzle pieces made and they all link together, linking the four of us." Lucy and Charlie's link side to side as do Vega's and mine, but then our pieces fit into Lucy and Charlie's connecting us as one complete shape.

I hold up my wrist to show Lucy mine charm on a bracelet.

"Can I wear it now?" Lucy asks.

"I hope you wear it every day," I say, helping her remove it from the box. "Turn for me." The girls were treated to updos for the day while mine still remains down as Charlie likes it. I clasp the tiny catch and then hold my hands on Lucy's shoulders, aiming her for the mirror.

"What do you think?"

"I think I'll wear it every day," she whispers as though she's making a vow to me. "Can I ask someone to take a picture of us?"

"Of course," I reply, thinking she means sometime during the day, but she runs to the door and opens it for her cousin Sadie. Directing her teenage relative, Lucy returns to the bed and wraps her arms around my neck. Cheek to cheek, we sit while Sadie captures the images that I know Lucy will share on social media in a respectful manner. She's learned her lesson about the dangers of images and improper use.

When Sadie finishes, I press a kiss to Lucy's cheek. "See you at the end of the dock," I tell her, and she gives me a little wave before leaving the room.

My heart nearly explodes with nerves—good nerves—over sharing that moment with Lucy and sharing the rest of my moments with Charlie in only a matter of minutes.

Chapter 35

The Last Link

[Charlie]

Standing in my room, I straighten my already straight tie one more time as I stare at myself in the mirror. My eyes flit to the dresser where it all started. A woman in my bedroom. A ring stuck on her finger. The prophecy I felt at that moment as she quietly stole my heart with one look, and months later, I gave her the ring to keep forever. My grandfather would be proud, I hope. Even more so, I hope my grandmother is smiling down on me.

"I picked the best one even after I thought it was too late for me." Too late to love. Too late to feel this alive inside. Janessa does both—gives me life and love—and I look forward to every day being a new adventure with this woman and her kid. *Our* children.

I've asked my sister, Mati, to find Vega for me as I need a moment with her before the wedding. Moving to stand at the footboard of my bed, I lean against it while I wait on them, thinking back over the past few months. What a crazy ride it's been, meeting a woman and connecting so quickly with her, but it makes sense to us. We've both suffered through loveless marriages while being passionate people at our core. We need that other person to light our match and keep us lit, and we've found it in each other.

A short set of raps come on my door, and then it opens without prompting. Mati smiles at me as Vega enters. I've asked Mati to remain at the door to make Vega feel comfortable. While Lucy quickly warmed to Janessa, it's going to take more time for Vega to come to me as her separation from her father is a new wound.

"Hi there," I say as she draws near, looking back at Mati. As the one sister in the Harrington mix, she's been the staple female next to my mother for Lucy. Her recent return from a summer-long road trip has thrown her back into the position of token aunt although we seem to be adding new ones quickly: Letty, Roxanne, and now Janessa. "Are you all ready for today?"

Smiling up at me, she nods.

"You look beautiful," I tell her as she tugs at the skirt of her pink dress.

"Mom looks beautiful, too," she says, and I can't wait to see my bride. Soon.

"You still okay with me marrying your mom?" It isn't going to change much if she isn't pleased, but I want her blessing all the same.

"Yes," she offers with confidence, and I smile.

"I have something for you." Leaning over my footboard, I pick up the small box and hold it out to her. "Your mother is giving Lucy something similar," I tell her before she opens it. I allow her to unwrap it and then lower to my haunches before her as she tips open the box. "It's a puzzle piece. Yours and your mother's link, and Lucy and mine link, and then the four of ours clasp together, like those friend heart necklaces." I actually didn't know anything about such jewelry until Janessa came up with this idea. Then I hold up my wrist.

"Mine is on this leather band while your mother's is on a bracelet. We bought you and Lucy ones on a necklace, hoping you might wear them often."

Vega hesitantly looks up at me, and I wonder what she's thinking behind those eyes that match her mother's. So much has happened so quickly for her: moving, separating from her father, the loss of her grandfather, and now this. While I've pushed for a hasty wedding date, I've tried to keep in perspective the rush might be too much for a child of ten years old. Janessa assures me Vega is handling it all in stride.

"Will you wear this today?" I ask, reaching for the necklace, and Vega nods. I take it from the box and then fumble with the tiny clasp. My fingers shake for some reason. This is a big step. It's more than joining Janessa and myself but blending families. As Lucy and I have been alone for a long time, it's going to be an adjustment, but with the time we've spent together so far as a unit of four, I'm hoping it won't take much for us to link like the pieces of puzzle jewelry.

Once I have the jewelry on her, another knock comes to the door. "Daddy, can Sadie take a picture?"

Mati opens the door wider, and my daughter and niece enter.

"First, just you and Vega," Lucy directs, and I kneel beside her, putting my arm around her waist. To my surprise, she leans into me, and I risk a kiss to her temple. When she looks up at me, I know I have an audience, but I have something to say to this child.

"I'm not going to try to replace your father, but I want to be a dad to you in every way I can." Not knowing if she understands my meaning, she nods again, lowering her head, and then I see a tear. She's sensitive, I've learned, and I pull her to me, hugging tight until Lucy wanders over and wraps an arm around both of us. I wish Janessa could see us and be a part of this, but our time will come soon enough.

When I feel Vega pull back, I ask, "Who's ready to get married?"

"Me," Lucy cheers, but I look at Vega.

"Me too," she says, holding the puzzle charm in her palm as the necklace rests on her neck.

"Then let's get married," I tease, and Sadie snaps a few pictures of the girls and me while my sister, Mati, swipes at her eyes before winking at me.

As I near her before exiting my room, she stops me with a hand on my arm. "You're so good, Charlie." And for once, I take it as a true compliment.

+ + +

I patiently stand at the end of the dock, waiting for my future wife, and then I'm not so patient when I see her appear. Even though her brother offered to give her away, she walks alone down the dock. She told him she was giving herself away this time—wholeheartedly, as well as in body and spirit. Zander might have mentioned that was too much information, but from what I've learned of him, he'd like the same thing. Janessa's mother cries tears of joy, but I assume sadness mixes in as Henri isn't present to see his daughter's happiness.

And Janessa is happy, as am I.

"Hi," she softly says to me as she meets me at the end of the decking.

"Hi," I whisper back to her. The preacher stands before us while only our family and the closest of friends gather on the yard near the water's edge.

While he begins in typical fashion, and we both know the ceremony will be short, I'm ready to share with Janessa something I've wanted to tell her.

"Janessa, with this ring, I give you my love and devotion. I promise to be faithful, honest, and true to you, believe in you, and support you." I reach for the engagement ring I gave her and continue. "With this ring, I gave you a treasure, valued in my family as the engagement ring from my grandfather to my grandmother. He liked to say it never mattered who was first because the winner was the last. The last person you kiss. The last person you bed. That's the person you see with the light of a new day and at the end of one, and that person lasts the rest of your life. I look forward to you wearing this ring…" I pause as I begin to slip the formal gold band down her finger. "Representing the most important love in my life and keeping it here forever." I finish slipping the wedding band on her finger to butt up against the engagement ring.

Janessa curls her fingers into mine and then holds up a gold band for me.

"While I don't have something of equal sentimental value, what I do have for you is my heart, my body, and my soul, all for you. I look forward to a partnership, a friendship, and most importantly, the love relationship we share now and will continue to share in the future. This is the start of a new adventure, a great adventure, and I'm so happy to have you at my side for it. You are the diamond in my life. The solid rock I plan to lean on but also hold up, and together, we will be invincible."

She squeezes my fingers, and I forget to wait. I lean forward and kiss her. It's soft and too brief before the preacher clears his throat.

"Just a few more lines, and then you can kiss her," he teasingly warns.

While I hear the words, and my brain processes them, none of them need to register. I know how I feel about this woman whose eyes are latched onto mine, and we sheepishly smile at one another, the heat radiating between us. If the preacher wasn't present and the family wasn't gathered, the best way to solidify our vows and commitment would be in another manner. Janessa must sense my thoughts because she squeezes my fingers, hinting at later.

Later.

Like the rest of our lives together.

Epilogue
Wet Reception

[Janessa]

When the short ceremony finishes, Charlie leads me from the dock to the pool patio where we plan to host a small dinner. His brothers, however, are eager for pictures.

"Step back a little bit," Billy calls out as his daughter is situated to take our photo near the pool.

"Just one little more," Giant encourages as Charlie holds me and shuffles us backward. My heel clips on the edge, but Charlie tugs me into him.

"Almost," Billy states.

"That's enough," Charlie calls out and then stomps his foot. Only, his own hard-soled shoe catches on the edge of the pool, and he tips. Gripping me, he tilts, and within seconds, we're going over.

When the water hits me, I scream under it, my dress instantly plastered to me. Charlie drags me upward, and I'm certain between my makeup and hair, I'm a mess. Charlie's suit is soaked, and my dress is ruined.

"Goddammit," Charlie calls out, pushing at the water to splash his brothers who bend over laughing. "You'd think they'd grow up."

"Never," Billy bellows, still laughing his ass off. "You'll always be the kid brother. Welcome to the family, Janessa."

"William, what did you do?" Elaina Harrington cries out, coming to the edge of the pool and staring down at us.

"Why's it always me?" Billy snorts.

"That's the same question I ask myself," their mother retorts, and I can't help myself. I start to laugh as well. With everything ruined, there isn't much else to do, and Charlie looks at me. His lips slowly curl.

"You didn't plan to ever wear that again, did you?"

"Never," I whisper about my beautiful dress. Charlie reaches out for me, and in the middle of the pool, he kisses me hard.

"You're going to wear only this tonight," he playfully warns, pressing at the rings on my finger.

"Promises, promises," I tease.

"Can we come in?" Both girls stand on the edge of the pool, primed to jump with their pretty dresses and fancy shoes.

"No," Charlie and I say in unison. Then Charlie pushes back his hair. "Bathing suits first."

The girls look at one another and run for the house, and I glance at Charlie. "Well, as long as I'm already wet, might as well stay in." He shrugs off his jacket and walks it to the side of the pool. Lowering for each shoe, he tosses them onto the concrete. Then he removes his socks and helps me to a seat on the edge of the pool.

"You're a good man, Charlie," I tell him, looking down at him in his soaked dress shirt and ruined suit pants. I recall the day his child ran to him, waterlogged in her bathing suit, and he lifted her like he didn't have another care in the world than to catch his daughter. He's caught me as well. The gold band glitters on his finger as he covers my knee with his hand and tips up for another kiss.

"I might be good for you, but you know I love to be bad *with* you."

I smile, as I do know how bad he can be.

We hear whoops and hollers as the girls run to the pool, dropping towels and things as they near it and then leap. That's how I feel about my life. It's been a big leap. The move to Blue Ridge. The faith in myself. The job with Parks and Recreation, and my love for this man.

And it's one jump I'd take all over again.

Watching Charlie splash the girls and toss them around the pool, with a party celebrating our happiness on the pool deck, I never thought I'd be so happy myself, and I realize I'm right where I was always meant to be.

With Charlie.

Thank you for taking the time to read Silver Mayor.
Please consider writing a review on major sales channels where ebooks
and paperbooks are sold.

Want a sip of Charlie and Janessa in the future?

SILVER MAYOR BONUS

Want to read the next Harrington brother to fall in love (again)?
Silver Biker
A marriage in repair when James Harrington once had it all and wants
it back again.

Flip the page for a sample.

Read where the Harringtons were first introduced in *Second Chance*,
Mati Harrington and Denton Chance's friends-to-lovers,
second chance romance.

+ + +

A sip of *Silver Biker*

Chapter 1
A Reintroduction
[James]

As I sit in the Ridged Edge, a biker bar just outside town, my vision glazes over. I've had one too many again tonight. I'm loose limbed and spineless but not past the point of remembering who I am. I can't forget myself although most days I wish I could.

James Harrington.

That's my name, my birth right, and my curse. I didn't always hate being a Harrington. At one time, I took it as a privilege. I used it to my advantage. But a name doesn't stop you from losing everything.

"Why the scowl, honey?"

The biker bitch on my lap cups my chin and forces me to look at her. I'm not about to tell her my woes. Few people know the truth and that's the way I like it.

Trixie. Trudy. Tabby. I can't remember her name and I tug at her hip. She's wearing the shortest of short skirts in black leather and a white top cut so low her red bra hangs out. Her thick ass presses into my thigh. She's unfamiliar in so many ways. She isn't the woman I thought would be sitting on my legs at my age. By forty-eight, I believed my life would be many things. None of them hold true. What a fucker I was back in my twenties. My thoughts want to wander to the past, but I refuse to let memory traipse there. There's no point in pulling up history.

"Thinking about how'd I get so lucky," I mock of myself, letting her believe it has to do with her on my lap. She's a brunette with brown eyes and it's all wrong. I need to keep it that way if I want to make it through the night with her. I don't, actually—want to spend the night with her. I'm not happy being with other woman, but I am a man. I have needs and I try to give what I take. The tongue works wonders. Fingers too. But there's a part of me that doesn't belong to anyone else but one woman.

And she's gone, fucker.

It's all my fault.

"We should get out of here," the babe whispers in my ear. Her voice is wrong. Smoky and rough, she sounds as tough as she probably is. It's a hard life being a bitch to a set of bikers. Rebels Edge. We aren't the worst bunch out there. We aren't one-percenters although the club had been at that level long before me. Something happened along the way and it whittled down to more a group of lost souls finding one another. We ride. We drink. We fornicate.

Such is my life now. The life I didn't think I'd ever be living. However, I love my brothers-on-bikes.

"Not quite yet, honey," I tell her as she licks the shell of my ear. I'm being hosed down by the saliva and lapped like the kisses my pouch Silver gives me. A lick from my Siberian Husky might actually feel better.

"Ranger." The call of my biker name from Justice, the president of our club, and one of my best friends forces me to look up. "I think this one's for you."

His silver topped head tips toward the front door of the bar and I squint. The brightness of blonde hair from yards away beckons to me like a beacon across a lake, but I can't make out the rest of her body as she stands before the front door of the bar like she isn't certain she should be here. Perhaps she's wondering how she got here.

Join the club sister.

Then again, don't. Whoever she is, from this distance, I can tell she doesn't have a stitch of biker babe in her. Something just doesn't feel right about her and tells me I'm correct in my assessment.

"Nope. Not my type," I say to my old friend, turning my gaze back to him and then offering a kiss to the jaw of the woman on my lap. Justice snorts and shakes his head side to side. His arms cross over his solid body. He's been acting all kinds of weird the last few months. Now that he's getting his dick dipped on the regular to one woman in particular, he's mellowing. I'd tease him it's old age, but I know the real source of his content. He's in love.

I shiver with the thought. I'd been there once—only once—then I lost it all.

Maybe the chick by the door is lost. Happens on occasion. Someone's driving toward Blue Ridge, up here in the Smoky Mountains of Georgia, and she gets lost. She hasn't quite made it to town and doesn't realize she's only fifteen minutes outside of it.

Keep going, honey, I want to holler. *You'll get wherever you're going soon enough.*

Blue Ridge is my hometown. Born and bred here, I knew I'd spend my entire life near this town. After what happened here, I'll never leave. Never.

"Wouldn't be so sure about that," Justice states, chuckling to himself and pulling me back to the present. The lost woman finally walks to the edge of the bar and pauses at the structure. It spans the length of one wall. The rest of the room has tables scattered here and there. I'm sitting near the pool tables toward the back of the place. I'd just won a game and somehow the woman on my lap is my prize.

I'm not getting laid, but I'll be getting long overdue head.

"What do you know?" I snap at my leader although it comes out more a slur. I'm feeling so good, really relaxed. I'd like to think the ease will allow me to stick my dick in someone random, but I know it won't. This bird on my lap could sing pretty, smell sweet, and tease me in all the right ways, and I still won't being going where I can't bring myself to go.

It isn't that I can't get it up. It's that I don't think I deserve to sample the pleasure.

"Ranger, you're asking for trouble." The tone of Justice's voice raises the hackles on the back of my neck. With my hair shorn short to my scalp, highlighting the hints of silver I've become speckled with, it doesn't take much for those fine locks to prickle. His voice has me on edge.

"Trouble is my middle name." I snort.

"Peach is your middle name," a feminine voice says, and I choke on air. *What the fuck?*

"You're a peach," I retort, squinting at the figure who has moved closer to my perch without me noticing her. The comeback is intended to be flippant and flirty, but my tongue swells the second I've said it. The air around me stills. Sound disappears. The woman on my lap feels like the weight of the world. I only have eyes for the woman standing two feet away from me.

Blonde hair bright as lemonade, sapphire blue eyes, and a body like an hourglass, I can't believe I didn't recognize her at first. However, I am drunk. Or I was. I'm sobering up real fast. My leg begins to bounce, making the woman on my lap jiggle and she lets loose a vibrating giggle drawing awkward attention to herself. She sounds like a child on a kiddie ride, only I'm not offering free trips on the James express.

"Peach," I whisper, not certain the nickname leaves my lips. I continue to stare at her, disbelieving she's standing before me. *She's still so fucking beautiful.* The glare in her eyes assures me she's real, and she's staring daggers at the woman sitting on my legs.

In a show of possessiveness and bitchiness to the max, the woman kisses my jaw, licking along the hard edge and scraping her tongue against the silvery stubble. Her eyes remain on the peach before me.

Fuck.

"James." The blonde bombshell speaks. I'd recognize her voice anywhere. I hear it nightly in my dreams, reaching out for it to drown out the other noises that haunt me. The screams. The scrapping. The silence afterward.

"Evelyn." Her name is sharper on my tongue then I intend. I'm pissed she didn't call this year. She owes me every May. She promised that one concession.

"You gonna join us tonight?" The bitty on my lap teases of the woman before me who looks ready to stake me on a skewer and roast me over a fire.

Good, let her be angry. Let her be anything other than emotionless.

It was all your fault, my conscience reminds me.

I sit taller in my sit, shifting the woman on my thighs who has a firm grip on my neck at this point.

"No, I don't think I'll be joining you this evening." Her sharp tone displays how unimpressed she is with this situation. Once upon a time she was impressed with me, though. She thought I was the shit, and she was my sweet peach.

James and his Giant Peach. My mother loved the irony of it.

"Evie," I hiss. Her nickname falls on deaf ears as the beauty turns away from me. My eyes fall to her firm ass, still tight in skinny jeans. My mouth waters and insides stir in a way they haven't for years. Justice steps back with a broad step. He stood beside her, ever the protector of the underdog, although I'm not certain who's the underdog in this scenario—her or me.

As she walks away, the soles of her shoes clacking on the tile like the ticking of a stopwatch, I sigh uncertain if it's relief, frustration, or fear.

"Who was that?" Trixie-Trudy-Tabby asks, her voice incredulous at the sway of hips walking away from me once again.

I answer on an exhale.

"My wife."

Continue reading Silver Biker

More by L.B. Dunbar

<u>Sterling Falls</u>
Small town. Big heart.
Seven siblings muddling their way through love over 40.
Sterling Heat
Sterling Brick
Sterling Streak

Parentmoon
When the mother of the groom goes head-to-head with the single father of the bride.

<u>Holiday Hotties (Christmas novellas)</u>
Holiday novellas certain to heat the season.
Scrooge-ish
Naughty-ish

<u>Road Trips & Romance</u>
3 sisters. 3 destinations. A second chance at love over 40.
Hauling Ashe
Merging Wright
Rhode Trip

<u>Lakeside Cottage</u>
Four friends. Four summers. Shenanigans and love happen at the lake.
Living at 40
Loving at 40
Learning at 40
Letting Go at 40

<u>The Silver Foxes of Blue Ridge</u>
Small mountain town, silver foxes. Brothers seeking love over 40.
Silver Brewer
Silver Player
Silver Mayor
Silver Biker

<u>Sexy Silver Foxes</u>
When sexy silver foxes meet the feisty vixens of their dreams.

SILVER MAYOR

After Care
Midlife Crisis
Restored Dreams
Second Chance
Wine&Dine

Collision novellas
A spin-off from After Care – the younger set/rock stars
Collide
Caught

Rom-com standalone for the over 40
The Sex Education of M.E.

The Heart Collection
Small town, big hearts - stories of family and love.
Speak from the Heart
Read with your Heart
Look with your Heart
Fight from the Heart
View with your Heart

A Heart Collection Spin-off
The Heart Remembers

BOOKS IN OTHER AUTHOR WORLDS
Smartypants Romance (an imprint of Penny Reid)
Tales of the Winters sisters set in Green Valley.
Love in Due Time
Love in Deed
Love in a Pickle

The World of True North (an imprint of Sarina Bowen)
Welcome to Vermont! And the Busy Bean Café.
Cowboy
Studfinder

L.B. DUNBAR

THE EARLY YEARS
The Legendary Rock Star Series
A classic tale with a modern twist of rock star romance and suspense

Paradise Stories
MMA romance. Two brothers. One fight.

The Island Duet
Intrigue and suspense. The island knows what you've done.

Modern Descendants – writing as elda lore
Magical realism. Modern myths of Greek gods.

About the Author

www.lbdunbar.com

L.B. Dunbar loves sexy silver foxes, second chances, and small towns. If you enjoy older characters in your romance reads, including a hero with a little silver in his scruff and a heroine rediscovering her worth, then welcome to romance for those over 40. L.B. Dunbar's signature works include women and men in their prime taking another turn at love and happily ever after. She's a *USA TODAY* Bestseller as well as #1 Bestseller on Amazon in Later in Life Romance with her Lakeside Cottage and Road Trips & Romance series. L.B. lives in Chicago with her own sexy silver fox.

To get all the scoop about the self-proclaimed queen of silver fox romance, join her on Facebook at Loving L.B. or receive her monthly newsletter, Love Notes.

+ + +

Connect with L.B. Dunbar

www.ingramcontent.com/pod-product-compliance
Lightning Source LLC
Chambersburg PA
CBHW060911210726
48293CB00006B/2055